My
Jewish
Face
&
Other
Stories

My Jewish Face & Other Stories

Melanie Kaye/Kantrowitz

First Edition
10-9-8-7-6-5-4-3-2

Spinsters/Aunt Lute Book Company
P.O. Box 410687
San Francisco, CA 94141

Cover and Text Design: Pam Wilson Design Studio
Cover Art: Hilary Mosberg
Cover Color Separations: Henrietta Boberg
Editor: Joan Pinkvoss
Production: Eileen Anderson
            Martha Davis
            Joan Meyers
Typesetting: Joan Meyers and Comp-Type, Inc., Fort Bragg, CA

Printed in the U.S.A. on acid-free paper

This book is an Aunt Lute Foundation educational project and
was supported by a grant from the National Endowment for
the Arts.

This is a work of fiction. In no way does it intend to represent
any real person, living or dead, or any real incidents.

Library of Congress Cataloging-in-Publication Data

Kaye/Kantrowitz, Melanie.
    My Jewish face and other stories
  by Melanie Kaye/Kantrowitz. — 1st ed.
      p. cm.
    ISBN 0-933216-72-6 : $19.95
    ISBN 0-933216-71-8 (pbk.) : $9.95
    1. Women, Jewish—Fiction. I. Title
PS3561.A888M9 1990
813'.54—dc20   90-9427

The author wishes to acknowledge the publication of some of the stories in this collection in the following journals and anthologies:

"Jewish Food, Jewish Children," *The Tribe of Dina: A Jewish Women's Anthology* (1st pub. as *Sinister Wisdom 29/30* [Montpelier, VT, 1986]; expanded revised edition, Boston: Beacon Press, 1989); "War Stories, 197-," *Sinister Wisdom 33* (1987); "Janey," *Sinister Wisdom 31* (1987); "For Her," *Hurricane Alice* (Spring 1988); "Our First Talk," *Sojourner* (February, 1988); "Burn," *Country Courier: Special Edition on Vermont Fiction* (March 25, 1988); "Vacation Pictures," *Lesbian Love Stories* (Freedom, CA: Crossing Press, 1988); "My Jewish Face," *Sinister Wisdom 35* (1988) and *Response* (XVI.1-2, 1988); "Some Pieces of Jewish Left," *Bridges: A Jewish Feminist Journal* (Spring 1990).

Grateful acknowledgement is made for the use of excerpts from *The Runaway Bunny* by Margaret Wise Brown, pictures by Clement Hurd (New York: Harper & Row, 1972).

ACKNOWLEDGEMENTS

From April to June, 1987, I lived in Taos, New Mexico, on Leibert Road in a small adobe house, #8 of the Helene Wurlitzer Foundation for the Arts. Before April I had written mostly essays and poems; only a few stories. By mid-June I had written drafts of what became most of the stories in this book. Though I would rewrite for another two and a half years, it was the uninterrupted space and time that allowed me to explore this aspect of my writing, and I'm very grateful to the staff of the Wurlitzer Foundation, especially Henry Sauerwein, the director.

I also want to thank Perle Olson, former director of the Adult Degree Program of Vermont College, for continuous support leading to a full-time job which made it possible, as these things ironically go, for me to take an unpaid leave so that I could go to Taos and do this work; and the New York State Council on the Arts, for a Writer-in-Residence Grant at the Schenectady Library, which supplied the funding for my time in Taos.

I thank those who were part of the Harlem Education Project in the early sixties; Marsha Hudson, who introduced me to women's liberation, and the members of the founding Women's Caucus of the department of Comparative Literature at UC Berkeley; the Portland, Oregon lesbian/women's community for the home I made with them for seven years, and for the work we did together. This work, these communities taught me about human possibility, and I owe these people much of whatever optimism and vision have carried me through bitter times. I thank the Jewish Caucus of the National Women's Studies Association for providing a contentious but loving annual *mishpocheh* (family).

I have many women to thank. Linda Vance for picking up the pieces in spring 1987 and for reading many of these stories again and again and again. I thank my sister Roni Natov for her sustaining encouragement; Margaret Blanchard, for nourishing criticism; Bernice Mennis, for loving friendship; Diane Nowicki, for empathic response, and for her dazzling use of language; Amy Kesselman and Vera Williams, for being their inspiring selves; Dino Lucas, for her love and her toughness; Kathy Saadat, for saying to me "you were the one"; Enid Dame, for early useful feedback on "Some Pieces of Jewish Left," the editorial collective of *Bridges* for feedback at a later stage, and Clare Kinberg of *Bridges* for her enthusiasm; Ellie Siegel, of *Sojourner*, for felicitous editing of "Our First Talk"; the women from WRAC, the Iowa City Women's Resource and Action Center, for caring reception of some of this work; Toi Derricotte, for her honest self and knife-sharp words; Suzanne Skea, of the Vermont College Graduate Program, for her indefatigable efficiency and her loyalty; Tess Zimmerman, of the Vermont College Library, for emergency research; Elana Dykewomon, for succeeding me as editor of *Sinister Wisdom*, thus allowing me time to write my stories (may someone relieve her as competently soon); for assistance in final proofreading, Helen Caudill and the incredible Patti Casey; Joan Pinkvoss, for delicate, insightful editing, and for giving me my head on almost every single point; finally, Irena Klepfisz, for reasons too many to name, but among them, for encouraging me to value my own prose and my own experience.

I also want to thank a number of women whose belief in me has often made up the slack for my belief in myself: especially Gloria Anzaldúa, Nancy Barickman, Carol Beatty, Evelyn Torton Beck, Beth Brant, Jane Bryant, Judy Chalmer, Marie Colandrea, Sharon Fitzpatrick, Esther Hyneman, Sharon Jaffe, JoAnn Koepke, Cindy Lanane, Helena Lipstadt, Laura Markowitz, Judy Waterman, Fauna Yarrow, and my aunt Edna Kanterowitz Meltzer.

It pleases me to write these acknowledgements, though I am certain to have excluded—from forgetfulness, or because I haven't yet understood their contribution— many who should be named. I wish I could thank by name every one who has said to me, in person, by letter, by rumor or innuendo that my work mattered. This recognition has mattered a great deal to me.

for my mother
Violette Wolfgang Kaye

in love and struggle

The future was already there; it was a matter of having the courage to announce it. How much courage?—I don't think we had any idea.

Nadine Gordimer,
The Late Bourgeois World (1966)

Jewish Food, Jewish Children

jewish food,
jewish children

1.

When you are around them your Jewishness becomes
an obsession, a connection, but different from what it
is when you are away: what sets you apart; your
consciousness. When you are around them your eating becomes an act of hostility, appeasement, but
never what it is when you are in your own home:
pleasure; nourishment; a meal. Jewish was always on
their lips—still is—yet they take it for granted, while
you are always asking inside your brain like a tic *is she
Jewish   is he Jewish   am I in doing/thinking/believing this
just like a Jew?*

Which Jew?

And eating. Always they said in words gestures
and just plain food stuck in front of you or cleared
away: *eat/don't eat   eat/don't eat   eat/don't eat.* You have
learned to do both when you choose in spite of them,
but here in their home in the city, half your learning
slips off your shoulders like a sweater slung carelessly
for momentary warmth. You feel it go and you think *o
jesus*—you have lived away from Brooklyn too long.

2.

And she is 63 this woman and her husband is ill, some
would say senile, and the doctors say dying, never sick
a day in his life except such bad colds daddy gets and
then five years ago it started—blurred vision,
forgetting—had the customer given him a five or a
ten, had he added the tax on already, even the name of
his high school—and *food:* crumpling dropping spilling
dripping; and missing the toilet when he pees.

She cleans up. All her married life she has cleaned up. For her, for all of them, the future begins to be measured by, *how long does he have?* For him, the future has vanished, he knows and doesn't know, but he has stopped looking ahead, and besides he only ever planned for next season's buying and when to have sales, when to phone "the girls," he would say, the ones who owed on their charges. He would call and urge them to make "small but regular payments," and your whole life when you hear about cheap Jews and Shylock's throbbing pound of flesh, you will think of the block-printing on 5 x 8 index cards, one for each customer, with the columns drawn in neatly with a ruler, and never a penny interest. He paid the bills promptly in cash, bought little, borrowed nothing, and saved, against old age and no pension he saved, building his future and hers and, for the first eighteen years of your life, yours, from Brownesville to Flatbush, and finally when you and your sister were long gone, built across the water to Manhattan, the Village, their dream. Where they live now. Where he is dying.

Where the mother is close to everything she loves, films galleries shops gourmet stores Sunday music in the Square, everything she had longed for and taught you to long for, CULTURE, meaning Western Europe, highbrow, never the *shtetl;* never Brownesville. So what was the thread that joined him to her, Brownesville to Washington Square? There was dancing which they both performed with grace and in unison, what a couple they made. There was class tension and class attraction, he, to the lady, the pretty one, flashy; she to the one who knew it all, the handsome one, the socialist. But for you, born nearly two months after the camps were opened, one month to the day after Nagasaki, three years before Israel could give the Jews a home, what seemed to join them was pride and horror.

Pride: in the Jews. Einstein was a Jew; Eddie Cantor, Arthur Miller, Sam Levenson, and they talked of Adlai Stevenson in such tones that years later you insist to your soon-to-be ex-husband, *Stevenson was a Jew, wasn't he?* Pride: in the values of the Jews: family Jewish men don't drink (a lie but what did you know? *he* didn't) we don't bend our knee even to God (so what the gentiles did in church seemed servile). When you took dance classes for six months and never thought to mention that your teacher was Black, the mother felt she had achieved something, you didn't understand what. When you walked on your first march, ban the bomb—they told all their friends. And when you went to college, that was the real delight, to get A's, to become an intellectual, as they had not, could not. You were their chance, and if you flubbed it when you ate and ate and ate, cut classes and slit your wrists, still you recovered and so did they.

3.

But before you were young, they were young, there was the depression and there was the war, which these first generation spared American Jews waited out, in fear, in isolation—in Wilmington, Delaware to be exact, where she was pregnant and got screamed at on the bus for causing the war—*you people are so pushy*—and he worked in the shipyard hooking up electrical wire and breathing asbestos that would later cost his life. Was now costing his life.

And the war was the horror, the other thing they shared. You always knew, cannot remember learning. Always to know they killed the Jews. Always to picture bodies with no flesh on them. Always to imagine the thinnest possible soup with grease floating on top. Always to know Nazis were evil incarnate, worse than what gentiles called the devil, and never to buy

German, always to shun the sound of it, so different, they would insist, from Yiddish which the mother did not know and the father rarely spoke but in phrases, tender or humorous, *sheyne meydele, meshugene, yenems hintn iz gut tsu shmaysen* (someone else's behind is good to hit).

But growing up he was law, money, power, the boss, grouchy and pompous because outside the store he was no one, but you didn't know that yet and you loved to go to the store with him Friday night, secular *shabes*, in Bay Ridge, selling to gentiles who bought like crazy at Christmas. You would sit on the high stool covered with bright orange vinyl, writing up sales receipts with the carbon paper placed just so. You belonged here with your aunts and cousins and he had to claim you; you were proud and stayed proud until after high school when you jumped class and learned to see him through the eyes of the class you were climbing into. He was no one.

And you were no one too, but from the mother, a vibrant wild girl whose energy and ambition run high in your veins, came the will to be somebody. She herself became the perfect salesgirl in the store— glamorous, gossipy, an eye for the latest thing—the perfect wife at home, though each Saturday when he was at work and she and the daughters were not, she wound up to a frenzy of shrieking, smacking, grab- bing clotheshangers and hairbrush, beating you and your sister till the backs of your legs rose in welts and she broke into shame and sobbing, and you would say you were sorry for making her hit so you could get out and go to the movies.

And in between she would work clean and cook. But the food, the food: salmon croquettes, clam cakes, casseroles, cream puffs, sweet and sour meatballs, and then, through the years, as you and your sister left and money was looser, escalating in gourmet finesse, spinach crepes, sole amandine, souffles and

vichyssoise and chiffon tarts. O the visits were filled
with food.

4.

And when you call to say you'll be late, driving ten
hours down from Maine where you live with your
lover in a log cabin, no electricity no running water,
and once in a while you cook rice or cabbage soup—
when you call to say you'll be late, her first words are,
I'll wait dinner. And when you say no, don't wait, she
hedges, and you arrive to a perfect plate of chicken
marinated in soy sauce with bean sprouts and corn
kept warm and do you want herb dressing or roque-
fort and the red wine saved special.

   Eat   eat   as fast as your little fork can move.
The mother smokes, one after another. You can listen
or you can talk. Talk. For him, the sick father who can
only sometimes focus, you talk about a book you've
been reading about—for a change—the Holocaust.
"Daddy, it said at first no one knew, only Hitler and
Himmler and a few others," and he comes alive arguing, "Six million Jews, how could they not know?"
You try to explain—"But the killing came later, at first
it was just hate but not killing, who could imagine
such a thing?" Still he insists, "Six million, they
knew." For the first time ever you don't try to prove
you're right. Besides, he's right too. Keep talking: as
long as it's Jewish, he'll stay alert, listening, interrupting, being a know-it-all, forgetting a word or a thread,
spilling his coffee, but hanging on for life.

5.

And the mother cooks and serves. This morning it's
raisin bran, she tries to give you a bowl of it while you
talk on the phone to your sister and she, jealous,
bangs kettle and cups around the kitchen big enough

for one. "I only give him half a cup of coffee," she's saying, "whatever I give him he doesn't finish, and he adds half & half like it was going out of style."

You hang up the phone feeling hateful, protective of the sick man referred to always as *he*, as you were never permitted to do, always say *mommy* and *daddy*, so that now you and your sister always with the luscious taste of conspiracy ask *have you talked to them? what does she say about him?* . . . . You wonder, is there a Jewish law you'll discover one day, a Talmudic commentary to explain this prohibition against parental pronouns, maybe a law for each prohibition, a few misplaced commandments preserved in genetic memory—then you would understand who they are, who you are, and why things were forbidden, like spending Sundays with friends instead of family, like eating supper with no potato, or later, like taking pictures in the 4-for-a-quarter booth with your blouse unbuttoned to show your recently acquired stuffed with tissues bra, for which, when they found the pictures, you were severely smacked.

6.

From the sofa where you sleep, where you should be clearing away bedding but instead sit lazy, reading yesterday's paper, slightly sick from the mother's cigarette smoke, you hear familiar tones: hers, anger simmering beneath forced sweetness; his, bossy, snappish, *get me my sweater, my coffee, my pills*.

Your guts rumble, stab of pain. In your life, in the cabin with an outhouse, at the campsite where you lived in a tent all summer, when you sleep in the truck pulled over to the side of some back road, you forget how many years you spent wrapped around pain in that sacred room, but here not 24 hours, it sets in and you head for the toilet. You enjoy sitting there—*is anyone in?* they will ask, over and over, him, her, your sister, maybe a guest, and the answer will be the same: *yes, yes.* Your childhood ploy: for comfort, privacy, and revenge, a weapon: against his bossy rules, his heavy worrying presence; a wall: against her tightness, control—everything in its place at its time, now we get up now we dress now girls time for supper, she the clock; you, the clock watcher, clenched against compulsiveness learned in this house, the tightness you detest in yourself, you sit on the toilet reading the paper, gut cramping against knowledge you can't afford to feel yet: He is dying and will be in pain. She is rageful, deceitful, and in pain. You are their child.

You're reading an article, a reprint from a journalist who entered the camps in 1945, he talked to a Czech Jew named Helen. Helen said mothers had been given the choice of staying with their children and getting gassed, or going to work and leaving their children, who would get gassed either way. It got around to the six-year-olds, there were terrible scenes between children and their mothers. One child was so angry that even though her mother changed her mind and stayed, the child still wouldn't talk to her. You, in pain on the toilet, ponder the gesture of staying, the option of leaving; the force of the child's anger.

7.

And a little while after they eat breakfast, you, having refused the raisin bran, are hungry, go poking around the refrigerator and come up with—pickled herring in cream—"ok if I eat this?" "It was for later," she says, "but ok—maybe I'll have some too, do you want some?" she asks the father, and there you are, the three of you, another meal, onion rolls, sliced tomato, it is delicious. "Honey, your napkin," she says to him, reaching across to straighten the napkin, automatically brushing crumbs from his lap.

She turns to you. "Did I tell you about my party?" she asks. "This summer I had such a party—for spite. Lois had a party and didn't invite us. The only ones she didn't invite. I was furious—not that I think much of her but everyone else was invited. Except us."

The mother lights a cigarette and looks sideways at the father. His head droops forward, he stares at something you can't see. You're angry. You can imagine people are inviting them less these days.

"So," she continues, "at the end of the summer I got an idea to have a party and I invited everyone, and I invited Lois. I got some zucchini artichokes pineapple pieshells mushrooms marzipan" . . . the list is mouthwatering, endless, but it ends. "And I was so relaxed," she says, "and everyone told me it was perfect, I should open a restaurant, everyone ate till their tongues swelled."

You remember marriage. Cooking. The perfect dinner party, passing the fresh-baked fruit bread again and again, urging everyone to have more, more, till Bob Weed with the glasses and thin dark hair to his shoulders said *no thanks* with an edge in his voice. *Mommy,* you think, *I no longer cook for men, I no longer eat till my tongue swells.*

She brings out coffee and cake, excellent coffee which you pass up—colitis—and Entenmann's danish, only fair but you eat it anyway. There is more to the story of the party.

"So when Lois came to say goodbye, I told her, 'Lois, I know you didn't invite me to your party and I just wanted to say, I know it was an oversight and I have no bad feelings and I want you not to have any bad feelings either.' And Lois went *heh heh*—she's such a jerk." The mother drags on her cigarette.

The father excuses himself and walks crookedly to the bathroom. The mother stands, follows him down the hall, tossing over her shoulder, "But, you know, I didn't want anyone to feel bad."

You sit, touched by her loyalty to him, embarrassed by her spitefulness, her pretense: to shame by being good. Something in this goodness shoves you, the daughter, into guilt: whatever anyone sacrifices, you must swallow. Her words come from your mouth with a certain inevitability as you fetch your lover her vitamins, make her tea, fuss and bother, care for her in that least personal sense of caring, do all this when you are angry because you are angry and then say, "I only did it because you said you wanted it," or—better yet—"I made you tea even though you always make just for yourself." Don't look at what you earn in your own mind, points for endurance, the sense of worth this gives you: power of the victim, trapped into it, and here at the source where you learned it—

Crash from the bathroom. You run to see. He's pulled over the bathroom shelf, broken the stained glass tissue holder she made last summer, carefully piecing together the blues, the ambers. She's looking at the broken tissue box, not crying but with a thin shake to her voice: "I can make another." Something grabs in your throat. She's locked up with him crashing into, peeing on, grinding food into, disrupting her world: the apartment.

"Go on," you say, "I'll clean up the glass."

You fetch the broom and dust pan. You want your lover here to rock you to tears, release. You're remembering, just before you got in the car to drive down here you drank tea together, huddled close to the stove, and she told you about a man who had fought in the French Resistance, a friend of a friend's. The Nazis tortured his six-year-old daughter. It worked—he betrayed his comrades. The comrades were caught and killed; the fighter and the little girl, released. Stunned, you asked, "What was their relationship like after that?" "He left," she tells you, "the daughter was raised by the mother, in England. He went to Barbados and lived alone, he saw no one." You agreed, how could he have stayed to watch her grow, asking, was she worth those lives, that betrayal? You had thought him brave not to kill himself, but now you wonder how he lived. Life seems suddenly fragile, like a glass precariously balanced, tumbling and crashing, at least let there be a daughter to sweep it up. Is this my gesture, so slight, fit for the century's last flutter? Daddy, mommy, did they betray themselves, was it for me?

8.
And where, you think later, at dinner, was he during the party given to spite Lois? Enjoying the perfect food, the perfect spite? Did he sit in a comfortable chair and eat what she brought him, dripping sauce into his lap, staring vaguely at who knows what? Did he wander puzzled, unfocused, through the company, sometimes chatting, sometimes so off the wall people would get fidgety, not know how to respond, as for example right now, as the mother goes into rhapsodies about Judith Jamison's dance solo, the father interrupts knowingly, "Didn't I give her a sweater two years ago?"

But this is the last meal of the visit, fish baked with grapefruit and banana, it is delicious. And time to leave, to drive north, get home by sunrise, but not before ice cream cake. The father puts spoonful after spoonful in his mouth, and so do you, slurping in delight, with two cups of tea, and some thanks that the mother puts the cake back in the freezer instead of leaving it melting on the table for you, the daughter, to poke at with a fork until there is nothing left.

It's not that I don't like the idea of raising my own food: a vegetable garden free from poison, fruit trees and vines, meat animals to use every single part, and a goat for dairy. I have at times participated in a small way in this cycle, feeding the chickens table scraps plus their own egg shells, baked first to destroy germs. (Is it a New Age sign that I feel dowdy saying the word germ like I believe in it?) I have carried water from rain barrels, mixed compost and chicken shit for the garden, dumped woodstove ashes in the outhouse to keep it fresh. I have done these things with pleasure. I have even read with interest about digging clay, about pigments found in plants, rocks, earth; about clipping sheep and carding the wool and spinning. I have thought longingly about building my own house, and have helped, in small and awkward ways, other women build theirs.

I like all this a lot. But it doesn't feel natural.

What feels natural is sidewalk. In the beginning was sidewalk and then a tree broke through. You walk blocks to the park, a breach in city discipline. Grass runs riot between the paved paths, and the lake where you rent pedal-boats for 50 cents an hour is crammed with teenagers peddling away. Kids feed bread to the ducks and watch them duck, like their name. It's only natural.

Natural is peaches, plums and red red tomatoes from Tony the vegetable man who drives through the neighborhood on Thursdays, though only a few years later tomatoes will come to the A&P in little plastic crates covered with cellophane. Natural is also canned stringbeans and boysenberries in heavy syrup; frozen corn, frozen french fries, frozen fish filets in a cardboard box with a picture on it of fish filets. You hate vegetables and fish, and love french fries and boysenberries, not to mention fried chicken tv dinners. It's only natural.

What else is natural? Old grey stone four-floor walkups and, once every few blocks, a fancy new red brick building with an elevator, front door buzzers, and lots of glass. Radiator heat is natural, and you know this has something, unspecified, to do with coal because the coal truck comes twice each winter to dump a mountain of shiny black lumps on the sidewalk. Flat metal doors rise up from the sidewalk and the super shovels the coal deep inside. Every building has these dangerous metal doors, you could be standing on them when they open, or if you don't look where you're going, you could plummet into the basement's deep hole.

Every building has a basement with mysterious smells and sounds. The furnace rumbles, the washing machine sloshes and overflows. When you are five you get lost in the basement looking for John the Super, who is naturally your hero, and you fall asleep behind the dryer. Your parents have half of Brooklyn out searching until John finds you, but all you remember is waking up in your bed and they're talking about eating out, the world's biggest, rarest treat, so naturally you want to go too.

Every building has a super who is in charge. If you play in the courtyard, the super might yell at you. But if it's your own building and something is wrong, you tell the super, he will know what to do. He could be Black and young, like John, or white and old, like Eddie next door. But if he's old he smells like whiskey. John knows everything. He teaches your mother to drive, he answers every single one of your questions, and he lets you come along when he makes repairs. It is not natural that he moves and is gone. No one moves, hardly. What's natural is to live in the same apartment your whole life, like Mrs. Larue and Miss

Dock in 3-C upstairs, they have the same blue-white braids pinned up on top of their heads, even though Mrs. Larue is tall and a widow and Miss Dock is small and round. Every day you bug them with questions until they give you two chocolate chip cookies and you go outside to play potsy, punchball or A-my-name-is, naturally with a Spaulding, pronounced spall-deen, the pale pink ball which everyone knows bounces best on sidewalk.

But if you're not playing ball, or following John around, or bugging Mrs. Larue and Miss Dock, naturally you're reading: backs of cereal boxes, other people's newspapers on the subway, and books books books from the library, four at a time and ten for summer. When you shove a book at your cousin come to play, and she complains, you snap, can't she read?

Natural is your parents working six days a week, except seven for Christmas and Easter. Natural is writing sales receipts, straightening and folding the underwear, wiping the glass jewelry cases with win-dex and a soft rag. Natural is varicose veins from standing ten hours a day. Natural is counting every cent that comes in or goes out, saving for when you're old, spending any available money on health, educa-tion and culture, like a cabinet position. Natural is renting, not owning. Apartments, not houses. Land is unnatural and buying it even more so.

Natural is taking the subway *Towards Coney Island*, to the end of the Brooklyn world, which *is* the world, the train rising up into the sky while Brooklyn rushes past. When at last you arrive, you eat a hot dog with sauerkraut that makes the roll soggy. But if it's summer, you get off the stop before, to find a patch of Brighton Beach not claimed by someone else's blanket. When your mother billows the soft faded brown and white flannel over the sand to lie in the blissful sun, you naturally snake your way through a

million bodies to run shrieking with joy into the
crashing waves of the vast green Atlantic.

inviolable space

You wanted your own room. With a door you could close.

You're talking to a new friend about why you left home when you were 18. "It was crowded, I had to get out."

"What do you mean by *crowded?*" your friend, a Black woman from Alabama, asks.

"Four of us in a four-room apartment, my sister and I shared a room."

She laughs, not unkindly. "There were eleven of us in a four-room house."

So you were lucky. Luckier than millions; luckier than most. You've known this all your life. It doesn't change the fact. You wanted your own room. You wanted some boundary, maybe drawn by some magically intervening grownup, Glinda the good witch in *The Wizard of Oz: Here,* she'd announce, marking the ground with a wand so long she doesn't even have to bend over, *this space is yours.*

There's the fake leather diary Aunt Etta gives you every single Hanukkah. It locks with the same key as every other fake leather diary in the nation. This constitutes some protection, but not enough. But you are sly. You're not allowed to close the bedroom door, so you hole up in the bathroom. You're not allowed to lock the bathroom door but you do anyway.

Open up, someone yells.
I can't, it's locked.
I told you not to.

I forgot.
So unlock now!
I ca-an't, I'm in the middle.
It's the surest defense you've ever learned.

The bedroom, aside from the door you're not allowed to close (and it's years before it occurs to you that this is odd), is full of Naomi and her phone. Which she pays for with her afterschool job, thus circumventing your father's political but also, face it, pathological aversion to phone company profits. AT&T represents everything his kids take for granted that he managed fine without.

But Naomi's hooked on the phone. Every night all week, Naomi talks on the phone while you sprawl across your bed and do homework, then fall asleep to the buzz of Naomi's phone voice. Saturday mornings, seven, eight o'clock, you wake to the buzz punctuated by an occasional snort of laughter. The buzz continues for hours or until interrupted by your mother winding up for a Saturday morning showdown. Needs have an absolute hierarchy, by size places—the Three Bears except there's four of you: first comes your father (often as interpreted by your mother), then your mother, then Naomi, and at the end, Vivian: you. Your mother needs a spanking clean apartment. Naomi needs to talk to her friends. You need to daydream and read, to float in unstructured time. Sooner or later, it erupts. You take this for granted.

Weekend nights Naomi's out, the bedroom's all yours, but it feels eerie, you have no habit of solitude and the opportunity's so fleeting, why bother to learn? Instead you choose TV or, if your parents have company, you hang out with them, eat and make conversation. Everyone says you're so smart, so amiable, such a lovely daughter. Every minute plotting your escape.

h a r l e m   s u m m e r

She was fat. That's the first thing, though it was important only on the outside. Inside—meaning, inside the movement—it didn't matter. There was one place it didn't matter.

he gave her valium, dexedrine, and a diuretic

That spring she had tried to kill herself and he, she was told, was saving her life. Picture her, seventeen, with her long brown hair, "blond" her people called it, and not until she left New York for California three years later would she discover that, in reality, both her hair and her skin were quite dark. She brushed her hair often and wore it pulled back with a clip or twisted in a bun, to be loosed at crucial times, usually involving men. So there was the hair, and orange lipstick, and a pale blue arnel dress, sleeveless, self-belted, with pleats. It came with a matching jacket and was made for women fifty years older than she was, but it's what fit.

That spring every day after work she'd stop at the Horn and Hardart and pick up a loaf of raisin bread and some peanut butter. She would carry these things on the subway in a brown paper bag back to her parents' apartment in Brooklyn and hide them in her dresser drawer, to eat secretly in the morning and at night. The skin on her arms and back was scabbed and scarred, as if time not spent eating was used to claw at herself, drawing blood.

he said, why do you pick at yourself, you think it'll make your parents good and miserable?

That summer she volunteered with a group working in Harlem. A hard worker, good with the children, reliable with their mothers, she always did whatever she'd agreed to and was astonished by the points this earned her. To her it was just bare minimum, but she'd worked for a living and many of the other white kids hadn't. She was working as a file clerk at the Motor Vehicles Bureau, way downtown. All day she collected piles of files from the various baskets and carried them into the dingy little alcove where she filed them alphabetically one after the other until they were all gone and she had to go collect more. At 4:45 she'd take the elevator down to street level and, breathing hot city air, she'd walk towards the subway. She learned the subway map by heart. She'd ride hanging onto the strap or, if blessed, sitting, nodding out on the little straw seat, the best seat because you didn't have to share it, no pressing thighs to contend with. Standing, sometimes she'd feel men pressing their things hard against her, disgusting and shameful. Somehow she had caused this. Or imagined it.

he said, there's no such thing as wanting sex too much—like money, there's no such thing as too much money

At 135th & Lenox she'd get off the train and come up for air, sweltering and moist that Harlem summer, the year before the riots. She must have attracted notice, she was white, but she was too young to feel scared. Didn't her presence indicate her good heart? And maybe people took it like that, because nothing bad happened to her, and she'd arrive at the tutoring center to work with her student, Thomasina Cook, only two years her junior. Thomasina would show up with her friends Julie and Gwen and they'd *kibitz* (her word, not theirs) the entire time she tried to work with Thomasina on her algebra. Thomasina didn't give a shit about algebra.

Thomasina stopped coming, and Sammy showed up, thirteen, with medium brown freckled skin and startling blue eyes. His little league team needed uniforms, and someone had suggested he write to local businesses for contributions. But Sammy couldn't read or write. He came to the project for a tutor, and he got her. Within three weeks he was reading, the whole little league team were her fans, and she had discovered it was easy to teach reading when the person thought there was a reason to learn.

By the end of the summer she was working several times a week with the five-year-olds, meeting in the apartment of one of the children's grandmothers, writing words they wanted on large cardboard slabs, following the practice of Sylvia Ashton-Warner teaching Maori children in New Zealand. These five-year-olds proudly took home their cards with words like *monster, antenna, saccharine* (which she used in the hot tea she always drank with Mrs. Leed when she'd first arrive from work, and they were fascinated by the bubbles it made. Pralie even asked for the word *effervescent,* off the saccharine bottle). The children returned to Mrs. Leed's with their tattered cards memorized, ready to dictate stories which she would write down and type at the project office and bring back for them, to use as texts. They told stories about their lives and imaginings—the dead man in the vacant lot, the block party, the monster whose home was the empty refrigerator carton, on which Pralie had printed in clear block letters BOX.

They were planning a public school boycott for the fall. In August they organized a special freedom school, with Black history and music and African dance, and meetings with parents and children about pushing on the Board of Ed to include these subjects and to integrate the schools. She teamed up with a lively seven-year-old, Lenora, dressed immaculately, her braids done up with red barrettes. Lenora could read already, fast, and they wrote a play together about Harriet Tubman. Lenora said she didn't want to go to school with white people.

"Why?" (The dominant sentiment at the time was integrationist, except for the Muslims; Black Power was two years away.)

"My daddy told me all about white people, how they so mean and ugly. If they come into my school, I jump out the window."

She thought for a minute. Finally she said, "Lenora, I'm white."

"You not white," Lenora responded as if it were the most ridiculous assertion.

"I'm not?"

"No." Lenora's scorn was affectionate. "You sort of pinkish brown."

The truth of this silenced her. Lenora looked at her confusion, seized her hand and began to drag her across the room, looking for something, a stack of paper on the table. Lenora picked up a sheet. *"That's* white," she said.

"Have you ever seen a white person?" She was beginning to understand.

"No."

Lenora's wisdom, Pralie's story about the monster in the box, buoyed her. So did weekend workdays, when project volunteers and community people would turn out to collect trash, build shelves, turn a junked-out basement into a classroom. So when they were organizing a rent strike on 132nd & 7th and needed people to hand out leaflets, she was there. A picnic? Creating a community library? She'd be there and they learned they could count on her, she learned she was being counted on, and the fat, the pocked skin, the blue arnel dress didn't matter. She didn't lose weight but the raisin bread and peanut butter slid away, an outgrown habit.

he said, do you think niggers like fat white girls?

When he said that, her stomach turned over. Why did he say that *word?* Was it to shock or shame

her? It was wrong. It was disgusting. She felt implicated because her parents were paying him $10 an
hour to save her from suicide and madness.

But is that what she thought? Was that why she
felt comfortable in Harlem? It was true that at the
first party she got asked to dance, and there was a
man she spent the night with, fully dressed, after
heavy kissing and breathing such that her underpants
the next day were stiff. Jimmy. She was afraid of
Jimmy (all over Harlem white girls were fucking, she
knew that).

*he said, you're ashamed of your body, show me your breasts,
come on*

She refused. He was her *doctor*. He shouldn't be
asking to see her breasts. He gave her the creeps. Her
skin, she noticed, was healing.

And the summer wore on, sweaty on the IRT,
Lenox Avenue line. Sometimes if she got off work
early she'd go to the cheap foreign films at Bleecker
Street or the Thalia, gobbling them up like the books,
James Baldwin, Gunner Myrdal, John Howard Grif-
fin, the Port Huron statement from SDS, films like
Black Orpheus, Forbidden Games, Bicycle Thief. Then she'd
get back on the subway and ride all the way uptown,
buy something to eat, usually ribs or chicken from
one of the stands on Lenox Avenue where they were
beginning to know her and say *hello*, and nobody
stared at her for eating when she was already fat. The
Muslim on the subway corner, somehow looking cool
and dry in a dark suit, would say *hi, blue-eyed devil* and
get her to buy *Mohammed Speaks*, the paper. They knew
her and she felt like she belonged to a life larger than
herself, a life in which change swooped down and
transformed people's lives because they were
together and could not be defeated. Didn't they sing
We Shall Overcome?

he said, aaah (the sound was like 'a' in jack, 'a' of dispar-
agement, not of gratification), every 20 years, 30 years, people
think they're going to change something—does anything change?

She didn't want his voice. She knew she was
looking at two ways of life, maps of two countries,
two planets, and one was staid, familiar, what everyone knew and was supposed to believe—*aaah, you get a*
decent job, you marry someone who'll be nice to you, not
drink . . . .

The other beckoned to her from her parents'
stories of the thirties and strikes, of Spain; from
Howard Fast's early novels (he had not yet written
the later ones), stories of Clarence Darrow, Paul
Robeson, men who did everything to fight injustice
(she had not yet discovered women). The children and
how they learned was change. The rent strike, the
community library in Mrs. Leed's apartment, that
was change. (And she didn't yet think it but somewhere she knew: she was healing. That was change.)

She did not know how to reconcile these stories,
these facts, with this doctor. She knew she should
stop talking to him about change. Maybe he had saved
her life but he didn't understand what was healing
her. She knew that whatever reconciliation took place
between her survival and the larger revolution would
take place inside her, without his knowledge or co-
operation or even comprehension. His maps were
stupid and useless. This summer she was in Harlem,
learning the street signs, tracing a new map. Anyplace
else she might wander for the rest of her life would
have signs written in different languages, assuming
there were any signs at all, but the map was drawn
that summer and it was hers.

he said, next week, same time?

Yes, she lied.

manhattan lay before me like the world

It was inevitable. I left Brooklyn.

My first apartment—I was eighteen—consisted of four dingy rooms on a back alley. My half of the rent was $41 a month, and I had my own room. Three locks on the door? Empty bottle crashing through the window, glass shattering into my bed the night before New Year's? Never mind, I was awake at 3 a.m. when it came crashing through, awake with my roommate Susan, laughing and smoking dope and there were no parents.

No parents. At first I knew only the absence of control, freedom to poke, to play with my time, food, waking and sleeping, what I saw breathed ate wore thought about. NO ONE COULD TELL ME WHAT TO DO. For months I put nothing on the walls in that apartment. First I had to discover blankness, a wall empty until I chose to fill it. Later I brought home postcards from the Museum of Modern Art: Van Gogh, *Sunflowers* or *Starry Night* and a Renoir nude whose body, soft, round, and luminescent looked something like mine. I put these cards up on the wall to entertain myself and to inform my guests of my cultural breadth. Plus which, with the Renoir, to remind them I was beautiful in some century.

My love affair with Manhattan began before I moved there. I was working several days a week in Harlem, and I deliberately chose to attend City College instead of Brooklyn to spare my parents' feelings by building a case of convenience: "I need to live closer to school and work." I saved my money, wrote down every subway token, every pack of gum. I could not say, *I need freedom. I need to get away from you*.

The city *was* freedom. In the city women and men my age slept together without getting married. People had parties with drugs. There were museums, libraries where I could read and listen to records for hours. Bookstores stocked poetry, philosophy, novels from Europe in different translations. Movie theaters ran foreign films in black and white, three for a dollar: *films*, not movies. About class struggle, sex, defiance; about ordinary people who didn't understand the sensitive suffering few. I wanted to belong to the sensitive suffering few. I could not bear to be identified with where I came from: Brooklyn, the clothing store my father and aunt owned where the whole family, including me, worked vacations and summers. Sensitive souls did not live in Brooklyn, nor did their families sell ladies' sportswear and lingerie.

My first home was on Central Park West and 105th—pre-gentrification, this part of the Upper West Side specialized in luxury buildings alternating with rattraps. I lived in a rattrap, but I was free. Free to hop on the subway, zip, the Village to Harlem, free to walk the endless crosstown blocks or the choppy numbered streets that whizzed by under my cheaply shod but strong feet. Manhattan lay before me like the world.

My mother called it *dangerous*, but I knew nothing would happen to me, and nothing did, though my building averaged one mugging a month for the entire time I lived there. She said I wouldn't eat properly, and she was right—this was before food stamps—but I never went hungry. Susan Blitzer and I stocked up on cans of Campbell's soup, Wonderbread and margarine, spaghetti and canned tomato sauce. (Our idea of cooking was frying onions for the spaghetti sauce.)

Susan and I met through her *roommate needed* ad on a Columbia bulletin board. She was older, twenty-three, small and thin, but we sort of looked alike, with our dark skirts, black turtlenecks and tights, long brown wavy-to-frizzy, depending on weather, Jewish hair. (We shared tips on how to make it hang smooth and straight.) An accountant's daughter from Long Island, her parents sent a modest monthly check and paid her expensive tuition at a small private college. I took notes in City College classrooms crowded as high school, resting my notebook on the wooden arm-shelf, my coat plumped up on my lap. I envied Susan her luxury education but not the strings attached to her parents' money, tugged during shrieking phone calls or the rare visit home.

We began with no expectations and hit it off instantly, soon spending hours at the table—the kitchen itself was nothing but a path between creaking appliances. The table was always heaped with papers, books, shopping bags, and evenings we'd clear a little space and drink cup after cup of instant coffee, reporting the events of our separate days. Here I learned to smoke. Here she'd test me on Latin translation and I'd critique her oral reports. Here we'd analyze in minute detail our not-that-frequent sexual activity, compare the men we slept with, vie with each other to define them by catchy phrases based on style of fucking, physical attributes, or memorable remarks. We listed these phrases on an empty pizza box, and they became our private code, periodically invoked and capable of reducing us to gasping tears: *dead fish* (we howled with laughter), *is it in yet?* (more laughter), *"was it good for you?"* (weak and wheezing by now). These raucous sessions were often far more fun than the sex itself, which we pursued largely in a spirit of curiosity and adventure; sex was what you did if you were free, rebellious and grown-up. Neither of us had done it enough to find it repetitious, though a couple of times right in the middle I found myself weighing which aspect to name this one by—*polka dot boxer shorts* or *"squeeze my balls, honey"*?—selecting for Susan, my excellently critical but supportive audience.

Who lived in our building? Students, like us. Old people, who didn't leave when most of their cohorts went—where? To Miami, their children, "rest" homes? And the former luxury apartments, one to a floor, huge, with views overlooking Central Park (never mind the muggings) and cheap—these were inhabited by families with young children, for whom I babysat as one of the ways I earned my living.

One of these families was the Johnsons, Marianne and George. Marianne was French, in her late twenties, and she had clearly married George, her fortyish American businessman husband, for his money and passport. Yet she hated the crudity of America, the difficulty finding decent food, wine, clothing. I had just read *Madame Bovary*, and I knew Marianne wanted to have an affair and maybe was having one. I'd show up to babysit for her three-year-old, Jean-Jacques, who had the reddest cheeks, the orangest hair, the bluest eyes—beautiful Jean-Jacques who could scream for a solid hour and who was so used to getting his way that my attempts to stand firm threw him into an existential crisis, *who are you?* he'd scream, *who am I?*

Marianne was never ready, but since she counted my hours from the time I showed up, I didn't mind. She was lonely for company and would lead me into her bedroom, plunk me down on the bed, and serve me drip coffee (which I was too callow to appreciate, it seemed bitter) while she'd parade around in front of me in her lace bra and slip (I was not too callow to notice how her breasts filled the lace cups and swelled above them). She'd take the glass stopper from the perfume bottle, inhale and sigh, and dab some perfume behind each ear and between her breasts. Once or twice she came close to me, so I could smell the perfume mixed with her own smell, and ran her wet-with-perfume finger along the back of my neck. "A delicious scent, no?" she'd ask, and I'd respond, "Yeah, really nice." She'd pull on black patterned stockings, a tight skirt and equally snug sweater, deep blue or red and scooped low to show off the swelling breasts. Her cheeks would be touched with blushon, her lids with blue or mauve, her lashes with dark black. ("You 'ave the most *byootiful* lashes," she'd tell me, singling out my single seductive feature. "Such lashes I would die for.") She'd stretch her mouth wide for the white lipstick undercoat, then the deep red-brown on top. "You look really pretty," I'd say, and she'd answer, "I'm going shopping, what does it matter?"

Then she'd leave, in a whoosh of perfume and lipstick smells, and I—wet and dazed—would imagine Marianne in a room with her lover, pulling the curtains, stripping off the sweater, unhooking the black patterned stockings, and I would tend to the monstrous Jean-Jacques, screaming by now for his mother.

That was Marianne, but there was also Mrs. Wisensky, who lived on the 6th floor—there were seven—and had lived there, she told me with her old-world accent, *almost twenty years.* Since 1946: this building was her first American home; she was, I realize now, a Holocaust survivor. Mrs. Wisensky was plump with dark hair she set daily in pin curls. Her lips, in the era of pale and pearly, gleamed dark red. She could have been 60 or 40, everyone over 25 looked the same to me.

There was Alfred, pale and blond as his Minnesota origins. I met him at a moving sale on the fifth floor and for two months he was oddly devoted to me. He'd take me out to eat (I would have gone out with Dracula for a meal in a restaurant), leave flowers and cookies in front of my apartment door with curious creepy notes, typed, like fortune cookie secrets—*Have you thought about your day's heart?* one asked, and another remarked, *Crossing the channel we find passion in the ice cold water.* Most spectacularly, Alfred would substitute for my broken alarm clock, showing up at my door in his pajamas at whatever time I'd request. He never entered my apartment or invited me to his, and I never pushed it, something about him made my skin crawl. Susan and I speculated endlessly about Alfred: he lived with his mother, no one had explained sex to him, he was waiting to propose, he had a girl back home . . . . One day I realized I hadn't seen him for a while and when I checked his apartment, he'd disappeared.

There was Theo, my first good look at an apolitical, unconflicted member of the upper class. He had an "income"; he needed to prove nothing. Theo had slept with Susan the year before I moved in, then switched to her then-roommate Priscilla, whose comings and goings were surrounded by mystery. (Priscilla had been beautiful, rich, suicidal; had disappeared suddenly with a small suitcase, and neither Susan nor Theo knew how to find her, though her parents had long since come for her things. I was the sane little drudge slated to replace Priscilla.) Now Theo went with Hattie, a beautiful young Black woman from Georgia, a nursing student, who worked five nights a week doing home care to make her expenses, while Theo, a Yale graduate, piddled away on some religion or philosophy dissertation.

Once Theo threw a party, with nothing but Budweisers and potato chips (I had hoped for more, given his income). Someone played over and over a new song, *C'mon Kitty, tell us about the boy from New York City*. Hattie kept hugging Theo, tugging him to dance with her while she sang along, *ooh ooh Kitty*. Theo was definitely not from New York City, but he was slick and he had swept Hattie off her feet. She told Susan she loved Theo but she knew he'd never marry her. I wanted to shove his long-legged grace, his sockless loafers, his perfectly faded levis down the elevator shaft.

And there was Marty Rothman in the apartment next door. Marty was a mediocre graduate student in English at NYU. He was short, very thin, waxy pale, with black hair which, had he grown it, would have bushed and curled about his head, but he kept it absolutely flat. We borrowed everything from Marty: coffee, cigarettes, cans of soup, his typewriter, a TV he himself had borrowed, and, above all, books.

Susan and I made fun of Marty. We said he was "faggy," which didn't mean gay (though we were, neither of us, above scorning deviation of any sort). No, Marty was determinedly, obnoxiously, repeatedly assertively het. He talked about sex continually, how he'd just gotten it, how he had to have it; regaled us with stories of sexual conquest.

The one that sticks is how he learned to like cunnilingus. Let me say I have never and still don't like this word, though I too have learned to like the act, going and coming, as it were. But the word in a man's mouth made me shudder, even then. I listened with sick fascination. He had always been squeamish about the taste, the smell. (Inside I was a hot tight ball of shame; outside, I lit a cigarette, Winston in those days, like Susan.) He had a date and when he showed up at her apartment, she was just getting out of the shower. I think there was a part about a floral douche. The point is, he tried it and, he said, *I developed a taste for it*. My response was complicated by the fact that he was telling me this story, I was sure, as a come-on. Men who ate cunt were supposed to be in demand. I put out the cigarette and stood up. *Well, Marty, gotta study*. He never pushed, I'll say that for him.

I'll say something else. I used to study at Columbia's Butler Library, because it was closer to my apartment than CCNY; because I liked to pretend I belonged there, with the oak and mahogany and open stacks; because I wanted to meet men with grace and money. Walking home meant crossing some of the most dangerous territory in the city, Columbus, Manhattan Avenue, now gentrifying at the speed of light; then, full of drugs, mugging, rape too, though we never said the word—admitting you were afraid of rape was like announcing you were virgin and proud.

Once I was coming home at ten at night, cutting over to 106th Street, the wide one—we didn't mention rape but I wasn't stupid—and staying close to the curb so I could run into the street if necessary. Someone was behind me. I stepped into the street, visible for blocks, and slowed down. No sound. He was waiting. I took a breath and began to run, not home—still blocks away—but to the *bodega* open late on Manhattan Avenue, between 106th and 107th. I was no runner and my arms were full of books, but I ran and he ran after me. Even now I need to convince you, myself, I didn't invent him. I was being followed. I ran to the *bodega,* pulled the door open and shut behind me.

The owner, a middle-aged Puerto Rican man, looked up, politely surprised. A woman came out from the back room. "Yes?"

"You have a phone?"

She shook her head, "No pay phone, on the corner," she trilled her *r,* "one hundred seven street."

I stared at her, the room went dark and light again. "Please," I whispered, as though my request were dangerous and not the man in the street. "Please, I'm being followed, there's a man out there. I have to call someone to meet me."

She came up close. Scent of rosewater, like my grandmother. "Yes, yes," she patted my arm, "here, the phone." She took me to the back room, gave me a chair, shouted in Spanish to her husband. He stuck his head out the front door, to look around. I dialed Susan. The phone rang and rang. I didn't have money for a cab, and besides, the idea of getting a cab in that neighborhood was ludicrous. I dialed Marty.

"Sure," he said, "I'll be there in five minutes," and

he was. When we got home he fed me brandy, the first time I'd tasted brandy, and he said, "Listen, any time you need to walk home late, just call me, I don't mind." But if he didn't mind, I did: I was leery of owing Marty anything.

Why did Susan and I call him "faggy?" Maybe what we meant was "pretentious." He affected a British accent, wore suits and ties almost always (he supported himself with an office job, so he could go to school nights), constantly quoted 18th century poetry, which he had chosen to specialize in because there would be jobs in it—naturally enough, hardly anyone could stand it. To me this seemed unbearably crass. People who didn't count every penny, make and remake their budgets, were unimaginable to me, but I also did not understand Marty's concern with survival. I expected my current financial status to rise automatically, like cream, as I moved through school; what was he so worried about? Most damningly, there was nothing natural, sexy, raw about Marty. He was the Bronx trying to be Oxford, a decidedly unhip aspiration in my judgement (I was Brooklyn trying to be Manhattan). In short, I was eighteen: nothing came easier to me than contempt.

Once I was over at Marty's watching TV, a murder, my favorite kind—he was in class, as usual. When he got home, he offered me a glass of wine, Beaujolais—I had never tasted it before. The movie ended and I glanced over at Marty. His mouth was trembling. He stared into my eyes, his face utterly open: the first genuine emotion I'd ever seen on his face. I didn't want to see his face like that. *Night, Marty,* my voice came high and quick, as I moved towards the door, *Thanks for the TV.*

The next day, when Susan got home, I'd tell her about Marty's latest come-on. We'd drink coffee together, laughing about who could we find for poor, desperate Marty. I'd leave out about his face.

But right then I just walked across the hall from Marty's apartment to mine where no one was home and no one could tell me what to do. I made myself a cup of coffee—it never kept me awake then—and sat alone at the kitchen table for a long time, smoking, dreaming, floating in my parentless freedom.

when   words   are   seeds

1.

Nothing grew from seed in the city. Everyone emerged suddenly, full-size, ahistorical. At parties, meetings, bus stops even, I'd mix with people I'd never have met growing up: people from Gainesville, Florida and Scarsdale, New York, Port Elizabeth, New Jersey and Montgomery, Alabama, not to mention Harlem and Bed-Stuy.

Each weekend we worked at creating a small park designed by Dan, one of the project organizers. The plan was to take a vacant lot piled high with rotting garbage, and turn it into something beautiful for the whole block to use: *today, 144th between 7th and 8th; tomorrow, all of Harlem*. We piled and hauled, piled and hauled, and under Dan's direction we built swings and seesaws from splintery scrap wood sanded smooth; planted scraggly little trees and papery tulip bulbs. My focus that summer was on Marcus, with his knockout gap-toothed smile. High school dropout poet and editor of the project newsletter, he spent hours welding metal sculpture that doubled as a jungle jim. The whole bus ride home from the March on Washington, Marcus and I necked, but after that he'd only toss me a cool hi.

I'd wander over to the project office. There was Harold the rent strike organizer with his small repulsive goatee. The whites of his eyes were yellow and his intensity scared me. One sweltering evening Harold gripped my hand so tight I winced, but would not jerk away. "All my life I been looking at black," he crooned. "Now I want some white." I admired Harold's tireless courage, but his longing turned my stomach, a sickish desire I was somehow responsible for, even though I knew there was nothing personal about this. It was as if huge masks had dropped before our faces, binding us to some painful and grotesque dance.

Men. Where were the women? Students and fresh graduates, mostly white, came to work in the project. Pinny from Radcliffe, with her cascading laugh and quick pat on the arm, whose real name was Elizabeth Mary. (She was the first in my experience of a long line of upper class WASPs whose family named them one thing and called them another, and who felt somehow confident enough to impose their odd family nickname on the world.) Pinny's grace and warmth fascinated me, but I was too young, awkward, and infatuated to penetrate the wheel of activity that surrounded her. Laura, a Detroit Jew, Bennington dropout, with huge compassionate eyes and dancer's walk, was easier; and Amelia, who was Black and sported a then-daring "natural." Amelia went to City College, like me, and we almost shared an apartment except no one would rent to us. She dated the white boys in the project. But the young neighborhood women mostly stayed away from us.

Powerful older women walked right in, women like Miz Orrie with thick bifocals, shoeblack hair and queenly bearing, women who could absorb almost any activity into their sphere and still be in command, who mothered us as they mothered entire neighborhoods. Miz Orrie owned the candy store where I taught kids to read and write, and she made them hop with *please* and *thank you* and *you talk to your teacher with respect.* I had taken to sitting crosslegged on the floor or clumsily submitting to dance lessons—the monkey, the jerk, *loosen up Miz Vivian,* they'd howl at my stiff shoulders. Anything to make them easy with the teacher. Besides I wanted to learn to dance.

I was having trouble with little Billy Rowlins, with his large solemn face, the worst eight-year-old anyone had ever heard of, wild in class, would not sit still, would not shut up, until finally I took him outside to the curb and laid it out. He had to behave or he couldn't come to class anymore. Billy sat stone face. My voice rose. What was wrong with him? Did he want to drive us all nuts? Why did he come to Miz Orrie's if he didn't want to be in the class?

Two huge tears ran down Billy's grave cheeks— from the scolding? the threat of getting kicked out? *Omigod,* I thought suddenly, *this is a child, an eight-year-old child,* and burst out crying myself. I put my arm around Billy and we sobbed together. Maybe I cried for needing so much to control him that I forgot he was a child. Maybe it was the sudden rush of helplessness. What did I know about teaching? What could I do for Billy? Transform his school into someplace he looked forward to going? Air his mother's stifling apartment, or fix the heat, come winter? . . . . I was naive but I knew I could fix nothing. Even this one child needed more than I had power to give.

I dug out a kleenex for myself and one for him. We blew. Then we traipsed back in to Miz Orrie's. Thus we bonded. Even the other children got that Billy had special rights in the back of Miz Orrie's, where he began to dictate slow but amazing stories for me to write down. Weekends Billy and I hauled garbage together.

And there was Charles, a pale thin white boy from Detroit with whom I fell and stayed in love for years, stunningly faithful considering the encouragement was so desultory. Charles hated himself, but I could never figure out why, since I adored him. He had dark very straight hair parted on the side and long enough to hang over his pale blue eyes, classic Irish, lapsed Catholic, exotic by Flatbush standards. Sitting or standing, Charles slumped, shoulders rounded, head slightly forward, a posture intensified by his habit of nodding in agreement or just to show he was listening. Which he was. Everyone loved Charles because he paid attention.

Charles had just dropped out of college for the third time, and I amazedly watched him bounce from job to school to some other job, never giving that much of a shit. Both his parents were lawyers. He had read everything, had been to Europe and all over the U.S. Once I asked him, "If you could live anywhere, where would you pick?" Asking felt heretical; as far as I was concerned, there was only one place to live: New York.

"San Francisco. It never gets really cold or really hot. It's right on the ocean and the coast is wild," he explained with huge hand swoops. (*Right*, I thought vaguely, *West Coast means a coast, an ocean*. Anything west of Jersey was Mars to me.) "The Pacific's dark blue, you know—and the hills, they're so steep they take your breath away. But the most beautiful place in the world is New Mexico."

"Isn't it desert?" I was mystified. Desert to me meant sand and cactus.

2.

Charles shared an apartment with Rudy, and sometimes with Rudy's younger brother Dan, who had designed the neighborhood park, and Dan's girlfriend Chris. Rudy was slight with light brown skin, chiselled dapper features, and a pencil moustache. Everything about him was quick, even his sharp brown eyes darted: Rudy thought, talked and moved twice as fast as the rest of us. You would never have picked Dan for Rudy's kid brother; he wasn't slow, but he was solid, well over six feet tall, a body you'd want on your side. His hands and feet were huge. He was darker than Rudy, his features fuller, hair longer and nappier, his speech, movements, deliberate, thoughtful. Everyone went to Dan for advice, which he would dish out solemnly, and then burst out laughing: *Aren't I full of bullshit?* he'd shake his head, *Do I know?*

Rudy and Dan were raised in South Philly by hard-working, churchgoing folk—a housepainter father who died of paint fumes and a nurse's aide mother who lifted and washed hospital patients into her sixties. They got their kids to college, where Dan studied architecture—he was still at Columbia when we met. Rudy had majored in science at Temple, and that summer he was inspiring kids all over Harlem to take apart clocks, wrecked motorcycle engines, anything with parts. He hustled five microscopes plus slides from NYU downtown, returning triumphant on the subway in less than two hours. He drove a van full of teenagers, including me, way up to Maine to watch an eclipse of the sun. He showed us how to protect our eyes with complicated cardboard-tinfoil contraptions.

Chris, a white woman from Connecticut, had dropped out of her elegant women's college. She was movie-star beautiful once you noticed, which her wire-rimmed glasses, baggy sweatshirt and jeans discouraged you from doing, a style I found utterly mysterious—in Brooklyn, we made the most of what we had. But Chris was morbidly shy, which she exhibited not by keeping quiet but by swallowing most of what she said. She and Dan were always moving in with friends and then out again. When they lived with Charles, I was afraid to drop in on him since I assumed they'd be in bed; I thought that's what you did when you lived together. I even hesitated to phone.

The summer before I finished college, I blew half my state-guaranteed student loan on a charter flight to Europe. Dan was working for an architect in London, I crashed with him for a couple of weeks, and then we traveled north. On the train to Edinburgh, we shared a compartment with a middle-aged English lady with tight grey curls and a face unlined as mine. Chatting the usual where were we from, where were we going, she turned to Dan and said, "You're not like the others, are you? You're so much nicer." She beamed.

"Excuse me," Dan nodded, casually standing to swing down his pack and walk out into the corridor. I fumbled for my plaid suitcase and followed, my face hot with anger, shame—his or mine? I felt his pride.

"That happens a lot," I said, not a question. I couldn't read his face. The British Isles rushed by the window. He jerked his head towards an empty compartment. "I can't ever be friends with someone white till we talk about it," he said, stashing our things in the overhead rack.

I felt embarrassed—I'd thought we already were friends. It took me a minute to realize he meant we were friends now.

As soon as we got back to London, I engaged in what I even then recognized as a protective sexual maneuver: while Dan slept, I let his roommate, a sophisticated pale Black journalist, whose people traced back to Reconstruction leadership in Missouri, seduce me. It was months before I told Dan about his roommate; years before I saw his obvious unasked question: *Why him, not me?* That had been the point, not to sleep with Dan. There was Chris—we weren't close yet, but I knew her. And, in another way, there was Charles. Sleeping with Dan would have been like giving up on Charles.

That winter—my last in New York—Chris and Dan lost their apartment. Rudy had returned to Philly to marry fabulous Terry, his childhood sweetheart. Charles was renting a room in some sleazy SRO hotel. So they came to crash with me and Susan. After a week on the living room couch from Susan's family's basement, they accepted my double bed, and I moved onto the couch. All winter the four of us worked, studied, came home nine, ten o'clock where someone would dish up sausage or spaghetti, maybe a bottle of cheap red wine. Dan used to get us hysterical with mock sermons, while skinny little Susan stepped into Dan's vast shoes and danced around the apartment to Smoky and the Miracles sobbing *Tracks of My Tears*.

That was the winter I figured out that couples who lived together were not constantly fucking, and when Chris and Dan found their own place I'd drop in on them often. They were the couple so grounded they drew us to them, especially Dan, with his welcoming grin: *Hey*, his face would light up, *look who's here*. They were so stable they always knew where everyone lived, how to get in touch. Several times I tracked down Charles through them, but that was after I'd left New York for good. Civil Rights had become Black Power, no longer my movement. All New York held now was friends, and I was twenty, new friends lurked everywhere. I chose the Bay Area, drawn by activism and by Charles' descriptions, and approached graduate school like a paid adventure, occasionally attending classes, sopping up high culture and Berkeley nuance like the greedy alien I was. I moved into a collective house with a lemon tree growing in the backyard—I had never imagined lemons outside supermarkets—and I sent home a number of postcards describing the miracle of a backyard tree with a ripening lemon.

Five years from the day I met Charles, I got married—not to Charles, though he showed up with Chris and Dan for the wedding party in my parent's same old Brooklyn apartment. I took note. It was 1969. Dan's was the only Black face at the party.

Afterwards, I cried for hours in the bathroom. Charles had gotten quickly drunk and gone off with his arm around my friend Eileen—*isn't she pretty?* he said over and over till I wanted to stab both of them through the heart with my mother's best carving knife, dangerously close at hand. Not only that, on his way out he untangled from Eileen for a minute to put his arm around me. *I never really told you how I feel about you,* he said. I had just gotten fucking married. Besides, I knew, even at 23, that Charles would have said this to me under no other circumstances. Still, three years later and twenty minutes after deciding to leave my husband, I was on the phone to Charles. We even slept together a few times, but it never took.

3.

The summer before I started teaching, I had an abortion, a million reasons why this was not a good time to have the baby I assumed I'd have sometime soon, and within a week after the semester started, I had left my husband. Walked out of a marriage and a fireplace-wood-floors house. We were all doing it, but some women who had gotten houses also had sense to keep them. Or take the cash.

I moved into a concrete box. Five apartments hid silent, invisible neighbors. Behind the door that became mine were four tiny box rooms painted white over orange to retain a slightly orange julius glow. No furniture. Living room filled with pillows, a borrowed mattress and several plants—one I called elephant leaf, high as my eyebrow; tiny baby's breath; three wandering jews, which I hated to hear named by others, but in my mouth the name was a blessing.

My time in this room was calm, sane, glorious even. I was a new teacher—part-time, I was supposed to be writing my dissertation—and I loved to prepare for class. I oohed and aahed over everything my students did, like a new mother entranced with her baby's smells. I basked in the late afternoon sun, listening to music. I saw the blank walls as a challenge, put up posters for women's liberation, including the famous *Fuck Housework!* and a quote from *Moby Dick*, illustrated by a line drawing of a huge foot slicing the water beside a tiny spiralling body. The text—*and Pip saw God's foot on the treadle of the loom and spoke it, and therefore his shipmates called him mad*—served as ammunition (you could hardly argue with God's foot) in support of visions that looked crazy to others. Like my choice of solitude and a box over a nice house and a decent husband who worked steady and neither drank nor ran around. That was supposed to have been plenty.

The bedroom sported another mattress, also on the floor, a tensor lamp and a TV I bought for $15 from someone leaving town. The tiny study was dominated by a fabulous desk left by the same person who sold me the TV. The desk depressed me with its dusty slate top. It craved important work. Going from bedroom to bathroom, I'd avoid the sight of the desk, the books neatly shelved, waiting for someone who didn't exist yet.

The kitchen and bathroom were another matter. In the kitchen I ate. Ate and ate and ate. Brought home Sara Lee cakes and half gallons of ice cream, bags of food which cost huge amounts of money I didn't have, from 24-hour grocers located strategically all over Berkeley and Oakland. I ate, stuffing it in at such a pace you'd have wondered, *what's the hurry?* There was no hurry: I was seeking the pace. Inside that pace was not an inch, not a second . . . to feel . . . what? Who knew? Against that terrifying vagueness, I ate, careful to drink fluids, to ease the evening's next segment: when every last speck of food was gone, I'd go into the bathroom and throw up.

Into the void, figuratively speaking. I was discovering the void, God's foot notwithstanding. My apartment was inviolable. No one else came there, unless asked by me. No one moved the cup from the sink, the toothpaste from the toilet top. No one took out the garbage or brought in a book of matches. Whatever happened there I made happen.

All winter I managed to show up for class reasonably prepared. I read and returned student papers. I met friends for various meals, talked on the phone occasionally. From outside no one would have imagined what I did inside my orange julius walls.

Some mornings I woke up, tongue swollen, head throbbing, and could find no reason to get out of bed. I'd tell a friend I'd phone, and wouldn't. I'd plan to audit a seminar related to the dissertation I was supposed to be writing. I'd even get dressed, change my clothes three or four times in an agony of self-consciousness, step out of my box apartment into the street and start toward campus. I'd cover a few blocks before figuring out that the day was 20 degrees warmer than my wool skirt and sweater could tolerate. The sun closed in. I was sweating. I could barely move. I turned around and walked home, very slowly. To my car, to the market, to the kitchen, bathroom, oblivion.

It wasn't just the void. When I left my marriage, my fantasy about Charles, the one good man, had sustained me. But Charles, with all his kindness, felt overwhelmed by me. He wasn't enough, was how he put it, though I of course understood that I was too much. I would have gone on trying to contain myself, but he wrote a short note honed to zero ambiguity.

So there I was. I'd had an abortion, left my husband, given up finally on Charles: all things the women's movement had in one way or another made possible. I was newly single, heterosexual, and most men made me feel bored or homicidal. In my CR group we were reading about lesbians—not hot wet desire but the sensibleness of it. How it suited women's liberation. The very sensibleness made me nervous. Over afternoon coffee Pat would sigh, *I wish*

I could find a man like you. We'd laugh. The next night at dinner, I'd be saying the exact same words to Louise. We all said it.

4.

And there was Clare. I met her in a CR group, and when I had announced at my first meeting—to my own surprise—that I was thinking of leaving my husband, Clare had put her arm around my shoulders and said, "Me too!" so emphatically we burst out laughing—though she didn't leave for years. By then, I'd lost track of her and only learned that she'd moved to Sweden with her daughter Mira because I eventually became lovers with a woman whose daughter used to play with Mira.

Clare was beautiful. Like most women, perhaps especially Black women living in a mostly white world—her father was a doctor and she had been raised upper-middle class, always the token—she thought she was ugly. But listen, I mean beautiful. Cashiers in supermarkets would ask for her phone number, even when she bought pampers. When Clare smiled not just her mouth but her eyes, her whole face lit up, and three feet around, the room was radiant. Her hair was always covered with bright scarves tied in back—purple, magenta, seagreen prints. Beneath the scarves her hair was natural, meaning not an Afro and not straightened. Only in extreme intimacy would she take off the scarf so her hair showed. We became best friends and she took off her scarf in front of me maybe four or five times: showering, dressing, and once in grief, when I called it a *shmate* to make her laugh.

Clare wanted to be a writer. She didn't work outside the home, she and her stodgy lawyer husband had agreed she'd get to write for two years, one of which had expired, and she hated herself for not writing more. But in our CR group, she read a poem about herself, her mother and her daughter, a cycle of restraint and disapproval that made me gasp.

Spring came after months of bleak rainy isolation. For 13 months women in my department had argued, fought, petitioned for, and finally won a women's literature class, and I got to teach it. That first day the room was packed with women, half of them non-students. They didn't care about grades and credits. They were looking for women. Class time filled up with discovery—de Beauvoir, Woolf, Angelou (first mention of daughter-rape), Giovanni, Plath, Toni Cade (not yet Bambara), Tillie Olsen, Shirley Williams, Alta (*euch, he said, yr having yr period*), Judy Grahn . . . . And spilled over. We met at night, different apartments, potlucks, picnics, seven women made a film together and showed it all over the West Coast for the next couple of years. The energy was extraordinary.

Clare had joined the class to glean inspiration for her writing, and we began hanging out in earnest. She helped me prepare for class. We talked continually about the readings. We shared journal excerpts. We found countless excuses to be together amazingly often, considering I worked for a living and she had a husband and child.

In the civil rights movement I had been close to several Black men and many children, and had admired a couple of the older women. But between me and most of the women my age was an edge and the edge was the men. Clare was the first Black woman I loved. She was more than used to whites, but I was her first Jew, her first shopkeeper's kid. We told stories endlessly. From Clare I learned about being a doctor's child and driving across the country to visit your grandparents, knowing there was scarcely a place where you could pee, eat, or sleep, because of segregation. She had spent her junior year in Sweden. "I felt unaware of color, they just treated me like a person. You know how rare that is?" In turn she pumped me for tales of the claustrophobic Brooklyn apartment, of the little fat girl who refused to stop healing.

Talk talk talk. Intense, constant, primal. We laughed raucously, or in silent, side-splitting spasms. We held hands across the kitchen table. We fussed with each other's sleeves and collars. We sprawled on my living room mattress. She'd stroke my arm or my back. I'd lie with my head in her lap while she read out loud poems by another woman we'd never heard of until that moment. We could not keep our hands off each other—her husband joked that we were glued.

On my way home from Clare's, or after she'd left, the mattress still warm with her body's imprint, I'd zip over to an all-night market. Once—with great difficulty—I talked to Clare about what I called "gorging." I didn't know the word *bulimia,* or that other women did it, or that ten years down the road it would achieve disease status. I expected disgust, criticism. How can you be a radical and waste food? How can you be attractive and throw up?

"Doesn't it hurt your throat?" she asked with characteristic sympathy. "I hate to throw up."

It was the end of one of those long June days just turned dark. I was walking by People's Park, which a couple of years before had been liberated, as we said; then reoccupied. This was some kind of celebration, people were drumming and chanting. I could smell dope and cheap wine. Orange fire blazed from trashcans. My husband and I had been to People's Park a few times in its heyday—once I even baked cookies and brought them to a community garden work session. I don't know what I'd expected, but people were busy working, sweating, backs or knees bent. I felt stupid with my cookies and husband and graduate school.

Now the faces close enough for me to see them were all men. Where were the women?

"Hey, honey." Someone passed me a joint, white hippie, bony, scraggly beard. "Aren't you scared being here alone, a chick like you?" His hand ran down my arm, brushed my breast—I had not been touched there for months. Disgust fear longing rose simultaneously—

"Keep your hands off me," I sneered, my arm swung out to block his.

"Look bitch," he snarled, "you think I want you, fat ugly broad like—" I didn't wait for the sentence to end, I turned and ran out into the darkness, clumsy, sweating, stung in spite of myself *fat ugly you think I want you.* I'd heard it before, the white men's line, while the Black men went, *you prejudiced?* You were just supposed to fuck them, that's all, whenever they wanted—fuck now, fuck often. Meat. I knew all this, why was I shaking?

Five minutes after I got home, Clare called. She wanted to stop by on her way home: "I'll bring ice cream."

"Yay, Clare," I hung up. I knew ice cream now meant throwing up later, but then what didn't? We stuck the ice cream in the freezer and sat at the fold-down kitchen table to smoke the roach left over from the bony hippie—somehow I'd ended up with it. I was telling Clare about him, the edge of violence, everything but the lurch of longing, and suddenly I felt it. Through the eyes. Between me and Clare a sexual flash passed across the table, through the eyes, palpable as heat, as the familiar groin thrill contraction *omigod,* I thought, *I got turned on to Clare.*

I had no idea whether she'd felt it too or noticed anything. I could not be acting normal, I was babbling about something, she was looking at me funny. I stopped.

"I better go to bed," my voice sounded hollow and my laugh false. "I'm exhausted."

"Ok," Clare looked startled but recovered instantly, and goodnatured as ever stood up to leave. But when she went to hug me, "night," I pulled back slightly and lost my balance and we both laughed a bit forced, and she left.

Then I remembered the ice cream. I was embarrassed to have sent her home without her own ice cream, but of course I ate it, the whole half-gallon, spoon after spoon, and threw it up, still cold and sweet.

5.

It was summer. I'd been offered a teaching job in Silver City, hundreds of miles away. I was no longer casual about leaving friends. And Clare—I couldn't imagine it. On the other hand, I had groomed myself through nine years of higher education for a teaching job, and I knew you didn't live somewhere because of your married friend. The moment across the kitchen table I chalked up to strong dope and "not being myself." July raced by. I was trying to write my dissertation; restless days, jagged nights. Between food, speed and marijuana, I was almost never just alive on my own steam. One morning after a night up late with food of every description except healthy, I heard someone knock. I was groggy, my throat felt like it had been sandpapered a couple of layers down. I pulled on a t-shirt and jeans and staggered to the door. Clare and I never dropped in on each other unannounced. But there she was.

We looked at each other for a long minute. Then she stepped inside and burst into tears. "Jonah's dying," she said. "He has cancer." Jonah was her downstairs neighbor, a poet, and, I realize now, gay, though that was never said. *Cancer?* Jonah was our age. I put my arms around her. I could feel her ribs shake as she sobbed. I caught words, *pain   wouldn't   should've made him doctor fault should dying* Then she pulled away for a second. "He's the only one I feel close to besides you—you're leaving, Jonah's dying. How am I supposed to bear it?"—her words collapsed into my neck, more sobs, *selfish Jonah ashamed alone*. He was dying.

I held her very tight, her body shuddered against mine. *My neck is wet with Clare's tears,* I marveled. After a while I got the toilet paper and she blew her nose loud, like a honk. She gave a little snort of laughter. She took off her scarf and hunched on the mattress on the living room floor, spent and miserable. I stroked her hair.

"You took off your *shmate*," I said, and she snorted a little more. She looked at me, face open as a child seeking solution from some omnipotent adult: God's foot; Glinda the good witch.

"Have you eaten breakfast?" I asked. A level I could handle.

"No."

"I'll make you toast." But of course I had no bread, no food at all, having eaten everything the night before. I had to get something for Clare. "Wait here," I said, "I'll be right back."

"I don't need anything," she argued, but not so forcefully as she might have. I ran down the block to the diner.

"Toast," I said. "Buttered toast to go," and ran back with the toast to Clare, who carried on over the toast like it was Marie Antoinette's cake: "It's delicious, mmmm, just what I needed," until finally I said, "Clare, it's just white bread toast," and we burst out laughing at the tender non-solution to inalterable pain.

6.

A couple of weeks before I moved to Silver City, I ran into Dan on Telegraph Avenue. We hugged, a bit tentative—who knew what a few years had done to anyone? He had come to teach at the University, Chris and his mother Ella would join him in the fall.

Then he said, "I just claimed Rudy's body."

"You *what?*"

"I just got back from Philly, I had to claim his body."

Rudy. Dead. He had become impossible, abusive. Terry had finally taken off, escaping what Dan called *insatiable despair*. "No reason, just angry, Black and angry, nothing had gone the way we thought, no revolution . . . . He quit his job. He fought with everyone. He stopped writing. Stopped answering the phone. Finally, I flew back to Philly to see what the fuck was going on, couldn't find him, flew back home and there's a letter from Rudy saying, *Check the river, brother, I'm there*. Flew back again, and he was. Drowned in the Schuykill."

He shook his head. "I don't forgive the world, but I don't forgive him either. He could've hung on. He had me and Chris. He had Ella. He drove Terry away or he would've had her too. Where were his guts? *Where were his guts?*"

I'd never seen him so angry. We stood in the Berkeley sun, almost ten years after we'd quietly stormed out of the train compartment together. I wondered, was it guts? What part was men and women, black and white? Why could Dan always make me feel loved? How had Terry known to save herself? Why had Dan survived and Rudy gone under? *Why him, not me?* I thought of Rudy's quick-silver energy, the eclipse he taught us to see without danger.

7.

Summer ran out. I moved to the new city, new job, new apartment with friendly neighbors. Within three weeks I'd jumped into bed with a woman. I felt like I had landed on a delicious, frightening planet Earthlings didn't know about and couldn't understand, though I tried to write Clare about it. (I thought but did not write, *wait till I see you*.) She wrote back about her baby, her boring husband, Jonah who got sicker and sicker and died before Halloween.

Thanksgiving I went home to Berkeley, but it no longer felt like home. I eyed my friends with suspicion. They were straight. Were they? I went to a meeting of my old CR group and everyone had questions, but Clare, like Abou Ben Adhem, led all the rest. *Do you hate men? Do you hate straight women? Do you want me to be a lesbian? Do you want to sleep with me?* This, in front of nine other women. We had little time alone. I was impatient with her grief about Jonah, with her continued marital complaints—*Men!* I thought, contemptuous as any convert. Besides, I had earned my own living since I was eighteen years old, including through my marriage, and I had no children. I simply didn't grasp her sense of economic dependency. I just thought she was bourgeois. When she told me the thought of being a lesbian frightened her—she already felt so marginal and alienated—I heard this as criticism, that I was weird.

I returned to Silver City, my new life. Clare's letters were short and superficial, boring even. Where was she in those letters? She promised to visit, but her family kept asserting needs, and I felt hurt and judgmental.

My coming out euphoria had crashed on the genuine difficulty of creating any intimacy and I felt, again, alone. Teaching full-time demanded nightmarish guard duty against exposure as a fraud. Every class took days of preparation, and I had, in all, 112 students to whom I felt compelled to compensate for every cruel or indifferent teacher they'd ever had. I slept three hours a night, and slid again into a cycle of

speed, food, vomiting. Somewhere around March I
fell apart, crawling out of bed to teach, coming home
to soak in the huge tub I shared with two other
apartments. I stopped writing letters, turned off my
phone and waited for equilibrium to re-emerge.
When it did, I reached across a small chasm to phone
Clare.

*The number you have dialed—525-7737—has been
disconnected.* No new listing. Disappointed, a little
relieved to put it off, I assumed I'd run into Clare
sooner or later. It was a while before I heard from the
woman whose daughter had played with Mira:
Clare's stodgy husband had joined some ashram,
Clare and Mira had gone to Sweden. No address. She
wanted a clean break.

By now Mira is a grown woman. Clare must have
grey in her hair. I became a writer and wonder if she
did too. If she still wears scarves. If she still feels "just
like a person" in Sweden. If if if . . .

. . . if I could see her now, I'd bring her toast,
lightly buttered. Then we'd sit on something soft in a
private timeless room and talk talk talk until we
figured out what we wanted from each other.

8.

Chris joined Dan in Berkeley, and with Dan's mother
Ella, they worked hard at family, made once more a
home where friends gathered. Dan taught
architecture, Chris trained as a carpenter. Together
they rebuilt a Berkeley dump into an airy open space
with a huge round kitchen table. They had a baby—
Chris proudly showed pictures of the home birth—
and buried the placenta in the yard to nourish a young
tree, an African tradition. They nursed Ella through a
slow decline.

But when I visited, something was off. We talked,
we all talked, but I sounded like a leaflet—even I could

hear it but I couldn't stop. I wanted to hang out with Dan and drink cheap wine like we used to, but I sensed the edge of sexuality that had brushed our friendship, saw his charm rooted in an ease and confidence Chris simply lacked, noticed the space he occupied. I channeled what I had to Chris. Dan would drift off to bed, sullen and rejected, while Chris pinned me with need: in her carpentry collective the only het, in her family the only white, in her life the one who wasn't Dan. I'd leave drained and invisible. They had been my friends but I didn't want the weight of their symbolism, or the task of critiquing their feminist consciousness. It was easy to lose contact.

Years later, living in northern New Mexico, which was not sand and cactus but pink-brown rock, shadow, and in April a million furious blooms—the most beautiful place I'd ever seen, as Charles had promised—I dreamed Chris and Dan had split up. When I dropped a casual note asking how things were, it was Chris who answered, and it was true. Dan had lost his job and had turned first bitter, then strangely mystical: *He was consumed,* she wrote. She sent me a picture of their teenage son, whose custody they shared. And she told me what I'd never known, that it was the postcard I'd sent when I first arrived in Berkeley—*There's a lemon tree in my back yard with a lemon on it!*—that had planted the first seed of California in their hearts, as Charles with his stories of the wild coast and breathless hills of San Francisco had planted it in mine.

Not until I write and read this story does it occur to me, in a flash of loss, that we might have sat around the huge wooden table and talked about it, us, what was happening, the sand shifting under our feet. Dan had taught me the opening line: *I can't be friends with someone straight until we talk about it.*

s h e   b e c o m e s   a   w r i t e r

It was the time. Just as we chanted *every mother a willing mother / every child a wanted child*, we considered every voice a needed voice.

I started writing when I still thought all we had to do, each of us, was articulate our own corner of experience and stick up for it. The rest would take care of itself. I believed that women wanted, needed me to write. God knows I wanted them, needed to hear their experience, my experience, any woman's experience given language. My friend Rosa and I wrote a song to an African chant. The first verse, classic in its analysis, went:

> *we've been fucked over / we've had enough*
> *we'll find each other / we'll break our chains*

But my favorite verse went like this:

> *we are all poets / we are all prophets*
> *we have our visions / we must cry out*

More and more of us wrote poetry journals stories, hundreds of women crowded into women's open readings. That's how I began to write. As if a million mamas crouched down to eye level while I took my first step, each of them crooning, *sweetheart, come on, I'm right here, you can do it.*

There was no one who said, *who do you think you are, anyway?*

> *who does she think she is? a woman*

But that's a lie. Of course there were people who said, *who do you think you are*, people who existed all around me and even in me.

> *who cares about your stupid life, your stupid boring*
> *life   all over the world are people more interesting*
> *than you*

or, alternately,

who cares about your stupid life, your stupid lucky life
all over the globe people suffer worse than   fight
harder than you

WHO DO YOU THINK YOU ARE?

I begin to recognize these opposing voices as a single voice

> *boring lucky trivial*

its true message

> *shut the fuck up stupid worthless bitch*
> *WHO CARES   about your stupid trivial*
> *boring life your stupid lucky privileged life your*
> *pathetic life your angry life your fat life your fat*
> *gluttonous life your jewish life your petty jewish life*
> *your lesbian life your sick perverted lesbian life your*
> *worthless   worthless   life*

The summer I crawled out of my bathtub, I moved to a shack in the country outside Silver City, to write my dissertation. My dissertation was the last labor of Hercules. It was my ticket to job security (ha, the big laugh was I got dumped by the English department and finished my dissertation in the same year). The dissertation was a mountain, sometimes rock and sometimes cotton batting, but it stood in the way of any other thing I might ever write or even do. I didn't believe I could or would complete it. Other people could do such things, but not me.

> *kept at it   woke   read   wrote   thoughts into*
> *words*

The shack had a name, Trillium, for the flower I'd never seen before and which I learned not to pick: they never grow back. My first day at Trillium my skin crawled. It was old, filthy with suspicious country dirt. Who knew what lived inside creaky rough wood only partly covered by cracked green linoleum; in the high hidden sleeping loft; in the outhouse: *if you eat meat,* the note said, *don't throw the scraps in the outhouse.* Why not?

By the second day, the stillness claimed me. Life was not worthless or stupid. It was summer and a plum tree in the front yard swelled heavy with tiny green plums so sweet and soft they were almost jam; the plums of my summers had been purple and thickskinned, bred to travel. I wandered around creaking the floor. To sweep I opened the door and whisked everything out: cobwebs (spiders had free rein along the ceiling and upper walls: the floors were mine), ashes, matchsticks, dead bugs, bits of catfood from Krupskaya, the black and white part-Siamese with the absolutely Siamese voice.

I'd wake in the high huge loft bed, Krupskaya nuzzling my face to let her out into morning. There were no locks. No one came uninvited. I woke and read, and after a while climbed down from the loft to fetch water from across the field, lugging the five-gallon jug in my backpack. My arms grew strong from the slight insertion of physical labor into my day. I'd rinse out the coffee pot, dumping the grounds into useful compost. There was a cycle of life and I was admitted. Even the ashes found use, to keep the outhouse sweet, and I carved a wooden holder for the toilet paper roll, and hung it with twine.

After the first coffee, I'd empty the chamber pot to air in the sun; heat water for washing, face first, then armpits, neck, the rest would wait for swimming. Then I'd sit at the desk, drink coffee and write. Slept, woke, read, made notes. Climbed out of bed to fetch water. Sat at the desk drinking coffee, pounding my Smith-Corona.

thoughts are words   finding the words

For a break, I'd pick plums or wildflowers or vegetables from the garden. It was solitude without prison, without claustrophobia. I was not obliged to wait until everyone else was asleep or busy so I could scoot by unobserved. At Trillium my space was the whole outdoors. Creatures went about their own business, passing across my field but demanding nothing. I was neither visible/self-conscious nor invisible/erased. I simply was.

I can't remember if I ever binged with food that summer, if I ever bent over the outhouse hole to disgorge what I'd swallowed. Somewhere the habit slid away.

> *the imitation leather diary with the lock anyone could open   pounds of food charging up and down her gullet   the door she couldn't lock   the girl who never learned to say no or yes because she got told   everything*

Around three in the afternoon, when the air in the shack was too heavy to breathe, I drove to the lake. I cannot for the life of me remember what I did for a bathing suit. There were no mirrors in the shack. I swam, lay in the sun rewarding my body for its labor, and after a while I forgot for hours, sometimes for days at a time, the critical appraising eyes that make the body a thing. I read wrote carried water swam. My body was where I lived, happily finding my muscles, my uses; my own weight.

> *her own names*

My own names. At dusk I'd meditate, letting the day's thoughts and images wrap me with a warm bee-like hum. Then I'd cook, plain but plentiful, eat from a bowl with chopsticks. I'd walk miles along the road and never see anyone, except I'd hear dogs yelp as if walking were criminal; some, unchained, ran up to me barking fiercely, their happy tails betraying them as a soft touch. There were no accusations. No one told me what to feel think say do. I'd walk for hours, circling the neighborhood. Then I'd sit at the desk again, and write

past reason past anyone's caring even her
own to become habitual to have words
ready when she wants them she wakes she
reads she finds words and uses them over and over
until they become hers

the fake leather diary the maps learned in
harlem clare's scarves i can't be friends until we
talk about it

This new habit.

muriel rukeyser you asked what would happen if
one woman told the truth about her life you said the
world would split open you were talking about käthe
kollwitz but was it true? then? now?

runaway bunny

My sister Naomi is about to drive her son Luke into town for the 11:30 bus to New York. Every time he leaves—to go to college, back to the city, anywhere—Naomi grieves. She cannot quite accept that he has separated and will continue to separate from her.

At least she's honest about it.

"I can't bear it." Naomi screws up her beautiful barely aging face. "I know I have to and I even know I will. But I can't stand it." She doesn't say this in front of Luke.

In my twenties and thirties I made sure never to put less than 2500 miles between me and my family. Now I live only five hours away, practically next door. I'm visiting for the weekend with my lover Kate, whom Naomi adores, at least partly because she is perceived as having stabilized me into regular visits. Right now we're standing around Naomi's kitchen with Mario, Naomi's lover, while she fusses over Luke, who's off in his room packing. She's trying to help him get ready.

"Ma, I know how to pack." Luke sounds more affectionate than annoyed. "Why don't you . . ." his voice trails off as Naomi sweeps into the kitchen. Everywhere Naomi goes, she sweeps, something about all that hair.

"I have to control myself," she says, "I'm getting on his nerves. Here." She hands Kate a children's book. "This is the one I told you about, *The Runaway Bunny*."

It's made of soft paper, for very small children. Kate takes it and flips the pages.

"This is ominous," she says.

"Ominous?" Naomi's incredulous.

"I thought so too," Mario smirks at Naomi. "Ominous."

"It's my favorite children's book." Her voice is slightly plaintive.

I take the book and flip to the first page. The paper is thick and durable, beautiful crayon drawings, bright colors.

> "I think I'll run away," said the baby bunny
> to his mother.
> "If you do I'll follow you everywhere and
> you'll never escape me," said his mother.

I get chills. Ominous is right. I have no children and have spent considerable chunks of my life trying to escape my own mother, who's having trouble walking to the corner by herself these days. Just this morning over breakfast I was encouraging her to take small walks, to concentrate on balance. *Notice where you put your feet, that's all,* I tried to sound reassuring. *Pay attention, you'll be ok.*

Kate grabs the book back. "Listen to this." She reads aloud:

> "I'll turn into a sailboat," said the baby
> bunny.
> "If you do," said the mother, "I'll become the
> wind and blow you where I want you to go."

"That's the key phrase," Mario's eyes light up a bit crazily behind thick glasses. "That's it, where *I* want you to go."

Mario's mother lives a good 1,000 miles south in Florida, in a small depressing apartment of which she is, from his perspective, embarrassingly proud. He's always buying vases, posters, dried flowers for her apartment, which he carries in a huge unwieldy package on his yearly visit. He has a daughter a little older than Luke who makes a living as a potter in Amsterdam, an independent young feminist; but he seems to

feel guilty. Maybe he thinks her distance means failure, like his from his mother.

"You don't like *The Runaway Bunny?*" Naomi is
wondrous, but distracted. "I *love* it, it's so comforting." Her eyes follow Luke, who drags his pack out into
the kitchen. It's nearly time to go. She's being brave.

"Look," Kate points to the drawing that accom-
panies the baby bunny saying,

> "I'll become a bird and fly away from you."
> "Then I," said the mother, "will become a
> tree where you'll land."

It's a huge green leafy tree in the shape of a
rabbit. The baby bunny is heading straight for it.

"Nowhere to run, nowhere to hide," Kate bops her
appealing head back and forth, Mario snaps his fingers, *"So high, I can't get over it,"* and Naomi and I, in
perfect harmony based on years of practice, chime in,
"So wide I can't get around it . . . ."

The song drags back adolescence in thick sharp
waves. If anyone had told me then that the lyrics
would one day evoke my mother instead of Arthur
Siegel, I'd have written her off as demented.

Kate's shaking her head. "It's so bizarre," she
says, "my mother's the one who ran away. Constantly." Her wild beautiful mother drank herself to
death in her mid-forties. She doesn't mention that she
herself had a baby at seventeen, a boy now slightly
younger than Luke, but her husband won custody,
she never sees him. All weekend I've watched her
watch Luke.

I reach for the book. On the last page, the baby
bunny, overwhelmed by his mother's persistence,
yields:

> "I guess I might as well stay with you," said
> the baby bunny.
> "Yes," said the mother. "Because you are my
> own baby bunny."

My mind supplies stage directions: He sighs *(I might as well stay)*; she gloats *(because you're mine)*. Suddenly I want to jump in my car and drive 75 miles an hour till I hit the Pacific Ocean. I don't understand how Naomi and I grew up in the same apartment, shared a bedroom all those years until I moved out. And kept moving. For a quarter of a century. While Luke was born and grew. While our father died of asbestos-induced cancer. While our mother survived breast cancer. Suddenly the thought of my mother living alone terrifies me almost as much as the alternatives:

> *ME: passing my days in her kitchen, my nights bedded down on her sofa*
> *HER: living with me and Kate, me defending against her with my entire exquisitely trained being*
> *again, HER: in a dread dread home where parents go and don't return, shrink and shrivel; "take me home," they plead sometimes, and you don't and you wake in the night sweaty and guilty, cursing the late 20th century that gave you possibility*

"C'mon Ma, I don't wanna miss the bus." Luke hefts his pack.

"Ohhh," Naomi sighs, wistfully self-mocking. "There's another one at three." She plants little kisses on his hand, and he laughs and pats her head.

"It's ok, Ma, I'll see you in a couple of weeks." A little older than Kate's lost son, a little younger than Mario's perhaps neglected daughter, he smiles, shy, excited. Anything, even this bus ride, could easily turn into an adventure. I know Naomi wants to hold him on her lap as if he still weighed 25 pounds, rock him, call him her baby bunny. But it's time to drive him to the bus.

War Stories: Silver City

dance on the face
of the earth

1.

Dance on the face of the earth, he said, the summer before he nearly died of a bleeding ulcer and I, about to dump him and return to women, ended up at the hospital fighting for his welfare-stamped life.

We had taken mushrooms, vile-tasting but deliciously shattering, somewhere along the Oregon coast. The ocean was dark and wild. Then we clambered up some dunes, the first dunes I'd ever seen much less climbed, and at the top we vaguely wandered until we were quite high over the beach, walking along a ridge of short shaggy trees. I could no longer see the water.

Do you know where we are? I never had a sense of direction and the mushrooms hadn't helped.

I think so. His calm in the face of uncertainty enraged me.

You think so? What if you're wrong? It was of course beginning to get dark, or maybe to storm. I imagined being on top of this mysterious ridge populated only by trees. And us. During a lightning storm. It was so high. The trees below me began to undulate and I realized I was rocking back and forth. I sat down hard.

I can't do it, I whispered, *I'm dizzy. I'll fall.* It was too high, the footing too delicate. I couldn't imagine how we'd gotten there or how I'd get down. I was too big to carry. The ground was too rough to roll.

Here, try standing, I'll hold onto you. His hairy little animal face beamed. *You love to dance, just dance on the face of the earth, come on.*

I looked out over the miles of dunes miles of trees and swayed.

No, he said, *just dance*. Suddenly I could and did dance down the side of the mountain, to the ocean, and home.

2.

In the first place, why had I stood on top of the ridge, stoned on mushrooms with a man?

A woman had dumped me. Allegra. A poet with a huge cloud of hair, a mother with two monstrous, small sons enlarging by the moment. I wanted her to swoop me up in her rich girl's arms, teach me about pleasure. Once she confronted me, her voice thin and critical, *do you want pleasure or escape?* she asked, and I realized I'd never made the distinction. Allegra had been raised on pleasure, or at least comfort, but when I knew her she could barely make a living. She loved women but needed men—or thought she did, which came down to the same thing. The last I heard, from a mutual friend who also loved Allegra and had taken her in during a homeless period, Allegra was shooting heavy drugs. So you can see why she needed men and men's money. When my friend and I loved Allegra, she was tall and strong, broad-shouldered, a champion swimmer, a product of generations of protein: an amazon. When she wore out her welcome by trading in my friend's camera for white powder, she was skeleton thin. I think of her now as probably dead or dying.

But that year I was thirty and the women's revolution was just around the corner. I loved Allegra like she was my good mother, which is what I wanted her to be. Everything I did I wanted to see reflected in her radiant face, building me out of sheer delight, *yes, my darling, you're wonderful, beautiful, perfect*.

Especially we were poets together. At poetry events we would read poems only for each other: my urban Jewish voice grounded in history, pain, apocalypse; hers, the voice of women who speak from inside the centers of power but have always kept separate, marked as crazy, as she had been and would be again, but not quite yet. She simply spoke, her voice a blade honed god only knows where but it didn't save her. That voice, clean, flat, incapable of hyperbole, seemed one with her pale blue eyes which spotted everything: *when I saw the plane take off out of the corner of my eye, I had an orgasm,* she wrote, for example. I never saw anything out of the corner of my eye, or had orgasms so unconventionally, and if I had done either of these things, I would have built a system from it, not tossed it off in a single line of a poem.

The first time we made love, which was also one of the rare times we saw it through, beginning to end, like real lovers, not like shallow frightened children, she lay back on the pillow, hair spread like an aura around her absurdly full cheeks, wide mouth broadening into a smile: *I want you to make me come,* she said, each word echoing down my sexual core so that ten years later, I hear her voice: I WANT YOU TO MAKE ME   COME. I wanted to make her come, and I did.

Should that have saved her? There was still her past as a beauty queen before whose strong shapely legs men flung down expensive carpets; my past as a grasping deprived child who needed to hang on tight. And there were real children, hers, boys. She could not sit through my meetings. I could not sit through her mealtimes, though one afternoon a week, like a dutiful divorced father, I took the boys to Herfy's for dry roast beef sandwiches I couldn't afford, sopped in gelatinous gravy. In the end we were neither of us confident enough to push past inertia, fear, awkwardness, to let her own desire pound the other's hot irrational pulse into a steady drumming; neither of us *butch enough,* I want to say, but a heavy femme would have done. Anyone who trusted how hot women

could be for each other, hot and steady. What can I
say? We were new.

3.

Him. I met him at Allegra's poetry reading. She and I
were separating. Allegra seemed to be breaking apart,
taking the bus daily to and from her job in a health
food store where the owners, luckily, were college
friends and made excuses for her. She was paring
away chunks of her life, including me, like parts of her
body, becoming thin, finding new magical solutions.
One day it was eating only wheatgrass. Another, tea
steeped for hours in the sun in a huge asymmetrical
glass jar she'd found in an antique shop and paid two
weeks wages for.

After the reading, several of us went for coffee or
wine at Saleri's, a large darkish restaurant of the
hanging ferns variety, and I sat there steadily miserable in the role of one of Allegra's admirers. A very
young man with long blond hair sat close to her and I
knew with the finely tuned sense of a lover that she
had, for now, chosen him.

Sitting next to me was a small, thin, bearded
hippie with thick glasses, sharp laughing blue eyes,
and small multidirectional teeth. He talked with his
whole body, his enthusiasm boundless, even innocent, but I would barely have noticed him except for
one thing.

"I read your poem in the *Journal*," he said to me.
"What a poem!" His eyes lit up and his voice rose.
"And I said to myself, I have to meet the woman who
wrote that poem."

I could stop right here, couldn't I?

So it began easy. There was no way I could bear
another woman, not yet, and I owed him nothing. He
cooked strawberry omelets, took me along on an
interview with Lacy Monroe, an old Wobbly who'd

been telling stories about working women for fifty years. He himself had written one magnificent poem with blackberries in the title about growing up dirt poor in rural Arkansas. This poem he recited by heart, his voice booming out of his slight body—slightly misshapen by childhood polio, I learned later. He hated the rich even more than I did, though he knew how to suck up to them. Most important he was not and never would be me. Or my mother. No blurring. The clarity was like watching a fine film: I engaged only skin deep.

4.

Skin came into it almost at once. On our second date, after the interview with Lacy, we went for coffee, and smoked his Lucky Strikes until he offered to give me a back rub. I knew what I was agreeing to, and it came easy, the difference in bodies amusing, oddly undemanding. As if he knew, and maybe he did, how I felt about male demands.

So then he walked into my life whenever I let him. I could take Allegra's monster sons to Herfy's, even sit with her while she endlessly rearranged the kitchen drawers and chattered about how she was getting her life together. She wrote poems from the corner of her eye; I wrote poems about lesbian love and revolution, as usual, and we read these to each other, sometimes even in readings he organized, and where he appeared not to mind the way she and I poured our words into each other. He told fabulous stories while Allegra and I smoked his dope and cigarettes, or talked endlessly, as if we were alone, but safer.

Then we'd go back to my apartment, he and I, and fuck, sweet and right on the surface. Once, stoned, riding him on the bathroom floor, I saw myself huge and naked like a great mother goddess; he, the small consort. Aphrodite and Adonis, Cybele and Attis.

"Um, I need to straighten my leg." His voice sliced into my fantasy. I was lying too heavily on top of him, bending his leg and banging his shoulder into the cupboard. He was embarrassed, but I wasn't.

5.

Aside from skin, I knew him through his stories. The army wanted to cap all his teeth, which were small, ground down, separate, and—many of them—rotten.

He said, only if you make them look exactly like they look now. So he kept his teeth.

He used to make his living as a petty thief, until he got caught for armed robbery—he'd fired into the air and never pointed his gun at the cashier, but this show of good will had impressed no one, and he did some time. After a year in prison, he escaped and hitched south hundreds of miles to where friends were trying to make a living from squash. Standing on the interstate, he suddenly remembered the draft resisters his friends were hiding. He weighed for several minutes the risk he'd be laying on his friends and the draft resisters. So he turned around and hitched back up again and turned himself in.

"Why?" I asked.

"I had no place else to go."

These tales of adventure and guts spun around me, felt more real than my own life, and, along with the comfort of his body, helped me past the mound of pain that was Allegra; her boys rising into their power, she herself, now with a new man on her arm, a lawyer, taking her to the best restaurants, where people would honor her as a woman of the privileged class. We saw each other less. We reminded each other of failure.

Sometimes with him I'd wake up sobbing or grim, and he'd hold me for a while, ineptly. Then he'd say, *why don't we go to* _____ —and I'd answer either *no*, with lots of reasons why not, or, once in a while, *ok*, and we'd pile into my yellow Toyota and take off. To Astoria, to walk in the damp sea air among the houses of fisherfolk and old Wobblies, where Lacy Monroe had inherited her mother's, grandmother's, great-greatgrandmother's iron spine. To Florence, on the coast, where someone he knew had a house we could stay in for free. That's where we took the mush-rooms, and he told me to dance and I did.

Once—and this was our last trip—I drove him to the southern Oregon mountains where he would plant dope, camp and tend plants all summer to earn his winter's livelihood. We crossed briefly into north-ern California, and the border patrol asked if we were bringing in any fruit, plants, or seeds. "No," we an-swered gravely, and then whooped out of the inspec-tor's hearing.

"How many times have we lied crossing the border?" he quipped in near-perfect dactylic pen-tameter. He made me stop while he wrote the line down; he was not one to let a good line pass. Then I left him in the mountains, drove back home and real-ized I had seriously healed. Allegra was a point of pain, a bruise; but I didn't need to touch it.

6.

I was ready for women again. I started a new job at a women's center. Every day I went into the office downtown and talked to women who'd been raped or beaten, to girls whose fathers/uncles/grandfathers/brothers/mother's boyfriends, etc., were raping them. I thought of what he'd told me about prison: he'd avoided being raped only because he knew some of the heavy inmates. "Otherwise, small and thin like this—" he gestured, "I was chicken," meaning not *cowardly* but *meat*. When he'd told me, I had been glad he understood rape like a woman, through vulnerability, but working at the center all I could focus on was: *he walked at night freely and we didn't*. His fear had been temporary, aberrational.

A month later, there he was. He'd hitched up to see me for a day. I was cheerful but clear that it should be one day only. There he was in my bed and I wanted him to be a woman. It was that simple. I was done with him. I told him and we both cried, pretended it would be ok, and drifted into anguished but young sleep.

About 5 a.m. he woke with blood in his shit. Bleeding ulcer, he'd had it before. I resented being bothered, began my morning rituals, coffee, cigarettes. I heard him phoning someone, *It's happening again, two hours, black, yes, pretty bad*. Then he hung up.

"That was Lesley." A friend who was a nurse. "She said I should tell you I need to go to the hospital right away." He stared apologetically at the nasty yellow shag rug.

"Oh sure, let me just . . ." I was ashamed, trying to cover, as if two seconds ago I hadn't been waiting for him to get his annoying self out of my apartment and my life. They took him into emergency and within fifteen minutes his arm was stuck full of IVs, fluid, glucose, blood, and I was talking to doctors as if I were his wife or mother, demanding information. They treated me like a pushy woman, which I was; tried with all their doctors' *we know bests* to disengage me, but I knew someone had to stick up for him, lie about payment, enforce accountability.

I thought of Lacy Monroe a lot that summer, a model of a woman who'd fought injustice her whole long life, and every part of me turned back to women. Every man I passed on the street was a potential rapist. The one in the hospital healing from horrible surgery was a temporary exception. Every day I left the office and in between work and meetings, I went to visit him, to oversee the doctors, to assure him I would not leave him when the truth was I had already left.

He nearly died but he didn't. They cut out part of his stomach and tied it up with a piece of metallic wire so clumsily that he had gut-wrenching pain for the rest of his life. As long as we stayed in touch, anyway.

The day I took him home, a Friday, I'd left work early and was driving him back through the streets of glorious September. The air was sweet with something, maybe just fresh rain, and I burst into tears.

"This has been so hard," I said, mortified by illegitimacy. I had no scars, had undergone no surgery, had not nearly died.

I brought him back to my apartment where a couple of days later I told him I would find him a place, but he couldn't stay with me. I could not bear men. I could especially not bear a man who needed me, needed care, need need need: I needed him gone and he knew it. Some rich friend of his sent a ticket to Hawaii, and I took him to the airport and gratefully guiltily sent him off.

So I could dance. Not with him down the face of the earth, but with women. At the bar with women, on the streets with women, in the bed of the next woman I loved, deep, hot and easy. So my life could stretch before me, clear, without contradictions. I didn't know yet about ebb and flow, that life is not a river but an ocean, fathomless, nothing if not contradictory, tugging you this way and that so you cry yes and no at the same moment.

for her

I don't know why I want to write this. Something about how close I felt to her. Something about feeling trapped when he asked *was she really raped?* and I wanted to scream *how dare you ask me that?* Instead I used my authority—as a counsellor on the Women's Crisis Line, for christ's sake—for her. *Yes,* I said, *she was really raped.* To make things easier for her.

She called in the middle of the night while I was sleeping at Jesse's. I pulled on a t-shirt and went into the living room to get the phone. It was hot, muggy.

Vivian, it's Elizabeth at the answering service, there's a call for you.

I rubbed my eyes, "Thanks, go ahead."

Hello? Tiny voice. Often the voice was small, timid, not knowing what to expect; calling from who knows what impulse, where they got the number.

"Hello, this is Vivian at the Women's Crisis Line, can I help you?"

I was raped, she said. She was crying.

"Are you someplace safe?" Always the first question.

Yeah, I'm home.

"Is anyone with you?"

Just my kids, the baby and Ricki, she's six. My old man went out looking . . . and her voice choked off into crying again.

"What's your name?" Everyone always cools out enough to say her name. It helps them calm down.

Didi. Sniff.

"Didi, my name is Vivian. Can you talk?"

Nothing. Sounds.

"Do you want me to come there?"

Could you? More sounds, sniffs. *The kids are asleep and*

Robbie, my old man, went out looking for him . . . . She was sobbing again.

"Sure, Didi, you stay calm, tell me where you are."

She gave me her address and directions, way the hell out in the new sub-divisions. I said I would be there in twenty minutes and another woman would come with me. Then I called Elizabeth back.

"Elizabeth, it's me, Vivian."

That woman who just called, she was upset.

"Yeah. She was raped. I'm going over there, who's on?"

Sarilyn.

"Okay, I'll call back when I'm done. Night, hon."

Night. You take care now.

Elizabeth and I had shared many a chat, often going into more-than-necessary detail. We'd never met, we just liked each other's voices. She cared about the women who called even though she only got to say, *This is the answering service for the Women's Crisis Line, hold on and we'll connect you with a counsellor.* She told me once, you hear their voices and you know. Or sometimes, she said, you couldn't tell but it's the middle of the night so why else are they calling? Elizabeth liked to work graveyard, she had young kids and it was easier to work while they slept.

I stumbled back into the bedroom and got under the covers. Jesse put her arms around me and I kissed her neck.

"She was raped," I said, "I have to go there."

"Where?" she asked, eyes closed, nuzzling into my shoulder.

"Doverton."

"Like the white cliffs," she mumbled. "I'll go with you."

We dressed quickly—it was past two when we left her apartment—and she drove my car through the hot, badly lit, dangerous-to-women streets. Usually whoever called just wanted to talk on the phone. Sometimes she'd come to the office, or we'd go to her. Sometimes (rarely) she'd want to report to the police and someone would accompany her. I had met hundreds of these women, but from phone voice to woman, I was always surprised. If she sounded like she'd been raped walking home it would turn out to be her boss, at night, after the kitchen closed down and she was going over the checks and cash register. If I'd assumed it was something from fifteen years ago she was just now remembering, the door would open to my knock and I'd be looking at a purplish swollen face, an icepack pressed to the lip. Sometimes the woman was twenty years older or younger than I'd imagined. I had stopped expecting anything in particular since I could never tell.

But I must have expected something because Didi shocked me. She looked 18 though she must have been at least 25; pale and delicate, slight, short silky blond hair, traces of makeup still on her skin, eyebrows. She was wearing jeans and a tank top, and a fat two-year-old was in her arms half asleep. "This is Vincent," she said.

The door opened straight into a small living room and I introduced myself and Jesse. Didi sat on the couch with Vincent. Jesse and I sat on the floor, making a sort of circle, but Didi stayed totally focused on me.

"Robbie's out looking," she said. "I'm afraid he'll get in trouble."

"You want to tell me what happened?"

"It was Robbie's friend. Buster," her voice cracked in disbelief. She took a deep breath. "I married real young. A biker too. Robbie's a biker, so's Buster, all of them." She shook her head. "My husband dumped me with a four-year-old and a newborn . . . ."

I flashed a look at Jesse and she flashed one back.

"One of the other bikers, an old guy, Graham—he sort of took me under his wing. He'd take me along on trips. He bought toys and things for the kids. Look, this playsuit," she gestured at Vincent's fat little body, "Graham bought this for Ricki."

I admired the playsuit. She needed time.

"I met Robbie through Graham. And Buster." I nodded. Vincent was sleeping now and she put him on the couch and lit a cigarette. Menthol. I took out my pack, I chain-smoked Camels and was always grateful when a caller smoked too.

"We've been together a year and a half, me and Robbie. It's okay, he's pretty good to me." Her eyes took in the living room, the green cheap but new couch she was sitting on, the blue and green shag rug, three-way lamp, stereo, TV. "Most of his money goes towards his bike," she added, "but I knew that."

I flicked my ashes into the enormous yellow-green ashtray. I looked back at her face. Her eyes were huge and dark, and I realized that my surprise was partly because I'd expected a more crumpled look.

"Anyway, today . . ." She let her head fall back as if to stare at the ceiling, but her eyes were closed. "This day seems a week long." She breathed in and out, deep and slow, long enough that I wondered if she'd nodded off. Just then she opened her eyes, still focused on the ceiling.

"Robbie was at work and Buster came by. For Robbie, he said. I gave him a beer, he talked for awhile. His old lady walked out a few weeks ago, I knew he was at loose ends. I never thought he was a bad guy." She began to sob again. "I never thought of him much at all." She caught her breath sharply and searched my face. "Do you think I did something?"

"No, he's the one who did it. Didi, he did it, not you. You have to remember that. He did it."

She nodded, blew her nose on a wadded-up tissue. "He asked if we wanted to go to the park, Ricki and Vincent and me. It was so hot, I said sure. The park!"

She lit another cigarette, dragged deep and exhaled. "We picked up sandwiches and a six-pack and we went to Eastland Park and found a place in the shade. I fed Vincent and put him to sleep. We were just hanging out." She stared at her cigarette, as if she'd forgotten what it was. Then she took a drag.

"We're sitting there, he told Ricki to go to the truck and get a certain cassette—he had a tape player. He described the tape very carefully to Ricki and, you know, she was proud because she knows how to read . . . ." She hiccoughed a little sob and sucked on the cigarette. "I remember thinking the truck was a ways off, I was worrying about her, but it was the park and the middle of the day, no one was around . . . ."

I lit another cigarette. The room was practically blue with smoke and poor slightly allergic Jesse got up to sit by the window.

"As soon as Ricki left, he jumped on me . . . ." I heard the shock in her voice, and she began to sob again. "Vincent woke up and he could see, the whole time . . . ."

She was sobbing deeply now and I got up from the floor and sat next to her on the couch and put my arms around her. I didn't usually. Women who've just been raped tend to be very particular about who touches them. Besides, as a lesbian, I'm cautious about who I touch—who wants that coming up in the middle of someone's rape trauma? But I could tell it would be okay to hug Didi. I stroked her hair while she cried and I felt the familiar jolt, the one I kept thinking I'd get over the way I'd gotten over my amazement that a man could take pleasure in forced sex with some woman he didn't know. That was sex to him. I didn't understand and I wouldn't ever understand. But I was rarely shocked anymore by street rapes, the rape while robbing, the hitchhike rapes: a different species, I'd tell myself sometimes, and if women were doing the classifying they'd define it that way. But what still shocked me was the men who raped women they knew. Weren't they ashamed? How could they function in a world that said hello, how are you, would you like a cup of coffee; where they knew your kids, your birthday even.

Jesse handed me some tissues for Didi. "Blow," I said and she did. "I didn't tell Robbie this part, I was too ashamed. I just said Buster raped me." She looked at the rug. "He made me take my pants down and he—put his face there and made me let him do it and Vincent could see. I was afraid to scream. I just kept begging him, *Buster, stop, Buster, please,* but he wouldn't stop."

She dragged on her cigarette. Her eyes were closed and I knew she was seeing a movie she was going to watch over and over for years. And watch Vincent, wondering if he remembered.

"He had me pinned—he must weigh 250 pounds. He did it for a long time. I tried to think about other things, I was scared Ricki would come back and she'd see too." She looked down at the rug again. "Then he made me do it to him. He shoved my face down on his—thing. I gagged. He made me suck on him. I heard noise in the grass and it was Ricki, her face looked all weird. She didn't say anything. I pushed at him and—" she burst out laughing "—I bit him." Jesse and I laughed too, a short spasm of a laugh.

"I *bit* him," she said again, shaking her head with delight. "He smacked me hard but he rolled off." The smile vanished. "Ricki was standing there holding the cassette. I just wanted to pull up my pants. He took the tape and said *thanks* and went off in the bushes to go to the bathroom. I wanted to say something to Ricki but I was too ashamed." She put her head back on the couch and closed her eyes again. "I didn't want to scare her." Pause. She was seeing the movie.

"He took us home. Like it was nothing. Like it was normal. He said *tell Robbie hello.* Then he left. I took a shower, a long hot shower . . . ." (Destroyed evidence, I thought wearily, but it doesn't matter, the cops would cream her: divorced, a biker's old lady, someone she knew, the park, the beer . . . .) "I fed the kids. I acted like nothing happened." She began to laugh again, a little hysterical now. I took both her hands in mine and looked right into her eyes.

"You got through it. You're very strong. You took care of yourself and your kids. You're still here. Don't you feel bad about yourself."

She studied my face. "I didn't know if I'd tell Robbie. I called Graham, he said to tell. I didn't say about—you know . . ." Her color rose. "Just that Buster raped me. I said that."

"He did, you know. That's rape. The details are your business."

"Yeah?" She looked relieved. "Robbie kept asking me over and over was that the truth, did Buster really rape me. He went over to Graham's. He said they'd get Buster. That was, I don't know . . . nine. I just sat here remembering. So I called you."

She had phoned around two. Five hours alone, remembering. "I'm glad you called, Didi." We were supposed to say that, but it was also true.

"I'm scared. Robbie took his gun. If they find Buster, they'll kill him. I'm scared they'll get into trouble." She crossed her arms over her breasts, rocking slightly. I looked from her face, turned inward, the movies again, to Jesse's face, attentive, carefully blank. The sound of a car drifted in the window. Robbie and Graham, home from avenging their collective honor. Buster back for a rerun. A woman driving to another woman's side to staunch some pain sliced open by some man. Or someone just run out of cigarettes.

Then it was quiet again. After a minute Didi said, "Listen, you want a beer? Some coffee?"

"Coffee would be great." Didi went into the kitchen and Jesse and I looked at each other. "I hope they kill the fucker," she whispered harshly, and I wondered what that would mean for Didi.

Then Didi brought the coffee and some cookies and emptied ashtrays and suddenly it was like a visit. We just talked, about anything, except every so often she'd say something else she remembered. And as much as it ripped me up to listen, I felt blessed. Like a magic trapdoor had opened, plunging me into intimacy with a woman I'd never seen before and probably never would again. Sometimes it was like that. She'd talk from her deepest self, no guard, no pretense, and I'd answer from wherever I could. That's what happened with Didi, some kind of love shimmering through the smoke. That was one blessing. The other was Didi's face when she said *I bit him*.

After about half an hour Robbie came home and of course it changed. Didi introduced us. His eyes took us in and I was afraid he'd get on her afterwards for calling up a bunch of dykes, but he just said, "We couldn't find him. But we will." He didn't put his arms around her or anything. She went into the kitchen to get him a beer and that's when he asked me was she really raped. I flashed all the angry colors of the rainbow—but to myself; to him I said yes, she definitely was raped and he should be very kind to her and gentle. Then Didi came in with the beer and we all lit up cigarettes except for Jesse, and after a while we left. I told Didi to call me at the Crisis Line if she just wanted to talk. I thought of giving her my home phone but I knew it would look unprofessional to Robbie and throw her rape into question again. She kept thanking me and I kept saying it was fine, I was glad to be there. I wanted her to know she had given me something too but I didn't know how to say that, especially in front of him.

Jesse drove us back through the still dark, slightly cooler streets. "How was that for you?" I asked.

"What do you think? You hardly know who to kill first."

I watched her profile in the dark car. That belligerent chin. "I love your anger," I said.

When we got back to Jesse's I called Elizabeth. "I'm back, same number. Any calls?"

All quiet. Lucky Sarilyn. You must be exhausted.

"Such fuckers. Her boyfriend's friend rapes her, her boyfriend doesn't believe her. He asked me did it really happen. Can you imagine?"

Yeah, she said, *I can.*

"She bit his cock, Elizabeth. That's how she got him to stop."

Elizabeth guffawed. *Yay, women,* she said, and then, *Go to sleep now, the phone's under control.*

"I know. Thanks."

Hey, what for? she said and hung up.

Jesse was already in bed and I climbed in and wrapped myself around her.

"Thanks for coming with me."

"Don't be ridiculous," she mumbled, tightening her arms around me so I could hardly breathe.

"I don't cry any more," I said into her neck. "Sometimes it scares me."

"I know," she whispered, rocking me as if I were crying us both to sleep.

war stories, 197-:

1. the day
we didn't declare war

We just weren't ready to kill, and anything else seemed too dangerous.

I remember the sickish feeling that descended on me, like fog rolling in, filling the room which happened to be my studio apartment where thirteen women sat around on what was available, mostly the bed and floor. I listened to each of them talk and I heard my own voice, but the words floated off into the fog, and I thought, *We're not ready. We're not going to pull this off.*

And I felt sick because I knew: If we weren't ready, who was?

We were at a pitch in those days, and no wonder. We had only recently concluded that a war against women had been going on for centuries, and rape was one of the major battle strategies. We assessed the effectiveness. Many of us had been raped, some on the street, more by dates or fathers or husbands, or some man whose car or back room you wandered into because you needed a ride or directions or just wanted a cup of coffee.

But it got worse. We were all afraid. Fear governed all our lives, limiting where we lived, what jobs we'd take, what hours we'd work; how late at night we'd go for a walk or catch the bus home from a friend's; whether we'd take a shower when no one else was around. That is, lucky women got limited; the unlucky had to face danger right through the fear. It was endless, when we started enumerating the ways this war affected our lives. We concluded rape was working: for them.

Because clearly it affected their lives, men's lives, too. Everything taught them that we had to be afraid and they didn't. That we got raped all the time and nothing could stop it. That we needed them to protect us. That rapists rarely got caught (except for Black men raping white women in the South—only everyone knew this probably meant Black men who made trouble for white men, or just Black men period; not protection against rape, but one more injustice to hack away at).

We started collecting stories of women fighting back. Inez Garcia, Joan Little, Yvonne Wanrow were our heroes. We knew it was not incidental that women of color were out in front being brave. We knew that each woman, by killing her attacker, had strengthened every woman's ability to resist violence. We'd comb newspapers, reading between the lines; like the Skillet Murder, a wife who creamed her husband, and the daughter maybe saw, and the wife's co-workers maybe helped, maybe tried to cover it up. That's the sort of thing we'd speculate about—what did the daughter, the other women, have to do with this killing? What would make a woman that angry, to slam him not only with the skillet but with several other articles of kitchen equipment?

And there were stories less needy of interpretation trickling in from other cities, stories of brave desperate women. We amassed names and wrote poems about them; we performed rituals honoring Jennifer Patri, Claudia Thacker, Francine Hughes (years before Farrah Fawcett played Hughes on TV as a pathetic victim pushed to a horrible deed. Our Francine Hughes was a tough cookie; that's why she's alive). Plus lots of women who never got famous: Wanda Carr, Marlene Roan Eagle, Miriam Grieg, Evelyn Ware, Gloria Maldonado . . . .

We learned the statistics of small, relatively safe Silver City, and—it's not that we were shocked or appalled. I'll speak for myself. It was as if a curtain of thick gauze had suddenly lifted and I saw very clearly in a harsh accurate light: *war*.

And to tell the truth, it's still accurate. But I don't know what to do about it, and this is the story of how I realized none of us knew. Because we were decent people. Because we were afraid. Because we could not trust one another enough to declare war back.

But it starts before that, in the early fall. I was working on the Crisis Line and so was my best friend Diana. On my shift I got a call from a woman named Miranda whose boyfriend smacked her around two or three times a week. She was eight months pregnant, and sick of getting beaten up. But she didn't want to leave her apartment and go to a shelter, which was what we had to offer. She wouldn't go. That was that.

It was Diana's idea. We called a couple of friends and suddenly The Godmothers was born. Why should Miranda have to leave her own home? We would go in and stay with her in twos, make sure she was safe. Miranda was thrilled. We felt tough, useful, bold and daring. So in a way we were undoing men's violence against all women by showing up at Miranda's with our sleeping bags, night sticks, and a new lock for the front door.

We weren't stupid. We had rules and believed in modest weapons. We knew that any place where a man used a gun or knife, we shouldn't be there, and neither should the woman, no matter how much she hated to leave home. And we insisted she get a restraining order against him, so he'd be violating the law just by showing up, and we could call the cops. But if what he usually did was get drunk and bullishly angry and punch her around—which was what most of them did—we figured he would not be prepared for "his" woman to have sober, determined help. We pasted a notice on the front door saying, *This house is under the protection of a restraining order and THE GOD-MOTHERS,* and it worked exactly like it was supposed to. Men were afraid of us. They'd show up at the front door, usually after the bars closed; spew obscenities at their useless housekey, rattle the doorknob, curse and mutter. Then they'd split. Every time.

Word of our successes got around, and our numbers grew. It seemed lots of women were angry and anxious to do something. Of course we made some women nervous, with our nightsticks, name (*Godmothers*), and attitudes. They would say the real answer was not violence but education. We'd point out that being prepared to stop violence was the opposite of violence, and besides, we were educating like mad. Look at the lesson we were offering these women's children, and their neighbors and neighbors' children: women stick up for women and keep men in line. We were cheeky and proud.

The only problem with the Godmothers was the time it took to be one, the womanpower needed to protect every single woman who called. Godmother-ing was hardly efficient: an average weekend's cover-age required eleven women willing and able to leave their own homes, families and lives to sit around a stranger's apartment in eight-hour shifts. Some improbable friendships were formed this way, and Miranda became a fiercely committed Godmother, staffing the phone while she nursed her tiny lump of a new baby. But women were burning out fast. Jokes about the logic of simply offing abusive men became standard fare.

Then, around November, Sarilyn got a call on the Crisis Line from a woman who'd been raped in Clinton Park over on the north end of town. Two men with a knife. She described them as twentyish, white, one blond, the other dark with long hair.

Have you reported to the police? We always asked.
No.

Do you want to? I'll go with you. We always offered.
But the woman didn't want to report. She was fifteen
and had lied to her parents about where she'd been. *I'd
be stuck in the house until I'm eighteen,* she said, but she
wanted someone to know what had happened.

Sarilyn talked to the woman for almost an hour,
comforting her, informing her of the various services.
Then she filled out the phone report, as usual.

That same week, Charlene got a call from a
woman who'd been raped in the park by two men
whom she described with some precision: in their
twenties, one blond with short hair, the other with
long dark hair and a half-moon scar on his left hand.
The blond one, at least, carried a knife.

Nobody had put any of this together yet, so
Charlene went through the usual procedure. This
woman was older, in her thirties. She'd been jogging.
She would not report to the police. *I'm not stupid,* she
told Charlene, *I'm divorced, I work as a cocktail waitress and I
know exactly how the police are going to treat me.* As Charlene
said afterwards, "I would have liked to tell her it
wasn't true, but I knew it was still goddam true."

I got the third call, two days after Charlene. This
woman actually came in to the office to talk. She was a
college student, studying for finals, she was very
upset and I referred her for free counselling. She
didn't want the hassle of the police. *Besides,* she said,
their faces are a total blur, and I hope they stay that way. She
was able to give a general description.

By the time we had our next staff meeting and
were going through the phone reports, there were
five calls from five different women who had been
raped in the same park by, barring extraordinary
coincidence, the same two men.

So we called the police. We knew that without
women willing to file reports—or, in police lingo, *no*

live victims—there would be no arrests. We demanded that they post the park with signs to warn women of the danger, and that they patrol, at least on weekends, when most of the rapes had been committed.

When I look back on it now, it's kind of touching. On the one hand, we had identified a war being waged by men against women, and, on the other, we were outraged when the police responded as every scrap of our analysis should have predicted. For centuries women who say they've been raped have been accused of lying by men. The women who'd phoned the Crisis Line were accused of lying by the police.

Why were they lying? Because if they were telling the truth, they'd report to the police. When we pointed out that by FBI estimates—not exactly a radical source—something like nine out of ten women don't report, they pooh-poohed it.

Or maybe, the captain of our city's finest explained blandly, as I sat on the other side of his desk during another useless meeting, *some of those women who answer the phone are—not lying exactly, but exaggerating a little, you know, to puff up the Crisis Line.* Women who report rape are routinely asked to take polygraphs—"lie detector tests." The captain suggested that the Crisis Line workers who'd reported the phone calls take polygraphs. Failing that, he was sorry, but the police had no basis on which to act.

All this talking took several days, during which three more women who called the Crisis Line to say they'd been raped described the same two men in the same park.

We did the normal responsible Crisis Line-type things. We called a press conference. We printed our own posters, to warn women and seek information. We held neighborhood forums, and literally dozens of women from the neighborhood called the Crisis Line to get involved. The Godmothers organized a huge patrol of women to march through the park on a

Saturday night with chants and flashlights: to shame the police as well as to keep the park safe, even if only for one night. And to give women a taste of power. From the cynical police point of view, Clinton Park was a hot ticket. From ours, women were responding to a dangerous situation with an authentic desire to bond and protect each other.

And while this organizing activity was going on, the Crisis Line was called by three more women who'd been raped, and in one case badly cut up, by the same two men in the same park.

That was the background for the secret meeting in my apartment. Many of us were Godmothers, but this group had no name. We were the hard core, though our discipline at meetings left something to be desired. Everyone talked at once.

"Can't we just patrol, I mean not sixty of us at a time, but, say, six?"

"Do you have time for that? What are the goddam cops for?"

"Not us, that's for sure."

"I have to get up early for work."

"Let's just kill the fuckers."

"We're not going to catch anyone—they'll just stay out of sight."

"They'll go to another park."

"Yeah, so we can start patrolling there. Terrific."

"Sure, let's devote our lives to park patrol."

"At last, another opportunity for women to volunteer."

In one corner they were cracking up, fantasizing about uniforms and a marching song, when someone asked, "What do we do if we see them?"

"What do you mean? We make a citizen's arrest."

"How do we know it's the right two guys?"

"That description is pretty fucking exact."

"It's not a photograph."

"Who cares?"

"I want to know how we bring them in. They carry knives."

"Yeah, do we hold a knife to their throats?"

"You have to come in real close with a knife."

"Maybe we should use guns."

"Knives are safer."

"Where you come from, Mars?"

"Who owns a gun?"

"We could just knock them out. With night sticks."

"Do you know how hard you have to hit someone to knock him out? I mean, without breaking his head?"

"So we break his head."

"What good does arresting them do? We don't have one witness."

"All those women who called."

"They won't testify—that's why the cops won't deal with it, Dumbo."

"Hey!" protested the woman being called Dumbo.

"Sorry."

"We could use a decoy."

"I'll be a decoy."

"It's too dangerous. They carry *knives*."

"So what are we saying, these two fuckers can go on raping to their heart's content and we can't do anything?"

"We could beat the shit out of them."

"We could tie them up and dump them naked in front of the police station, like in *Sister Gin*."

"Look, are they going to stand there while we tie them up?"

"They carry *knives*. What if they attack one of us?"

We all saw it at the same time. One woman separated from the rest, knife against her throat. Breathless, airless silence. There's no oxygen in the room.

Diana said it. "We can't do anything unless we're prepared to kill." That's when I looked around the room and saw the fog roll in. It was fear blanketing us, each one separately, pulled back from the others, each mind making its own horrible movies. I knew we didn't trust each other enough. Or else we just didn't have the training that makes you—makes men—able to take this sort of thing lightly. Look what they do to each other in war, for christ's sake, for no reason except someone tells them to.

No one could tell us to. No one could say it was okay. I looked at Beverly. She had worked at the post office for ten years, she was 28 now, paying the mortgage on her little house. Jesse made her living stealing, but she loved music, volleyball, me, and life. Even Jean, who so readily volunteered to be the decoy, wonderful brave Jean, had a daughter and a lover. A lot to lose. Could we make a plan and pull it off? Could we keep our mouths shut? Would someone drink too much, have bad dreams six months down the road?

Brenda finally broke the silence. "Yeah," she said, very softly, like a breath. "It could get there really fast." All our heads were nodding and the words after that were just words.

I can't remember how the meeting ended or what we decided. There were more press conferences, the neighborhood gathered hundreds of signatures on petitions, the police charged us with rabble-rousing, there was a demonstration in front of police headquarters, United Way refused funding to the Crisis Line, the mayor had to make a statement, and somewhere in there the calls about Clinton Park stopped coming, and, we assumed, the two men we didn't kill stopped raping women in that park and went somewhere else.

But I remember that moment, poised right at the edge where our theory had taken us; unable to leap. I have long since stopped seeing this in moral terms: was this the right decision or the wrong one? Could the large but amorphous women's movement have supported an underground, and were we weak and shabby not to be the first? History has its own logic. It's what happened. It's who and where we were.

And, you know, I've heard, through the years, stories of a rapist/killer in Seattle who the lesbian community went after, and it's true he disappeared from the news. I heard the same thing about L.A. Apocryphal? Who knows?

But I know this. Every time I hear about a woman who kills the man who attacked or abused her, and sometimes she lands in prison, or, in one case, a woman who killed another woman's rapist—she's doing time in Framingham right now—my heart leaps for her courage and for the simple fact that he can't do it again and every goddam man has to hear that and every woman has to know a woman did that. I tell myself few of us choose to be heroes. I hope, if I should be chosen by danger anyone with a scrap of sense and self-love would run miles to avoid, that I'll do my part as well as Inez Garcia, Wanda Carr or Gloria Maldonado did hers. But sometimes I grieve a little for us in the no-name group, that we couldn't give that to ourselves and each other. And I feel a little ashamed, like maybe my freedom, such as it is, is getting staked on someone else's bold, daring, per-haps imprisoned back.

2. the day we did

But maybe it didn't happen that way at all. Maybe it happened this way. Maybe a couple of us had studied self-defense intensively, and three of us had guns; Beverly had done target practice once a week for years. The women who knew all about the wisdom of you don't draw a gun unless you're prepared to kill said straight out: *We can't go into this unless we look very clearly at what might happen.* It was getting pretty hot in that room.

"The law won't touch them. We don't even have a choice, we have to use a decoy."

"What for?"

"So there's something to charge them with."

"That risks someone's life. What is this, *Be Fair To Rapists Week?*"

"So what are you saying?"

"They carry knives. They're killers."

"They haven't killed anyone."

"How do you know? Maybe they have."

"Great. Now we're dealing with hypothetical crimes."

"Hey—what do you think they do with those knives if a woman resists?"

No one answered. The words echoed. Pictures of women, men, knives, throats, blood hung in the air.

Finally someone asked, "You think we should kill them in cold blood?"

"Cold blood, hot blood, what are you talking about?"

"They're enemies. Treat them like enemies."

"That's how men talk."

"Who else ever gets to talk?"

So we went around some. Women said things like *it's wrong* or *then we'll be as bad as they are.* But when the logic was pressed, it crumbled. The clincher came when someone pointed out how elated we'd feel if two bodies matching those descriptions were to turn up in Clinton Park.

First, we talked about confidentiality and self-protection. While we agreed it would make a terrific self-defense case—either simple or complex, as in arguing that every woman was, in a sense, one's self, we were not anxious to be martyrs and especially not to do time or be confronted with a resurrected death penalty. That meant we had to keep our mouths shut and not get caught. But we wanted everyone to know women had done it, that was part of the point: to create a new image, in advertising lingo. We needed to claim the act. We decided on an anonymous flyer cleverly worded to credit and protect us at the same time.

What we agreed was this: those of us who had been very visible around the rapes, public speaking, meetings with the cops, would have airtight alibis. This meant Diana, myself and Charlene. All three of us balked at being left out, and besides, there was something about equal risk and responsibility that made us feel safer. But Brenda pointed out we'd be on the line soon enough, the first three suspects brought in for questioning.

We talked, too, about other women who'd been outspoken, women at the Crisis Line, a couple of women from the neighborhood who'd risen wonderfully into leadership, women who might also be suspected but who would not have the prescience to arrange alibis. We agreed that if innocent women were charged, seriously charged, we'd have to respond. *What if men were charged?* We agreed women had to get the credit. We'd bombard them with press releases. *Down to taking the rap ourselves?* Somehow we avoided this one, comforting ourselves with an obvious truth: the cops were getting nowhere with tight descriptions and a repetitious m.o. Where were they going to get with us?

"That's because they don't believe in rape. None of the women has officially reported."

"Yeah, well, these turkeys aren't going to report either."

This got quite a laugh. We began to feel better. We began to spill into the room all our scary images of revolutionary violence, mostly derived from books and movies, like *The Informer, Man's Fate, The Possessed.*

Idealistic, usually young, usually men, drawn to a cause, end up betrayed by their ideals, or—worse— corrupt, ruined, as *bad as the oppressors*. Was this automatic? We decided it probably wasn't. Anyway, the danger to us right now was not corruption but inaction.

So we planned very carefully. Jean would be the draw. She was willing, had superb outdoor skills and was used to being outside at night, and she knew how to shoot, though she was rusty and didn't own a gun. She and Beverly would take off immediately after the meeting to pick up Beverly's .38, stop by Sam's for a silencer we thought would fit (it did), and drive two hours to her cousin's camp in the eastern part of the state so Jean could practice shooting. Someone would call in sick for both of them at work. The other two women with guns would drive out the next day, to practice. Also the next day, Diana and I would go to the park to study the layout, locate places for cover, choreograph our moves. Thursday night Brenda, Lois and Jesse would walk every inch of the park. Friday would be the first try. By the time the meeting broke up, we were feeling much more in control, no longer so afraid.

Diana stayed for a bit after everyone left, Jesse with the others. "I feel weird," she said. She stretched her arms over her head and moved her torso back and forth. "Not to be part of the whole thing."

"Yeah, me too. It would be really stupid though." I had opened the window to smoke.

"You think we can pull it off?"

The phone rang and we both jumped. It was Jesse, calling to see if she could come back and stay the night. "That's okay, I just like her to know I have rights," Diana smirked on her way out. Jesse and I went directly to bed, I had to be at work early, but we made love anyway, much slower and softer than usual, as if this were the last time; as if we were each other's mothers, tending the body of a delicate newborn.

You want details. You want to know exactly what happened in that park. Fat chance. Here is the article from the *Silver City Herald*, November –, 197–.

TWO MEN FOUND DEAD IN PARK

The bodies of two men were found today in Clinton Park, according to police reports. The men, identified as Roger Allston, age 22, and James Johnson, age 24, had been shot with .38 caliber revolvers.

Morris Abramson, a resident of the neighborhood which borders the park, is reported to have found the bodies when his dog ran into the bushes and he followed. Mr. Abramson also confirmed a rumor, which the police have refused to comment on at this time, that a poster was pinned to the jacket of each man, stating that the dead men had attacked a woman with a knife, and that they matched the description of two rapists operating in Clinton Park. The poster, Mr. Abramson said, stated that women had killed these men to prevent further attacks against women, and accused the police of refusing to act.

Clinton Park has been the subject of controversy between the Silver City Police and the Silver City Crisis Line, the Crisis Line claiming they have received reports of rapes by the same two men from 11 women in a period of three weeks. The description of the two men, circulated beginning October 25, matches the description of Allston and Johnson.

Now you'll say, *You're just as bad as they are.* Like the
only other woman in the audience when I saw *Platoon.*
The day after battle, thousands dead, the innocent
young hero, barely surviving, spots the wicked sergeant, the one who massacred Vietnamese villagers
and murdered the decent sergeant in cold blood. Cold
blood makes everything worse, and it was bad
enough. The hero aims his gun at the fucker, who
clearly did not deserve to live and would do damage to
his last breath, and I'm sobbing *shoot, shoot,* but silently,
since I'm alone at the movies. He shoots, and from one
row behind me comes the sad, shocked voice of the
other woman in the dark theater: *Now he's just as bad as
the others.* As if the task were not *how to stop violences* but
how to stay pure—a little finicky for my taste.

So let's get some facts on the table, as they say,
like toast and eggs over easy, the yolks filmed over but
sitting up yellow and plump.

The rapes stopped.

The rapes stopped.

The rapes stopped.

Consider for a moment Silver City: the newspapers, the talk shows, the conversations at work, in
kitchens, on telephones, at diners and the
laundromat.

Consider the neighborhood around Clinton
Park. The women who loved to walk there and had
been afraid. The men who had jerked off thinking
about the women's fear.

Consider the women who'd been raped, by these
men and by others, realizing they were not part of an
endless chain of seemingly natural disasters.

Consider the women in the no-name group. The
boldness of the decision. The dignity and strength of
the act. The power of taking women's safety into our
own hands once we'd realized keeping our hands
clean was not our primary goal.

I know you don't want to hear this. You'd rather it was the other way. Sad but disillusioned. Power corrupts. Action is guilt. Victims are innocent. The oppressed, aware but helpless in their oppression, afraid of becoming as bad as the oppressor, refuse to fight for power.

I know you don't like this story. But it could be true.

our first talk: 1986

The thing is, I'd known Daisy for years. I was always running into her scrubbed face and neat blond head at demonstrations and rallies. We belonged to the same community in Silver City—lesbians and leftists— though we never socialized. I never even knew what part of town she lived in.

That was just it. Daisy and her equally scrubbed friends kept separate from the rest of us. They worked with us on political projects and were fabulously responsible, usually picking tasks that involved ideological content and gave them some control, but at least whatever they took on got done. If one of them said she'd contact ten potential speakers—no question, she'd arrive at the next meeting with a list of who and what and phone numbers and alternates.

They were also that other kind of responsible: stupidly proper, low on humor, politely appalled by any sign of wildness—the sort of folk who left me shaking my head late at night after a long embroiled meeting. My best friend Diana and I would be sprawled on her living room floor, getting stoned and analyzing every ten minute block of what we'd just lived through, as if living it hadn't sufficed. We would speculate about whether responsibility was inherently boring, or could you, could *we* survive with our humor and outrageousness intact and still get things done. Rebellion, creativity, a whirling energy were our battering rams against the status quo. We knew that rage and laughter were what attracted at least some women to meetings and kept us there, made us willing to put out extra, beyond jobs and home— though this was the mid-seventies and we were all getting by on part-time work or CETA jobs, temporary magic.

Sometime that summer a woman inspired by a Bay Area event suggested we organize a Take Back The Night march in Silver City. Enthusiasm was immediate and women gathered to plan. We called it Women's Night Watch and the poster, asking *When was the last time you walked alone at night without fear of rape or harassment,* made women burst into tears and show up in droves at the Rape Crisis Line to help work on the march.

Suddenly it was bigger than we were. Our crowd knew how to whip up enthusiasm, but we had no interest in city government, in structure of any kind. Thus we had not focused for more than three seconds on would-be solutions like better-trained police (corrupt racist pigs), or street lights (ridiculously tame), or guards in parking garages (implying women needed protection and, further, that male guards could provide it). Looking back, I don't know what we expected, but scorn was power. Women who thought everything was a pile of bullshit but knew their own rage found home in us. As for me, I was in rebellion against classical Marxism, but at my core I was a Jew and a millenialist: I wanted everything absolutely this minute. Anything less was a cop-out.

At the second or third meeting, Daisy, Polly and Suzy from Sister Comrades showed up. They all had faces that smacked of white picket fences: blond or at least fair; pale, medium-sized, with wire-rimmed glasses. Only Daisy didn't wear glasses. They seemed impeccably well-mannered, especially compared with some of us, whose favorite slogan of the season was *Off With Their Rocks,* which, prowling the downtown in groups of five or six, we would chant at the backs of lone men, watching tension tighten across their manly shoulders as their pace quickened.

Everyone knew that Sister Comrades were Trots. We watched suspiciously for signs of line-from-above, of Daisy, Polly and Suzy deflecting the march from its own direction. But this didn't happen. They asked, at their second meeting, if we were presenting the mayor and city council with any demands—exactly the sort of responsible politics we found so tedious and beside the point—and they argued cogently for making demands, even if only so we could say later our demands hadn't been met. I have to say they convinced me. Better yet, they said they'd write the demands, type them, and bring them to the group for approval.

Next week, they brought a dozen fine demands to the meeting. We suggested additions, like *free self-defense classes for women, women-only nights in the parks,* and *waiving no-pet restrictions in housing to allow women to keep guard dogs.* The Sister Comrades agreed that those were terrific ideas, and said they'd add them right in. No one would go for the *curfew for men* demand, but it got some applause.

So I ended up feeling okay about the Sister Comrades, though they remained in my mind as "they," undifferentiated, since they revealed nothing personal. None of them ever stayed after a meeting to go for a drink, or participated in the raucous gossip which is the lifeline of any lesbian community. Now, of course, it occurs to me how little any of us reached out to any of them, treated Daisy as distinct from Polly or Polly from Suzy. A certain wariness pertained on all sides, but they were the newcomers, and probably shy.

After that, we'd run into each other over various political events: a battle about racism with the owners of the women's bar; a new women's center; a rash of rapes in the city park. And all along they would be having their Sister Comrades forums, educationals on "The Election and the Working Class" or "Racism and the City Police." Someone told me one of their principles was that each member had to develop public speaking skills, and I cringed to think of these reserved colorless women holding an audience's attention. At the same time, I had to admit, whenever one of them spoke in meetings, she was articulate and to the point.

I never went to their forums. They were the sort of thing that put me to sleep. I already knew what I thought. My relationship to politics was as Bad Child, and the neatly pressed cotton shirts and Popular Front topics of these women made me feel instantly compelled to jump up shrieking *fuck you, off the pigs,* or twirl a bloody tampon by the string. Besides, having begun my political life in the ban-the-bomb early sixties, when you held demonstrations and nobody came, I could not bear being a too-eagerly-received new face in the sparse audience I imagined Sister Comrades drew. Yet the flyers for these events always touched me. There was something so wholesome about them, almost old-fashioned, like my parents' CP friends trying eternally to bring information to the people. I half-expected them to sing "This Land Is Your Land."

So we went on like this, working together on marches and conferences, responding to crises. Sister Comrades kept planning forums, "The Economics of Women's Liberation," or "The Grand Jury: Instrument for Repression," organized when a Grand Jury was expected to arrive momentarily in Silver City to attack the Black community's health clinic. I even thought about attending that one, but what interested me was protecting the clinic, not the predictable analysis I assumed would be warmed over and dished out.

Time passed. Things were getting tighter and nastier. In crisis, what we loosely called "the community" acted together, but less of us each time. We were all drinking too much, smoking too much dope, making love—who would say too much?—smashing monogamy and breaking each other's hearts, some-

times in the same flamboyant gesture, though more
and more of us were settling into couples. My particular contingent—mockers and scoffers dedicated to the
proposition that while revolution was not a dinner
party, neither was it a ladies' tea—was becoming iso-
lated, scolded by more respectable types: neo-conser-
vatives who urged us to grow up; about-to-become
heads of social-service-agencies-begun-as-women's-
liberation-projects who accused us of alienating
women, forgetting that it was our energy, humor
and, above all, candor that drew many women to the
movement in the first place. We did not yet know that
CETA money was like all government money in support of progressive projects—*get them hooked and pull it;*
that the world of work, time, survival, tension, rent
and dirty laundry would press down with more and
more force.

We did what movements do in such times: even
those of us familiar with history repeated it. We
attacked each other, called each other on smaller and
smaller points: did someone wear makeup, thereby
enjoying heterosexual privilege? (from the nothing-
but-flannel-shirts-&-army-pants-will-do faction—
quite large); was someone else going to college, trying
to drag herself up by her bootstraps without bringing
the entire body of women along? (another faction,
this one almost entirely composed of college graduates and dropouts from rich families); were some
women scaring off others new to the movement by
chanting at the second annual Women's Night Watch,
> *Rapists, hecklers, men who beat*
> *The women's army's gonna carve your meat?*
(from the respectable faction, already gliding towards
the seats of small power they would soon occupy,
some with integrity); was someone else too interested
in the bennies derived from lunch with the bank vice
president, insufficiently impressed with the need to
build collective power? (from the manhating wild-

child faction, Diana and me and our friends).

And women of color were getting strong against racism, pointing everywhere from women's studies reading lists to who was getting the CETA jobs. Some white women were digging in their defenses, and others—this was us—were so anxious to be the good whites that we mobilized our attacks against the other whites, not considering that perhaps our job was to struggle with them in kindness. Give people room to change? Allow for differences? We cornered one another in every aspect of our lives until AT&T was just the goddam phone company, we were the on-the-spot enemies, and it was easier for many of us to go elsewhere and hate whom we hated—bosses, rapists, boards of education—instead of women in our own movement.

I left Silver City, ostensibly because I fell in love but really, I had to get out. Diana and her new lover had taken off for Arkansas to grow soybeans. I felt trapped by too many sniping feuds and burdensome loyalties, too much acting and being reacted to according to type. And in the end I was a Jew in a bland, goyish city. I went, oddly, to a city where there were even fewer Jews; where no one knew me. I watched how women in the movement ignored me, and wondered if I had treated newcomers that way. I marched to Take Back The Night in this new city, and the organizers had changed the slogan from *Women Unite, Take Back the Night* to *Citizens Unite.* As if aliens were the problem.

I went to other cities and small towns too, moving often, collecting little, belonging nowhere, money tighter and tighter. Jobs grading papers, selling hot tools at the flea market, part-time teaching. Writing when I could, about Jewish as well as women's issues. I met Jewish married women who opened their homes and baked cakes and served coffee for me to talk with them about lesbian rights. I heard lesbians scorn me

for celebrating *pesakh*, "that patriarchal holiday."
Here, Chassids picketed a Jewish lesbian event.
There, a multiracial women's center invited me to talk
about Jewish women, "because it's important." From
Brooklyn, my parents sent their friend Charlotte's
obituary: it read like a history of the left. One minute
women cared about El Salvador. The next day it was
Nicaragua, and El Salvador slipped into file folders,
though nothing had changed. I watched a hit parade
of issues. Hardly anyone seemed to make
connections.

And always there were women scrambling into
the mainstream, shaping political justification for
whatever they were doing that minute, god forbid
anyone should honestly announce, *I just fucking feel like
doing this*. One woman actually wrote a three-part
article about reading books by men—as if claiming an
immensely daring act. A women's paper published it
too, all three parts. I saw feminists and lesbians hurt
and betray each other, no more but no less than
anyone else. It was all far more complicated than I had
thought. The only things that seemed simple were
kindness, and dignity, and life itself, delicate and
besieged.

It's not that I gave up on politics, which was—and
is—the only way I know to change what's wrong,
however clumsy and indirect. It's that I felt my heart
open and close in different places. Aged. Mellowed.
These are words some people would choose to describe what happened to me, but they describe wine
and cheese, not people. I was older, sadder, more
suspicious but easier on other people, obsessed with
time running out and the role of money in everyone's
life. I was kinder to myself. I noticed other people
more. I was exactly as angry as before, but simmering,
steady, a heat I could live with. I felt separated from
most of my generation, and my parents' generation
was dying, and the kids—who knew?

And after a while, years in fact, I noticed I had changed from thinking about Silver City as one which had driven me out, to missing the movement and community and years of hard trust born from common work and common goals.

And now there's a lesbian conference in Silver City, they send me a plane ticket to come speak. All day I've been running into old friends, sisters, comrades, ease of slipping immediately into political discussion. Was the agreement among us always so vast? Did we just focus at the wrong end of the telescope? Am I suffused in rosy visitor's glow? Gloria Reynolds, who served on the hiring committee when we were integrating the Crisis Line, who now heads the Afro-American Foundation for Economic Justice, grabs me in a huge hug, and we make a dinner date. A breakfast date with Brenda Levine, who worked on that first Night Watch march, and who helped raise money for my plane ticket; she's setting up low income co-op housing. I write all my dates on a matchbook. I feel welcomed home.

That night there's a dance, held in a gym in my old neighborhood, just off Cedar in the Southeast. I've had dinner with one old friend and am due to meet another, but I arrive alone and early and recognize no one. It's dark and the music painfully loud. I climb into the bleachers, just to sit in the darkness and feel myself nearly ten years older in Silver City. The music blares, and women, many of them in their twenties—and younger?—dance with that fierce energy I used to churn out every Friday night in the women's bar of this city. The last time I danced was at my students' graduation: time careening along, taking us all, one way or another.

At last the lead singer announces a break. I look around, eyes growing accustomed to the dark, using the strobe light to scan the faces. Next to me is Daisy.

"Daisy, hello," I say, surprisingly glad to see her. She's glad too, gives me a huge smile, and we hug sort of awkwardly in our chairs. She smells like peppermint soap. "I heard you were in town, how've you been? What's it like being back?"

"Exciting. So much going on." A friendly but stock answer—we never talked about what it was like being here in the first place.

But her answer is not stock. "It feels like that tonight, doesn't it? It's the conference. Maybe things will pick up from this. But it's been dead."

"Seems like big time to me. When I first came to Silver City I thought it was so small and dull—says something about my life now." The edge to my voice startles me: self-mocking. But Daisy smiles, and my heart beats open a fraction of an inch. "I miss it here," I find myself telling her. "I haven't been part of anything like this since, not with the sense we had then, of pushing limits."

"I know. It was the time." I can see into her eyes. Even in the dark, her face shines with a peculiar sweetness. She has freckles across her nose. How could I have thought she looked like Polly or Suzy? Her face is utterly her own.

"What've you been doing?" I ask. I'd heard that Sister Comrades had got its members to spy on each other. *Begin with Trotsky, end with Stalin,* was how my parents' recently dead friend Charlotte had explained Trotskyist politics to me, long before I needed to know.

"Oh, you know. I work in an office. We've been trying to organize a union. My big victory is they haven't been able to fire me." We both grin. "I quit Sister Comrades," she adds.

"I was just wondering . . . ." My voice trails off.

"I kept thinking we were the only ones with discipline, the only ones who took it seriously enough. We all thought that. But it just got tighter and tighter, everything had to fit, and boy," she gives a quick forced laugh, like a cough, "did it not fit."

I feel a lurch of identification so intense I'm stunned. Then I realize something. "I never saw you at a dance before."

"Oh no," that quick laugh again, "dances were frivolous. You were the ones who danced." Images of dancing, hot, stomping, showing up at the bar in threes or fives or even alone and you could dance with anyone, half the women in the room would be your friends or at least acquaintances: *sisters,* we said. But not Daisy?

She shrugs. "I still need to work politically, there's so much . . . damage . . . and danger. There's the union. I go to all the demonstrations, but . . . it's that other kind of work, that you give your life to . . . ."

Images of that first Night Watch, hundreds of us chanting *Rising Up Angry, Rising Up Angry, Rising Up ANGRY.* Images of the brave ragged rally to protest the Grand Jury that arrived in Silver City after all: the first multiracial coalition. It was so clear then, even Daisy and I, at opposite ends of something, knew exactly what to do and it was often the same act. *The Women United Will Never Be Defeated.* It's probably true.

"It's hard, isn't it," I say finally, "to figure out how to do it . . . ." I don't push naming what *it* is. I don't know what we share beyond the knowledge, acquired jointly with a few million others, of something more than daily existence, survival, the small self. Possibility: the winds of change.

"Tonight feels better, maybe things are picking up . . . ." Daisy's voice trails off, vaguely hopeful.

"And there are the kids, anti-apartheid stuff . . . ." Also vaguely hopeful. I feel like my parents or Charlotte, confused but willfully cheerful, looking to us, the kids of the sixties. The thought comforts and terrifies: *Did we? Will they?* I'm sure my eyes show something but Daisy doesn't look away.

A drumroll announces that the break is over. The music starts again at that all-encompassing pitch.

"Listen, I have to get some air, I can't take this music. It was really good talking to you." I pat her arm in its cotton shirt, my voice slightly wondrous.

"It was good," she nods. We hug again in our chairs, less awkward this time—smell of peppermint again, sweet and clean—and I get up to walk outside. I'm crying a little and I stand for a long time on Cedar Avenue letting the cool air dry my face. Teenagers are just getting out of the movies—*Return of the Jedi*—and I'm watching the traffic up and down the avenue, remembering when I was one car in that steady stream.

War
Stories:
the
Diaspora

janey

The dog's face was split in two. I could see the flesh
and bone and what was underneath the bone, and he
was still alive. Something, *an axe,* you breathed, had
split his face open, asymmetrical, Picasso, only the
eyes looked straight out at us. We had seen blood on
the snow-crusted road, tracked it over the drifts into
the grim winter woods of central Maine, thinking a
deer, some wild creature not properly killed, thinking
gunshot, never for a moment thinking *dog* or *axe.* The
eyes look straight at us and you begin to moan *oh god*
while I turn deathly calm the way I do and take your
arm and say, *that's all right* and then—*what should we do?*

Such pain, you say, *we have to shoot him.* I want to take
him to the vet but you, bitter, say, *there's no point, let's get
Janey's gun,* and then—*I bet George did it.*

Janey is our neighbor, our only friend around
here. Every afternoon we walk down the road to
Janey's to drink tea, sometimes with soda biscuits and
butter, really margarine. We sit around the old table
by the kerosene heater, and when one of us has to pee,
we leave because Janey's embarrassed that she still
doesn't have an outhouse, only a slop bucket. George
is her teenage son. He's quit school and steals small
from everyone, including us, but is on probation and
has promised not to again, though a few months later
he would steal everything nice we owned plus a full lid
of good dope, but we are at this point thinking he's not
a bad kid. We know Janey used to beat him, but now
he's too big. We know he has violence in him. They
live, Janey and George, with her brother John, who's
small and high-voiced, is called retarded, and Janey
gets paid by the state to take care of him. She always
calls him *Brother,* never *John.* Whenever we stop for tea

she chases him out of the kitchen and he hovers just outside the doorway—there is no door—*to spy,* Janey says, but we think just to listen—we are the day's news. It's clear Janey hits him when she's mad which is often.

We reach Janey's, the grey house, the tiny porch step, knock—I let you do the talking, your home, your people, and besides I can't imagine what to say. You begin: *Janey, we found a dog in your woods cut up and dying—*

That son of a gun is that where he went he was going after my rabbits and I wasn't going to let him eat my rabbits, no sir, I don't take that from any dog—

Janey, you interrupt, *can I borrow your gun to put him out, the pain must be awful.*

I'm out of bullets, she says, all reasonable. *Otherwise I'd have shot him but I just didn't have any bullets and I'll be damned if I'm going to let any dog come on over and eat my rabbits, he's been here before, that one, and I'm not raising those rabbits so some damn dog—*

Well, then we'll go on up the hill to get a gun, you say, *I want to put him out.* You are calm, friendly. We all agree it's a fine idea.

As soon as we're down the path from the old grey house your voice slams into me like a truck: *she has bullets, she just didn't want to use them up and she didn't use the axe because she was out of bullets, she did it to do it. She wanted to do it.* All the way up the hill you repeat, *she wanted to do it.* I'm stunned, an innocent. Janey.

We get your gun, an automatic. *Can you imagine,* you say, checking the clip to make sure it's loaded, *following the dog into the woods and doing that to him, can you imagine the strength, the rage?* I imagine nothing, I have no mind, no body, just motion and calm, but you tell me to hurry and I hurry.

We scramble over the banks again, easy to find, the blood trail but no paw prints, maybe she, maybe George carried the dog out here to die. It's illegal, what she did to this dog, yet I know we won't turn her in.

He's there, the split skull. The eyes.

Do you want to do it? you ask, meaning, shoot. I've never put an animal out. We agree you'll do it and show me how—for next time?—*up against the back of his skull,* you say—I am watching the eyes divided by a chasm of skull/brain/flesh, clear pink edges of the cleft—

Don't look, you say, *it'll splatter all over,* but my eyes are locked on that sharp pink cleft, an eye on either side. I can't look away but the brains don't splatter— later we remember: hollow point bullets open inside. The noise is not loud, the skull acts as a silencer, swallowing the blast.

He dies, quick as a breath. Relief.

You walk away. I check the collar, in case there's a tag. I want to tell the people, anonymously, their dog is dead so they don't look for him to come home, but there is no tag: a brown dog, shepherd-like, mutt— and a month later I would pick out from the pound a brown shepherd-like mutt puppy, never thinking once about this dog until I dreamed about my puppy with a split skull and I knew I had been wanting to expiate something, heal the memory of the split dog.

But now we just walk down to Janey's, we don't want her to feel shunned or shamed, don't want to acknowledge what happened either, because we don't want to deal with her, *how, why, Janey.* You say simply that we shot him, and she takes the big iron kettle from the woodstove where it sits all winter ready for tea and pours hot water over a tea bag in each cup, and we sit down for tea and make talk for a bit, and then we say, *well, time to get back.*

And walk up the hill again. You are still saying how Janey has this in her, you know it, and George wouldn't come downstairs while we were there, Janey said he felt sick and went to lie down, said he always feels sick around something like that. *Something like that.*

We open our door, varnished against the Maine winter, and go in. The fire's died out and dampness and cold fill the room. You walk the few steps into the bedroom—on our bed is the green and yellow quilt Janey made for us when we first moved in and had nothing, not even a good blanket, and you take the quilt from the bed, folding it neatly. *I can't sleep under this,* you say, and I know what you mean but am reluctant to abandon our pretty quilt, Janey, our friend. *I can't sleep under this,* you say again.

He lived upstairs—I meant to say, he *worked* upstairs, on the third floor, that's where his printing shop was, and I said "he lived" because we lived downstairs on the second floor in an office; but semi-secretly. No one was supposed to know. I was scraping by as a free-lance proofreader, she did a multitude of odd jobs, none of which required her to leave the office for more than a couple of hours at a time. So we were always there with two dogs; then she left and I was always there with one dog. Occasional smells of food seeped out into the hall, though we rarely cooked: there was only a single hot plate and no refrigerator. Besides, she craved the soothing atmosphere of restaurants, where someone else does the cooking.

The printer must have known we lived there because he was around nearly as much as we were, but he at least went home, nine, ten, eleven at night, to show up again early the next morning. Sometimes we chatted on the stairs. Our car had New Mexico plates and his daughter lived in Arizona. He and his wife had visited years before and were planning another visit that summer. He loved to discuss the southwest with us, to contrast it with mid-coast Maine.

"The sky's a different color blue out there, did you notice that?" he'd ask, and when one of us would nod, he'd warm to his subject. "You can see for miles, like your head was a top, spinning. You can see in every direction."

Once, after days of soggy April, we had a particularly animated exchange about the summer thunderstorms for which the southwest is famous, and the vast rainbow arcing the horizon as the skies clear.

Another time he mentioned that he always used to think domes were ugly—domes are common hippie houses in Maine—but he said, "If the sky out there doesn't look like the inside of a huge dome, I don't know what."

The printer was small, maybe five foot five, and he looked remarkably like a mouse, a grey mouse with glasses, somewhat bald, and slightly pouchy around the mouth and jaw. He always wore a hat—not a cap—when he went out, and a coat, not a jacket. He must have been in his sixties. His eyes behind the glasses were grey too, but piercing, eyes that had paid a great deal of attention to detail. But why am I telling you about the printer?

Mid-coast Maine is where we lived/worked in an old office building with pressed tin ceilings and a fourth floor, now gutted, with splintery rotting floors. Once it was a dance hall, like the uppermost level of every single building on both sides of Main Street, when Glen Hill was a granite boom town and there was work and money and good times. Now there were empty offices and store fronts up and down Main Street and not even one bar (a blessing, considering the propensity of the town's young male population to drink).

We moved into the office in September. Lest you feel sorry for us, let me say it had three rooms, radiator heat, and a toilet with (cold) running water, plus sidewalks shovelled and sanded, courtesy of the city, using the term loosely. The tin ceilings, originally designed to imitate molded decorative plaster, sported peaches, melons, and bunches of grapes, and the black and white linoleum squares covering the floors, though faded to charcoal and beige, were still elegant. All this for $150 a month; high living after a two-room log cabin with wood heat, no water, no electricity, no insulation, an often impassable road in winter, and mosquitos whining through the chinks in summer.

I am avoiding the point. The point is this: when we moved into the office we had been lovers for nearly five years, through most of which we fought bitterly, desperately—howling, screaming, sometimes throwing one another around, more often satisfying ourselves with intense audio effects. Most of the time we'd lived together out in the country with no close neighbors, and you can see what a blessing that was.

Here are our fights: her characteristic gambit was historical, the dredging up of everything I'd ever done wrong, the same poor little cluster of misdeeds which I would, clearly, never expiate, so why it took me all those years to recognize atonement was not in sight I don't know. My characteristic move was (and by chance it slant-rhymes) hysterical; the injustice of her litany never failed to unleash in me torrents of helpless rage so intense I am surprised I didn't kill her or myself. What finally pushed me to learn control was the night I put my hand through the office window. Blood streamed down my arm, biting wind rushed in through the broken glass, and I had to face the dangerous water I was trying to walk on— though, to tell the truth, the cuts were superficial, and the icy wind blew only in my fantasy, since behind the jagged window sat an intact pane of storm glass.

But the next time I felt that killing rage rise up in me—she had locked me out so that I was stuck on the narrow landing outside the office door. It was a harsh wet night. The upper portion of the office door was glass . . . . Guess what I wanted to do more than anything in the world. But I thought. I thought of consequences: of cutting myself, of needing to replace the glass; the expense, the embarrassment. Iron-willed, I cooled myself out. Then I tricked her into thinking I'd left and when she opened the door, I boldly pushed my way in.

But before that, while I was locked out sobbing on the landing, the printer came by from upstairs. The walls and ceilings of this building, while old and solid, were not soundproof. We could hear his printing press, the phone, conversations with customers. So we knew he heard our fights, vicious uncontrolled fights, fights between two women who were lovers in smalltown Maine, a Jew and an Italian, neither with a lick of verbal restraint.

The printer came by from upstairs. "Hello," he said, "nasty weather we're having." I murmured agreement. "Doesn't it make you miss Arizona—I mean New Mexico, that's right. The dry air and the sun, how it comes out and dries every speck of dampness. My daughter says it doesn't even matter if you put laundry away damp." And then he passed along downstairs, restraining himself, I could tell, from reaching further into his favorite pocket of southwestern observations which he obviously did not get to trot out nearly often enough. His vague but flawless tact awed me, and it was possible to hate myself less because a perfectly decent, reasonable and, above all, calm human being treated me as another being like himself.

The printer was always up there in his shop, even though we knew by the footsteps on the staircase how few customers bothered to climb the two long flights. I heard from my friend Sylvia, a bookkeeper who knew the dirt on just about everyone in town, that he'd been considered an excellent and reliable craftsman and had once done a thriving business. But now there were three other printers in Glen Hill, all with state-of-the-art equipment; one had even moved up from Boston to specialize in arty press work. Glen Hill was about to grow, and by the time I left, Main

Street would be showing definite signs of invasion from hanging ferns and primary color salad spinners.

But the town was growing in services, restaurants, tourist shops; not industry and not business. We used to wonder what the printer found to do up there all the time. His southwest stories suggested a deep fondness for his wife that precluded any suspicion that he was trying to keep away from her. We decided finally that the explanation was simple. He loved to print. He loved his equipment, however outmoded. He loved solitude. I used to envy his calm up there, the sanctuary of it, high above Main Street with only the ghosts of turn-of-the-century Glen Hill dancing above his head, executing who knew what intricate capers to who knew what high-stepping music.

And envied it more and more, as the velocity of discord increased between us, the fights, me hurling the beautiful wooden-with-leather-seat desk chair against the wall, denting the wall and smashing the chair arm; the screaming, the sobbing. The printer was the one who heard, even more than several waitresses in various local restaurants where we compulsively spent money we could not afford on the one somewhat reliable pleasure we could come up with. Unfortunately we often ruined this extravagance by fighting, and once we were crying so hard we had to walk out on an expensive dinner in one of the tourist restaurants that had just reopened after its seven-month winter break. I wanted to ask the waitress if we could take the dinner home, but I was ashamed to be caring about food at a time like that. It was a full year before I'd walk into that restaurant again, and then it was with Sylvia and her lover Florence, taking me out to dinner the night before I left Maine.

The waitresses by and large were kind, but they didn't have to listen to it day after day like the printer did. It was getting more intense. She wanted to leave.

I was stricken though secretly relieved, my ambivalence—and hers—reflected in the trading off we did for the next few months: I'd beg her to stay and she'd relent just as I grew resolute; then she'd cajole me into softening just as she was making plans to go. We finally agreed to call it a trial separation, knowing this was a lie, and at last I set a date: "You have to be gone by June 1st," I said. And she was.

What did they think, all over Main Street—the stores we frequented, the restaurants; one day we were almost always together, then I was almost always alone. She had vanished. I might have committed murder for all anyone knew. Aside from friends—and there were not many, ours was not the sort of relationship people got close to—not one person asked where she was.

Except the printer. When I said she had gone back to New Mexico, he happily launched into reminiscence: "Remember all the colors? I had no idea about the colors, all the things that live in the desert. Did you ever see a yucca plant blooming?" I nodded, remembering a huge spiny half-globe with a stalk coming out of the top. The blooms have the texture of tulips and hang off the stalk like ivory bells edged with rose. "I was just thinking about those the other day," he added without explaining why the yucca had come to him from thousands of miles away. "Around here, in the woods, even along the beach, there's so much growing you take it for granted. Everything has it easy." I thought of the Maine winters, but I knew what he meant: he meant water, lots of it. "In the desert, every flower that blooms is a tiny miracle, you know? Did you ever see the cholla blooming?" He pronounced it correctly: *choy-a*. "It shocked me the first time, that color, just blooms out of nowhere. Magenta."

Another time he stopped me on the stairs with a magazine picture of desert paintbrush. "Remember that one?" he asked. I did. Desert paintbrush is scarlet, you spot them a mile away. "What do you think of the color, think they got it right?" he asked, professionally concerned.

"You should have been a botanist," I told him, "you're really into this." He smiled his self-deprecating mouse smile. "Maybe I'll do that next. Yup, maybe I'll be a botanist," sounding the word like it was slightly unfamiliar.

It wasn't too long after that I heard the landlord had cancer, inoperable, probably dying, and sure enough the building went up for sale. Just a little more than a year after I'd moved in and now there were no vacant offices on the whole street. Downtown revival is what they called it here, as in scores of other American cities where it was or wasn't working. I was scared my rent would skyrocket, not to mention that a new landlord not sick with cancer might pay more mind to the tenant whose business was obscure, who no matter what hour of the day or night always seemed to be at work with her dog along, and who—when the realtor knocked at the door to show prospective buyers—would spend a good five minutes running back and forth before she'd open the door. (I was of course picking up or covering over signs of domesticity, which were many, including the new office-sized refrigerator and spice shelf.)

Around the same time I ran into the printer, on the stairs as usual, and he was nervous too. He'd been paying, he told me, the same rent for the last fifteen years, $50 a month. He figured anyone who bought the building would raise his rent to the going rate. He didn't spell out the implications, but we both knew there was no way he could afford to maintain his print shop with a higher rent.

It was a youngish couple investing cleverly in real estate who bought the building. They raised my rent a little, asked me to pay a reasonable share of the heating bill; and they chose, for the time being, to ignore my obvious domestic installation. But when I ran into the printer on the corner, one of our very few conversations not on the stairs, he told me his new rent was beyond his means. He said this matter-of-factly, and the details were filled in later by Sylvia the bookkeeper. Not only could he not keep the shop, he couldn't even sell his printing press, old and huge as it was. No one would pay to move it. Nor could he afford to move it himself, even if he had someplace to move it to, which he didn't.

So at the age of sixty-something the printer closed his shop. I saw him the day the moving men came to haul out such shelving and small equipment as he had been able to sell. "Are you feeling bad about this?" I dared to ask a Mainer, a man to boot.

"Well, it'll take some getting used to," he said. "The wife and I are driving out to Arizona, see the daughter. Then," he shook his head, "it'll take some getting used to, all right."

A couple of evenings later he knocked on my door and asked if I wanted any paper. "What?" I said, startled. "I'm closing the shop, you know, and there's a few boxes of good paper, no point in letting the trashman take it." I am a sucker for paper anyway, so I went upstairs with him, and not only were there stacks of decent white paper, there were smooth, sturdy gold-colored cardboards, rough-textured purple vellum, long strips of posterboard in rose and yellow and ivory. There were onion skins and cream-colored heavy stock bordered with red so dark it was almost black. I collected what seemed to me a huge quantity of paper. "Take more, I'm sure you can use it," he urged, piling my stack higher and higher until I had more than I could use in a million years.

Then he was gone from the building. He got a job working for one of the other printers in town, a much

younger man, nasty sonofabitch named Wayne who
took no pride in his craft and made everyone who
worked for him tense and miserable. My friend Dora,
who set type there and got paid exactly one-third of
what Wayne charged his customers for her work, said
Wayne was vicious to the older printer.

I saw him a few times when I'd stop by to talk to
Dora. He always smiled like nothing was wrong, and
we'd say hello and ask each other how it was going.
But he'd be bustling from one end of the print shop to
the other, carrying a stack of paper, a can of ink.
There was no way or time to talk about our common
ground, the building—my home and his old shop—or
the soft air and flat light of the southwest, where
scarlet paintbrush, ivory yucca and flaming magenta
cholla blossoms somehow find water.

b u r n

"Is the cream for a burn?" I asked, not right away.

She was a hitchhiker I'd picked up heading north towards the mountains from Escondido, my first day out of the house since I'd arrived last week. I drove along getting stoned, just looking at where I was, smack in the middle of sage-covered range, sky big as the planet, when I saw her stick out her thumb at the side of the road. Thin as she was, in jeans and a jeans jacket, I thought she was a small man and drove by—I don't pick up men anymore. But as I passed, I could see she was a woman so I pulled over, opened the window to air the smoke, and backed up as she came running towards the car.

I tossed my pack, the newspaper, the soup pot I'd just bought into the back seat. The joint had gone out and I didn't know what to do with it, so I held it in my left hand.

"Thanks for stopping," she said, "I gave up when you drove by."

"Where're you going?" I looked at her. She was young, twenties, with straight kind of stringy brown hair to her shoulders. White cream smeared on the tip of her nose, around her nostrils, on her chin. Her face was red. I wondered if it was sunburn, from skiing. Practically all the white people in Escondido had red-to-deep-brown faces.

"Just to the blinking light."

"Fine." I had no idea where that was but I was up for driving. Besides, she was the first woman I'd talked to in Escondido except for the cashiers at Safeway. I was curious.

So was she. "What's your license plate?" she asked. "It's green, like Colorado, but it's not Colorado, is it?"

"Vermont." Along the road was no longer any town, just range and sage brush and an occasional huge adobe with solar panels.

"Are you visiting?"

"For a few months. I only got here on Wednesday—in time for the snow." It was April and the sky had been dumping snow in a frenzy of last chances.

"I wish there was enough snow to keep the ski lodges open. That's where I work. They closed this weekend."

"Can you make enough to live off for the rest of the year?" On the lookout as ever for minimal labor.

"No, I usually work summers too. But last summer I couldn't find a job."

"What's to do here in the summer?"

"Beats me." We both laughed and our eyes met. Hers were blue, pale and clear.

"What are you doing here?" she asked.

"Writing." This took some determination. I know how it sounds.

"You came here to *write?*"

"There's a foundation in Escondido, they give you a house to live in so you can write, or you know, paint or whatever you do." I was torn as usual between pride and an embarrassment I've never pinned down. Something about privilege. Something about *who do you think you are, anyway?* echoing from a childhood among small shopkeepers in whose loftiest dreams I would teach other people's children to read other people's books. I looked at the half-smoked joint. I still hadn't figured out where to put it.

"Hey, that's great," she grinned. "I have a friend who writes plays and, you know, there's a place like that in New York. Their motto is, *we don't produce plays, we produce playwrights.* That's great," she said again, and her enthusiasm opened me. I felt suddenly happy. So I said the first thing that popped into my mind.

"Is the cream for a burn?"

She nodded.

"Were you skiing?" I looked at her again. Denim jacket over faded navy sweatshirt. She didn't look like the skiers in the tourist shops.

"No," she said, "a real burn. With lamp oil. It caught fire. I was in the hospital for a couple of days. That was only last week, it's amazing, it's nearly healed."

It was amazing. Except for the cream and the redness you wouldn't have known. "Did it hurt your eyes?"

"No, or my lungs. Took off my eyelashes pretty good, though, and some of my hair."

"At least that grows back."

She smiled and shook her head, as if to say, *really*. Really what? How stupid? How lucky?

I stared at the road. Grass and sage whipped by, the sky huge and pale, mountains straight ahead, dark and snow-topped. Quiet filled the car. I wondered who she was. How she lived. If she made it through the not vicious but definitely cold mountain winter with wood heat. I wondered if she lived alone. If she had electricity. If she read at night by kerosene.

I wondered how she had burned her own face with lamp oil.

Here goes, I thought. "How did you burn your face with lamp oil?"

She could not turn redder, but her eyes shifted, and I looked at the road. No blinking light yet. "I don't mean to pry," I lied.

"Well, it was the strangest thing. I was going to pour the lamp oil in the lamp—" her voice was tight, pitched high, words came fast "—and it just *spilled* on me. I knocked it over or something, you know, and then Pete, my boyfriend, was lighting a cigarette and I was—up in *flames*." She gave a short nervous laugh, and I kept looking at the road, but I couldn't swallow.

It was as if I forgot how to breathe. I saw the cabin.
Nearly dark. She gets out the red plastic kerosene jug.
Heavy, the kind you tilt to pour. I saw a man. Bigger
than she is, wouldn't take much. Probably drinking.
Probably smacks her. Probably—splashes oil on her
face and lights up?

My mind raced, inventing the speech I was about
to make. *Listen*, I'd tell her, *I'll help you. There are other
women whose men did terrible things to them too. There's places
you can go. A new life, a new country even. The ski lodges stay
open all year—only you don't even have to work, all the women get
to play on the slopes, to glide down the mountains. They say it's
like flying—*

Even in my mind, this sounded lame. Besides, it
was all a lie except for some places to go and the other
women getting abused by men they were supposed to
love. And how skiing's supposed to feel. I didn't know
where a battered women's shelter was, how far away.

And I was afraid of pushing too hard. So I said,
"It's your business, but I don't know how you could
spill lamp oil on your own face." Her breath went in
and out. I waited about a minute listening to her
breathe until I couldn't wait anymore. "What happened?" I put my hand on her arm. Thick with clothes.
"You could have died or been blinded . . . ."

She raised her chin. "Just some hair and eyelashes," she laughed abruptly, and glanced at me, her
face suddenly so bitter—as if her good humor had
peeled off with the burned skin—I almost shut my
eyes in sheer reflex. But I was driving, so I stared at
the road, and a yellow blinking light appeared out of
nowhere.

"Hey, here's where I get off." She had retrieved
her casual cheer. I pulled over and she climbed out,
genuinely smiling. "Good luck with your writing."

"Thanks," I smiled back, stupidly polite. I wanted
to say, *What about you?* To ask her name and tell her
mine, to say, *I'll help.* But in the second I paused, she

waved, turned to cross the highway and disappeared. That fast. I couldn't even see where she'd gone to.

I sat there in the car, staring at the half-smoked joint in my hand, wanting to crash full speed into the blinking light. Instead I floored the gas and squealed out from the side of the road, heading who knew where but it was north, towards the mountains and the snow—white as the cream on her burned face.

vacation pictures

We drive south through a Vermont blizzard that turns into vicious sleet in Connecticut, blinding rain as we pull into Brooklyn, where we sleep at Shelly's. Morning, by the time we've consumed several cups of coffee and pita bread fresh from the downstairs grocer, it's another goddam blizzard. You're pressing to leave now and I want to wait a while, so you passive-aggressive nag, *it's your turn to feed the meter.* I'm in the middle of talking to Shelly—*my* friend—and why the fuck are you so hellbent on measuring turns. I suddenly see our life together as coy, gamey and tightassed. I don't want to go with you. I want to stay in Brooklyn with Shelly.

So that's how we drive off on our vacation. We're heading south and get about thirty miles, as far as New Brunswick, New Jersey, where we are forced to pay $50 for a motel because driving's impossible, and the only good thing that has happened is the drive over the Verrazano Bridge, my first time—yours too, but then you are not a New Yorker. I am wondering if I am still, did the first twenty years mark me indelibly as I like to think, even now when people say I've barely got an accent anymore, and I don't know how to respond after years trying to shed it and more years trying to take it back.

Anyway, the Verrazano Bridge, silvery, techno-logical beanstalk, only we land in New Jersey and the expensive motel. We're both stopping smoking today after a solid week of puffing our brains out, and we are on edge. I don't want to go on this stupid vacation, I'm bitter and resentful, the time, the money. I want simply to stay home and get some work done.

All week before we left, snow and ice made our road virtually unpassable, and every day one of us stayed home waiting for Norma, the friend of a friend who was supposed to animal-sit the dog and four cats. The question was, would Norma's car make it up the road? But every day for a different reason she couldn't come. One day she got as far as the next town when her tire went flat, and another day her car absolutely refused, practically slid backwards down the hill. The last ditch hope was to see if snow tires made a difference.

All week, while you were getting more and more deeply depressed at the idea that we wouldn't be able to go, I was positively gleeful, trying to act subdued, until an hour before it was time to leave, we heard Norma's car chugging up the driveway, and I said to myself, *Vivian, for once in your life think of someone besides yourself,* and I tried to be glad for you.

And even am sort of glad, until you start being coy, measuring turns at Shelly's, insisting we leave right that second, right into a snowstorm that is dangerous and costs us extra money. We're irritable and I wonder how I came to be with you and how I will survive this vacation I don't want.

But the next day, the snow, if not entirely melted, has stopped falling and we keep driving south and by the day after we can see grass and then flowers. In January. We eat in diners where white people talk like the white parents I saw interviewed on the news when I was nine years old, *how do you feel about your child going to an integrated school?* Customers seem almost equally Black and white, the workers also mixed, not evenly but ten times more than when I'd worked in Virginia in 1967 teaching at a now historically, then totally Black college (and when I'd walked downtown with a Black co-teacher, male, who was not then but did in fact later become my lover, a car full of white men with that accent shrieked obscenities at us, and we ran back to campus, breathless and ashamed, because there was not one safe place downtown).

The third day from Brooklyn we come into Florida, shed our sweaters and corduroy pants, walk along the beach and feel hot sun pouring down over our deprived skin. Finally I am glad to be here. I sit in the sun to read the news for the first time in days and learn about a march planned in a county just north of Atlanta to protest segregation. I want to be part of it. History is happening and we are on a frivolous bourgeois vacation. I try to talk you into leaving Florida the next day to drive to the march. You, exhausted from endless weeks of work, relaxing finally into sun and sleep, refuse: you're not leaving. You say we'll never get there in time and if I want to go, I can. But I'm afraid to go alone (of course I don't say this), and I'll never make it in time driving by myself, and besides I suspect you'd be furious at me for abandoning our vacation. I give up the idea, blaming you for my passivity. We don't even fight about it, I just take your reluctance as law and resent it. You don't know how it sets you up in my mind as superficial and materialist: *a vacation,* I think scornfully, until months later we talk about it. You had not known how deeply I felt nor did I realize you were somewhat open to negotiating. Though I wonder still if this is revisionist history. I know how people use each other as excuses.

The truth is we've been together two years and we're right in between being new lovers and old ones. Will it stick? "When we were in Florida," months later you will say, "remember you worried that I thought you were weird and I worried that you thought I was superficial? The truth is, you *were* being weird and I *was* being superficial." When you say this, I will feel intense relief.

But right now you seem strange to me, except you can always make me laugh. You keep making the same jokes because they set me to gasping helplessly, convulsively, knowing I shouldn't, jokes about how ugly you are—which in fact you aren't—like *I'd better not go in the water, I'll scare the fish*—but funny. I want you just to be easy and accepting of how you look (so I can be easy and accepting of myself?). But you're not.

And I wonder: *Is this who I want to be with? Do I love you? What is love? . . .*

On Wednesday we take mushrooms together, a gift from a favorite student. I'm sitting on the blanket, frightened, the drug just coming on. You want to go to the bathroom a couple of hundred yards up the beach, but you say, *I don't want to leave you alone.*

The air is hot and visible. Words come strangely to my mouth, slow, as from some other larynx, some other brain center: *Yes, that's a good idea*, I smile weakly.

Vivie mustn't be alone, you say so gently sunglasses hide my tears.

Suddenly I love you. *If there were time, I'd have babies*, I say, profound and thick-voiced, grasping mortality.

After a while we walk into the shimmering Atlantic, circles of golden light dancing over the green transparent water. We play in the ocean, and fear stabs me, dispelling the golden light, the cool joy: *Will we drown? Is this dangerous? Will the car keys get stolen, and the car, our money . . .* and all at once comes a shocking thought and I say, speaking very slowly, and I don't think you realize what a bold thing this is for me to imagine: *I'm contemplating the possibility that the universe is not actively malevolent.*

Not *actively*, I'll think later, backsliding. But passively? The underlying principle is, after all, constraint, as now we have only three days left on the beach, lazy days, swimming days, walking days, shrimps and oysters and take-out from a Thai deli, and making love not so often as you'd think, considering it's vacation, but a couple of times anyway, and we are more or less liking each other (except once walking along the beach I'm trying to explain about a poem

I'm writing and you don't understand or aren't interested and I think, *maybe I don't want to be with her,* and am flooded by such terror and guilt I say to myself immediately, *swallow it, deal with it later).*

We drag the camera out only once, to a fishing pier, and when the pelicans swoop in close with their huge wings and expandable bills, you take pictures and I think, *If I could be any bird, I'd pick this one* —for the freedom of those vast swoops.

It's not until we're leaving that we take out the camera again. We check the corners of our little efficiency apartment to which I am by now fiercely attached, pack the car, and drive to the beach for our last walk before heading day by day back into hard winter. We're taking pictures of each other, I shoot as you walk towards me, the ocean at your back, your hair blowing. You're wearing a turquoise t-shirt with pandas on it, climbing bamboo. We are both especially fond of pandas since learning that all they ever do is eat bamboo shoots and fuck, continually. I try to imagine life without the need to dent some surface. I try to imagine I don't know I'll die sometime, maybe even soon, and you will too.

I take your picture as you walk towards me. You're laughing, the t-shirt is just a shade bluer than the ocean, a shade greener than your eyes. You flip up the t-shirt and flash your breast at the camera, mugging a wide funny mouth as if to get back at me for taking pictures of you when you think you are ugly and should not be photographed. In fact you are a beautiful and sexy woman, but there is nothing sexy about the gesture or the photo. It reminds me what I do and don't love about you and it's the same quality: you'll make fun of anything. I love how you goose the prig in me who learned young to shrink—along with my mother and all other women who married a half-class down—from my father's very occasional dirty joke; I hate how you sometimes seem to value or respect nothing. Sometimes your mocking voice seems crude, embarrasses me, and I look around to see who's listening. I hear the snob in me when I say this and am ashamed.

After the breast-photo and probably one or two others, you say finally, brash, the way you get when you're embarrassed and pushing ahead anyway, *I know you're above all this, but I'm still subject to vanity. Could you take a couple of me after I comb my hair?*

These words, and the sight of you, slightly embarrassed, combing your hair to pose, touches something raw in me. Your vulnerability, the simple thing you want: to feel pretty. Is that it? Or is it your failure to treat this want as I do, because I am not above it, in fact I am an extremely vain person, catching a glimpse in every store window or mirror I pass, checking, checking—how can you not know this? But I would never never ask to comb my hair. My vanity consists partly of pretending not to care, refusing to compete, take me as I am. How did I convince you I am above it and you should be embarrassed to want to feel like a pretty woman? I think of our familiar joke:

Two women, sitting up in bed, both speaking at once:
"But I thought *you* were butch!"

We resolve this joke intermittently by repetition, by making other jokes, by recognizing we are both butch, both femme, and it's the uneasy lack of distinction that sometimes catches us up in competition instead of compassion. I think of Otis Redding, killed in a plane crash that summer I taught in Virginia, his throaty sobbing voice instructing, *when that girl gets weary/young girls they do get weary/wearing the same old shabby dress*—image of a woman worn down by ordinary life which in no way cherishes her. Butch knows how to cherish: *try a little tenderness,* Otis urges eternally on my *Best of Otis Redding* cassette, and I pledge to try.

But something more. The loved one as all-powerful, needs nothing, gives everything. I forgot you are vulnerable. Forgot. It scares me, the responsibility of loving you, caring for you. I want only to be the frightened small one on the blanket: *Vivie mustn't be alone.* Must I be the large soothing one, the one who says effortlessly: *of course comb your hair, do whatever you want—I'll love you.* What if I fail, do not love enough?

You comb your hair and smile shyly for the camera, and no one but me (and other women who love you?) would recognize the smile as shy, but it is. In your smile I see my own tentative assertion: *here I am, am I pretty?* I feel pain for your vulnerability and your failure to see mine, and swimming around the tender place is the mirror we make for each other, even though you don't see it and I don't show you, around the raw, painful place which is not easy, accepting, natural, or anything but the cost of love.

my jewish face

*for the Jewish Women's Caucus of the
National Women's Studies Association
and in memory of Abbie Hoffman (1936-1989)*

It was the exact blend of rage and fun that got me
hooked on politics in the first place: deciding something had to be done, forming a group, and doing it.
Like Abbie Hoffman and Jerry Rubin—Jews and
Yippies—used to say, *Do it!* and if Jerry Rubin ended
up on Wall Street (a source of some humiliation to
those of us who measure Jewish safety by constantly
counting which side which Jews are on), Abbie Hoffman, as it turned out, had been plugging along underground all those years with his new name and plastic
surgery new Jewish face: still doing it.

We did it too—in this case, interrupted a performance we found insulting and made the audience to
some extent ours; a modest but thrilling feat. What I
remember most vividly, though, is not what we did or
even how I felt. It's Rae I remember and it's her face I
can see right this minute up on stage in front of the
cafe as the theater company was singing their stupid
finale. Because she was part of the company, one of
"them," and when it came to her part, she betrayed
them and announced herself.

The story doesn't start that night in the cafe. For
me, for the rest of the group it starts in the afternoon
around the lunch table. For Enid and Bonnie it started
the night before, when they had gone to the cafe to
see political theater. But for Rae it started when she
was an infant: orphaned, adopted, raised in a churchgoing family. At seventeen she discovered that her
grandmother was alive and a Jew, a survivor from

Hungary. Rae hitchhiked across the country to spend what turned out to be the last six months of the old woman's life with her. Then she hitchhiked back, came out as a lesbian, and hovered uneasily around her Jewishness like it was a gorgeous book in a foreign language. She didn't understand it but she craved it. She was nineteen, tall and large-boned with high Slavic cheeks, grey eyes, dark nearly straight hair. She joined the theater company.

It was her second show with them, early rehearsal. In one skit was a joke about the Holocaust, scraping the bottom of the bad taste barrel, and you're probably wondering about the joke; maybe afraid you'd find it funny. I wouldn't repeat it even if I remembered it, but it wasn't funny. In the same skit was a crack about animals looking Jewish. Each unfunny joke reinforced the other and Rae felt queasy. She said so.

The director of the theater company, a nubile man-loving sort of woman named Janet, ridiculed her. No one in the company stood up for Rae, predictably not even the one other Jew, who instead spoke the line that should be engraved next to (the by now somewhat hackneyed) *when they came for the x's I said nothing because I wasn't an x until finally they came for me*. The line I'm talking about is, *I'm Jewish and I don't think it's anti-Semitic*. So much for solidarity. Rae was nineteen and had been a conscious Jew for two years. She'd had no Jewish education, no exposure to Jewish culture or tradition, until the six months with her grandmother. In this she was not so different from a lot of American Jews, except for the six months part. She backed down and shut up.

And stayed shut up until that night on the stage.

But first comes afternoon, and at the lunch table Enid was upset. "It was disgusting," she gestured with her coffee cup, luckily almost empty. "There was a joke about the Holocaust and there was a woman wiggling around barking and meowing. The last line of the scene is, *She looks Jewish, doesn't she?* About the dog-cat character, whichever it was." Enid waved her cup again, this time in dismissal.

Bonnie took off her glasses and rubbed between her eyebrows. "The whole time I was saying to myself, *Is this happening, am I crazy?*"

"What was this?" Shelly asked. "A play, what kind of play?"

We were sitting in the stuffy cafeteria of a large Midwestern college campus. It was June and thousands of women from the questionably New South, the try-anything West Coast, the stiff calm towns of New England, the crumbling, yuppifying or occasionally renewing Northern cities, as well as from the bland flat heartland, had gathered for the annual feminist conference. A small group of us had coalesced just three days before in a Jewish caucus. We were wild about each other, saved seats for one another at workshops, met daily for lunch—we figured we'd get called clannish no matter what, so we might as well enjoy ourselves. One day Zelda and Penny led *midrash* about Ruth and Naomi—it was *shavuos*—and I had never known their story was connected to *shavuos*, nor that Ruth was a convert to Judaism and the mother of King David. As a lesbian with a gentile lover, I was moved by Ruth's devotion, a woman to another woman, and by the idea that someone could join a people through love. Zelda, on the other hand, hated the story, found the women weak and shadowy, cherished only for the sons they bore. She had been married for twenty years and kept an orthodox home, this Zelda. She preferred the story of Judith, who chopped off Holofernes' head. *Never pigeonhole anyone*, I reminded myself not for the last time.

Another day we sang Yiddish and Hebrew songs with vigor until we were grabbing each other's hands

for a jumping kicking line dance around the cafeteria
before the polite but appalled manager asked us to
stop. Yesterday at lunch we had talked about Israel,
the Palestinians, the Israeli peace movement, icy tension clamping down on everyone's temples as our
feared differences emerged. And there were differences. But we kept talking.

Today it had turned into a meeting about the
political theater Enid and Bonnie had gone to see the
night before. After two days of delicious Jewish pride,
one skit's throwaway insensitivity and contempt had
so stunned them that they had sat there quietly
incredulous. They hadn't even thought of telling
anyone. But at lunch Zelda casually asked what they'd
done last night, and then everyone was tossing questions on the table.

"This is supposed to be radical theater, like the
Mime Troupe or something?"

"Did anyone else seem upset?"

"What do you think they were doing?"

"What did *they* think they were doing?"

"Did you talk to the actors?"

"We went this morning," Enid said, "a couple of
them were there—"

"Yeah, they spared us almost thirty seconds,"
Bonnie cut in.

"We spoke with the woman who directed it,
Janet, she played the cat/dog creature—"

"What is this, *Animal Farm*?" Marian jerked forward, dislodging her breastfeeding baby's fat busy
cheeks. Lila wailed and Marian repositioned.

"Janet didn't know Nazi propaganda described
Jews as dogs," Enid went on. "She thanked us for
telling her, but of course she didn't *mean* anything by
it. The joke about the Holocaust wasn't supposed to
make fun of the Holocaust . . . ."

"What she *meant* . . . " Bonnie made a tight prissy

face and we all laughed, "was something like 'We're all Nazis' . . ."

"I can't stand that liberal bullshit," Shelly interrupted. *"If I'm Not OK You're Not OK Either?"*

Marian burst into song, the tune "Clementine"— *"If Everyone's Guilty, No One's Responsible,"* linking her arm through mine which dislodged Lila again (wailing, repositioning), but Enid kept on.

"She insisted she hadn't meant anything . . ."

". . . so we shouldn't feel anything," Bonnie snorted. "Then she had to go. She certainly wasn't about to change anything just because we were upset. She kept talking about artistic freedom, and—we understood—she was SO busy . . . ."

"She thought we were crazy . . ."

"Oversensitive," Bonnie corrected, making her funny little prissy face again, and we all laughed on cue, except Enid looked depressed and I wondered if she'd been called crazy a lot.

The cafeteria was nearly empty, the time allotted for lunch was over and I could feel a restless energy perched in the middle of the table. I have been an organizer on and off since I was seventeen and I recognized that energy. It was people wanting to fight back but uncertain what to do. I know when people want to fight but do nothing, everyone's sense of possibility shrinks up a little. That restless energy is my idea of sheer temptation, whereas blocking that energy—out of fear, laziness or just plain lack of imagination—is my idea of sin.

"What do you want to do?" I asked. The word *do* hung in the air, an odd moment of quiet.

Carla broke it. "We could go to the play and start a discussion when it's over."

"Tame, distinctly tame." Zelda wrinkled her nose.

"We could just interrupt the performance. We could give out leaflets." Shelly was getting excited.

"We can't get a leaflet together by tonight," I said automatically and instantly felt ashamed: Why was I offhandedly dismissing the idea? Who knew what we could do?

"Let's picket!" Zelda was piling her tray high with everyone's dishes. "I have to go do my workshop now, I'm up for whatever." Marian buttoned her blouse and tossed Lila onto one hip: "I have to get her to childcare. What about guerilla theater? Right at the entrance, we could do our own play." I resisted the impulse to say we couldn't get a play together so quickly.

But Bonnie and Enid were beginning to contort with self-doubt.

"What if we just took it wrong?"

"I can't remember exactly what gets said, what if we're being . . ."

"—paranoid?" I cracked, and we all laughed, rather bitterly.

"When are we sure," Shelly's voice dripped acid, "when they're marching us to the showers? Or do we say, *Well, maybe we need to wash.*"

But Bonnie and Enid were adamant. The responsibility was too heavy. They wanted the rest of us to see the play so we could act on our knowledge, not their feelings. We would attend the performance, paying for tickets—which annoyed the shit out of Shelly and me, but that's what people wanted to do—and when (or if?) offensive things got said, we would simply respond, thus forcing them to deal with our reactions.

So there we were, $6 a head. I have to say the show was unbelievably unfocused and just plain vapid. There was one skit about unemployment, a couple about TV and advertising—really bold subjects; one about American racism—unintentionally but distinctly racist; one about the Statue of Liberty in which poor Rae was the Statue, except we didn't know

Rae yet. She was just a large young woman, one of the actors. Half the jokes revolved around parts of her body. The overall message thrummed home with the subtlety of a buffalo herd was, *It's Your Own Fault If You Don't Do Anything* (definitely a variation on the *We're All Nazis* theme).

We sat in the audience waiting to be or not to be offended enough to do something: It. There was Janet scooting around barking and meowing and wiggling her small prized ass. There was the not funny joke about the Holocaust, and I said to myself in an affectionate but bossy tone, *ok, honey, you encouraged everyone else, you go first,* and I was on my feet asking in a very loud voice: "You think that's funny?"

Shelly said later when she saw me start to get up and heard the words come out of my mouth, her heart began to pound so fast she thought she'd have a heart attack. *It's really happening,* she thought, *now we have to go through with it.*

We did. Shelly spoke with a slow measured anger that was itself an irresistible force. "I have to say this very clearly, and I want everyone to understand it. The Holocaust is not funny. There is nothing funny about it." Dead silence while people combed the Holocaust for something funny. You could see them not coming up with anything.

"Do you know who's in your audience?" Marian was asking. "Maybe people who lost their families, or people who were tortured. You're supposed to be against torture."

"We are against torture, oh, of course," Janet the cat/dog nodded emphatically.

"But your jokes add to people's pain, people who've suffered what no one should ever suffer. Why would you want to make jokes about this?" Penny was asking with an inexplicably touching innocence. "People were . . . killed, tortured, right now it's happening . . . in Salvador. Now. You make it trivial, what they go through. Laughable. I know that's not what you want," she concluded sweetly.

"I'm not sure they don't want that," Shelly quipped under her breath, but I was crying. I was sure the audience too felt the gap outlined in neon between the cheap, shallow politics of the skits and the depth of these women.

Janet, deprived of some dignity by her tail and whiskers, kept repeating, "You don't understand what we're trying to do, let us finish, you don't understand . . ."

"It doesn't matter what you're *trying* to do." I put a hard edge on *trying*. "What matters is what you're doing. It's not working."

"We're on your side," whined one of the men who'd played too convincingly a creep pawing the Statue of Liberty. Several of the actors looked stricken, as if they couldn't believe our ingratitude.

"The whole point of political theater is that people shouldn't be passive," Carla waved her arms. "Why do you expect us to sit quiet and listen?" You could feel at least half the audience mentally nod, *Really!*

So the actors insisted on their intentions, we counter-insisted that intentions—in art as in life— were the least of it. Finally we agreed to let them finish the show in return for an open discussion with the audience as soon as the play ended. Which did not stop us—by now, imagine the adrenalin—from commenting loudly on anything that bugged us as the play proceeded.

Who remembers the rest of the skits? I waited for the show to end so we could discuss. At last came the finale. The cast gathered on stage at the front of the cafe to sing, each actor in turn, a verse about her or his character from the last skit. Each verse ended with the line, *see how you like my face,* sung three times, more or less musically. It was the turn of the large young woman who'd played the Statue of Liberty. She sang her verse like everyone else, concluding with *see how you like my face, see how you like my face*—she tossed her head, the words came through clenched teeth—*see how you like my* Jewish-looking *face.*

She was crying, that was why she had clenched her teeth. You could feel a wave blip through the other actors, like they hadn't expected it, and sure enough Bonnie whispered, "That didn't happen last night." The next actor took his turn on the song, the whole cast on-stage together, and the large young woman walked right off the stage behind the screen they all entered and exited from. The finale was just ending when she came back out and joined us in the audience right next to Zelda, who seized her hand and held on tight.

The play was over. There was weak scattered clapping. Then everyone started to talk. The cast charged us with censorship and with being deficient in our sense(s) of humor. We made all our points again, several times, and some new ones too, including Carla asking the company's one Black member how could *she* stand the show's racism (assuming no one else would mind?).

I watched the audience, mostly students from the college town, quiet young women, blabbing young men, a few women from the conference. The men were citing Marx and Brecht in sterile phrases which betrayed thin experience and fatal snobbery—college radicals whose underlying theme seemed to be not *We're all Nazis* but *Ordinary Working People Are Stupid.* Their language, their faces conjured up late-sixties Berkeley in such thick nauseating waves that I could only wish for my dead father's ghost to bellow disgusted judgement: *theory-schmeory* he'd say in a construction I only two years ago learned was Yiddish-derived. The same time Rae learned about her grandmother.

The next day over lunch we rehashed the details. We wondered about the young woman whose name we had learned was Rae. Mostly we were ecstatic, wanting to do it again and again, listing possible targets—

"*Fatal Attraction.*"

"Western Civ at University of Chicago."

"Bloomingdale's."

"The Unemployment Office."

Carla insisted she had done nothing wrong by making the one Black responsible for the whole company's racism—that's not how she put it, naturally. Enid brought up what everyone had noticed: she had not said a single word during the performance. She confessed that when we interrupted the play, she was mortified and hoped people wouldn't know she was with us. She said this with an edge of self-mockery, but the other edge was real discomfort—*we had gone too far.* Sometimes it happens. People pushed beyond themselves snap shut, a reflex of fear, resentment and guilt. After that they stop meeting your eyes and avoid you altogether.

Carla's defensiveness and Enid's alienation struck two sour notes, as if to remind us change comes hard. But everyone else was hooked on doing it: not a bad habit as habits go.

Word got around the conference. All day women asked about it and, better yet, spread fabulous rumors of Jewish women barring the theater exits (the size of cafe and audience grew sharply in these accounts) or forcing the entire audience into on-the-spot consciousness-raising groups. Someone had heard it was about Zionism and the PLO. A young graduate student told each of us at least twice she had never seen anything like it, members of an audience taking power from the stage. She was pink with inspiration.

That night was the final event of the conference,

a dance, and sometime towards midnight—I was
punchy with fatigue—I saw Rae heading our way
across the huge ballroom. She'd come to see us, so we
relocated around a table in the coffee shop while she
talked. For hours. That's when we found out about
her childhood, her grandmother, her shame about
knowing nothing Jewish.

"You think you're the only one?" Bonnie asked.
"Everything I know I learned in the last few years." I,
my cheeks surprisingly hot, nodded. I could tell this
made Rae feel better.

Finally someone thought to ask what had happened with the theater company. Janet the director
had been in a rage, especially at Rae, but also at two
women who'd tried to defend her. After nearly twelve
hours convulsed with fights, Rae had screamed, *YOU
may be a Nazi, I'm a JEW and I QUIT.* (We all cheered.)
Then she had gotten a ride over to the dance and here
she was. She wasn't sure what she'd do next, for work
or anything, but she was glad, she kept telling us that,
we shouldn't worry we had made it hard for her, she
was glad.

By now we were all crying and hugging. Then her
ride showed up, and we dug through our bags for
books, polaroid snapshots, our addresses, Jewish
strength we wanted to wrap her with, though the
truth is she had all she needed and more. "Don't
worry," she said again, "I'll be fine."

I *was* worried, that's the down side of doing it.
You make trouble and people get swept up into it and
then you leave and they're stuck with trouble. Rae
was out of a job, she had no Jewish family or
community.

But I looked at her face. She had herself. She had
been brave, and courage is a *mitzvah,* for her and for us,
then and now as I remember Rae standing on stage,
nineteen years old: those large bones, grey eyes,
straight hair. I doubt she often got spotted as a Jew,

and it seems she chose her Jewishness. When she was seventeen and found her grandmother. When she was nineteen, on the cafe stage. Maybe she's still choosing, in different ways, her proud angry Jewish face. Maybe I am too and that's why I remember.

Some
Pieces of
Jewish
Left

the woman in purple

I'm there shopping, me and the rest of Avenue A, when she comes into the store and right away she says, *Where's the manager?*

Where's the manager? It's Thursday, six o'clock, you think the manager works along with the shleps? She wants the manager.

She's not asking quietly, that's the thing, and she's a big woman. She wears a bright purple raincoat over royal blue pants. She has on those white socks with stripes around the top, and a red-and-purple scarf, kind of paisley, tied around her hair so you can only see a little bush in front, grey and curly. She looks about my age, early sixties, maybe a little younger, but her skin is very smooth, smooth and dark, not black but not white either. This neighborhood, she could be anything. Even without words you'd notice her because of her size and the colors she wears.

No one answers and she stands there in front of Cashier 9 where I'm on line. Again, bellowing this time: *Where's the manager?* I'm curious to see what she's mad about and the rest of line 9 is curious too. We kind of perk up a little and I exchange looks with the woman in back of me, a younger Black woman, about forty, wearing a very smart suit and high brown boots. Then I exchange looks with the girl in front of me, she has a sweet pink face and a very good baby singing to itself in the shopping cart.

The cashier is a young girl, maybe sixteen years old, blond. Her skin is having trouble. "The manager isn't in this evening, maybe I can help," she offers with such good manners I'm charmed.

We were here first whines the girl in front of me, a man's voice from in back complains *Great, she had to pick our line,* and someone else is shouting *Hey lady, wait your turn like everyone else.* Grumbling runs up and down line 9 and the cashier adds nervously, "If you'll just wait till I check these people out."

"Well, sure, honey, I can talk to you, but I don't think you can help me. It's about the mustard pot."

Wait your goddam turn, someone shrieks and I'm thinking, the mustard pot? This, the big mystery to talk with the manager about?

The cashier sticks up a *line closed* sign, smiles politely and checks line 9 madly through. Toilet paper in four-roll packs, loaves of bread, boxes of pampers and cans of beans glide along the counter. She's fast, this cashier. Meanwhile the woman in purple waits, purple arms folded across her chest, blithely indifferent to the hostile stares of half of line 9. I'm in the other half: curious.

I lift my sack of groceries, not so heavy since they put the seltzer in plastic bottles, but I'm not going anywhere yet. No one's waiting for me. I hang around.

Finally the line is cleared and the cashier turns to the woman in purple and says very sweetly, "Would you like to make a complaint or just pick out a new jar?"

"A new jar?" The woman in purple looks confused.

"Of mustard. The mustard."

The woman in purple laughs, a huge burst of laughter. "Aren't you a sweetheart. I didn't buy the mustard. I wouldn't buy Spengler's. Nobody should buy Spengler's. I want you not to sell it. Spengler's. In those little mustard pots." She pauses for emphasis. I'm not the only person hanging around, there are three or four of us. "You know where they make those little mustard pots?" she asks.

You can see the girl's mind working: *A nut,* that's what she's thinking, but she answers, "No I don't," with a smile obviously learned from her mother, meant to encourage the speaker to continue.

The woman in purple does not require encouragement. "They make those pots in Guatemala." She pauses again. No one gasps. *What's wrong with Guatemala?* I want to ask, but I'm embarrassed. Maybe it's like South Africa and I should know.

She continues, "The workers who make those pots in Guatemala, who are mostly women with babies that they carry on their backs or fronts, get lead poisoning from the paint they use on those pots."

Now I'm concerned. That's terrible. Besides, what happens when you eat the mustard?

"You know what they earn?" Pause. "One penny for every six pots. One penny." She looks around. *Goddam commie* mumbles a man with a perfectly bald head on his way out the door. There are seven of us hanging around now, a couple of younger people, the girl with the nice fat baby. One penny for six pots is a joke. How could you live on that?

"And you know what they get for those pots, here in this store? Look—go look at aisle 11, salad dressings." She pulls from her raincoat pocket a folded piece of paper, the white with blue lines notebook kind. "Spengler's Mustard, in glass jar (which is not exactly cheap I want you to notice), a dollar nineteen." The hand with the paper makes a flourish. We're waiting.

"Spengler's Mustard in the mustard pot, same size (or, to be exact, even half an ounce less) three dollars and twenty-five cents." She glances around triumphant. She's forgotten for the moment the cashier. "$3.25. Two dollars and six cents more for half an ounce *less* mustard, and the women in Guatemala get one-sixth of a cent for it!"

"That's disgusting," my voice surprises me. It is

disgusting. The girl with the baby is upset too. "And they get lead poisoning," she's saying, "what kind of company is this Spengler's?" which makes me think she's Jewish like me, despite the pink skin, always on the lookout for a German name.

A crowd is gathering where line 9 used to be. I hear someone snarl, *why don't you go back where you came from; always finding something wrong,* a man complains; and a woman next to me, young and pretty, mutters *can't even go to the fucking store without someone going on like anyone gives a flying fuck.* Her bitterness surprises me, not to mention her language.

The cashier bites her lip. "That's very interesting," she says, at which the woman in purple sneers, "Interesting?" with such disbelief that the cashier, who looks genuinely distraught, flushes and self-corrects: "It's terrible." She crosses her arms across her flat little chest. "I don't know what to do. I don't order the mustard. I just sell it . . . I mean people buy it, I can't refuse their money. I'd lose my job."

"I know, I know." The woman in purple pats the cashier's arm soothingly, "You don't order the mustard. That's why I wanted to talk to the manager."

A man from the crowd speaks up, the type you see in this neighborhood, once a week they take the kids to the park and already they're heroes. His skin glistens with health club exercise. He looks like he'd spend $3.25 for a jar of mustard. Sure enough, he starts arguing. "If not for the clay pots produced for Spengler's mustard, those same Guatemalan peasants wouldn't have any jobs at all, right? Right?" He looks pleased with himself and like being pleased with himself is a normal occurrence. Someone behind me mutters *asshole* which, I have to say, while I don't care for the language, makes a point.

The woman in purple is not fazed. "What are you, pro-sweatshop? You don't think people should get a decent wage for their labor? That's the argument capitalists always use to justify paying dirt wages: *It's better than nothing.*" I like the way she says *capitalists* like it's an insult.

"You can't judge third world countries by our standar—" he begins but the elegant Black woman from behind me on the line cuts him off.

"Don't give me that *our standards!* Whose standards you mean? Yours? Mine? Don't you think *cullid* folk want a decent life? Maybe you think we can't tell the difference." She glares at him and my dead Aunt Ethel pops into my mind: *Hatred is ice, not fire,* she used to say.

Shouts of *right on, sister* and *you tell him* echo through the crowd. The man turns deep red and shouts, "That rhetoric doesn't help third world people . . ." but the woman next to him, white, spiffy, and mortified, grabs his arm. "George, just shut up and let's get out of here." Shaking her head, she grips his sleeve and tugs him, still sputtering, out the glass door. I notice two of the other cashiers have joined us, and it crosses my mind that maybe nobody is left shopping anymore, they're all here listening about Guatemala and capitalism.

"It's not as if Spengler's is the only one." The person speaking is a fortyish white woman, very pale, the kind who didn't grow up in New York but has lived here for twenty years and works in the PTA and the block associations. They have very good manners, this sort of person.

The woman in purple pipes up, "She's right. Look around this store. Those grapes there are from Chile, you know they overthrew the legal president with the C.I.A. Our tax dollars. The other grapes, the ones not from Chile, they're from California. The grapepickers ask people not to buy because they spray the grapes with god knows what, something worse than DDT, and you know children work right along with the grownups, and pregnant women. And Nestle's, do I have to tell you about Nestle's?"

I'm getting depressed. Worse, I just bought grapes, I don't even know from which terrible conditions. "What are you supposed to do?" I ask no one in particular. "How do you know what you shouldn't buy?"

"I have a cousin"—this is the girl with the nice baby—"she goes shopping with a list three pages long of things not to buy."

"What if that's what's on special?" An old woman, nice and round, with black black hair.

"Yeah, what does she care, her husband's a doctor."

"That's the problem," beams the woman in purple, smacking her raincoat thigh. "Consumer boycotts penalize the consumer." (Does that mean I shouldn't worry about my grapes?) "That's why I want to talk to the manager. We're talking to all the stores. We figure if the managers all decided not to order what is really, to be honest, a stupid, dangerous and overpriced item, Spengler's might get the picture."

One of the cashiers speaks up, "Mr. Donner's only in from nine to five and he takes a looong lunch. But I don't know what kind of luck you'll have with him. You should hear him talk about unions." The girl next to her, another cashier, nudges her in the ribs and whispers something and they giggle. "He's a sleaze bucket," she volunteers and they giggle some more.

"Management always is," the woman in purple nods wisely.

The next time I see her is on the corner outside the Astor Place station and it's spring, a beautiful evening, still light at six o'clock. She's wearing the purple raincoat and with her is the Black woman who made the eloquent speech at the Avenue A market. They're giving out yellow leaflets and asking people to sign their petition. It takes us all a minute, but I recognize them and, miracle of miracles, they recognize me. I don't mean to imply I am mysterious, just hard to notice or remember.

The woman in purple reaches out her large soft hand with ink stains all over the thumb and first finger. "I'm Nellie Davros." She shakes my hand once I shift the groceries to the other arm. She can grip. "And this is Sondra Allen." I shake her hand too.

"I'm Ruth Schaffer," I say as if I think they're interested. Then I shock myself. "Why don't I help for a while and then you come over for coffee, I just live three blocks away."

In the one-second pause before anyone says *yes/ no, I can/I can't, here's a genuine or made-up excuse,* my face gets hot. I feel stupid, old, boring and humiliated to be caught thinking they might like to spend time with me. Then Sondra shrugs and grins, "I'd love to," and Nellie nods, "Why not?"

When I tell my daughter Nancy about this later she squawks, "What made you talk to them, Ma, they could be weirdos. Trots. Anything." Ethan, my grandson, glares at Nancy. "Ma-aaaaah," he says, sounding just like Nancy at his age. Ethan is thirteen and into being cool. I don't know how to explain to Nancy. Point out that her grandparents were socialists? Not to say socialists and Trotskyists are the same but both could get you in trouble. I don't say, *Nancy, the real reason I invited these women Nellie and Sondra is that they looked alive.*

"Watch Sondra," Nellie tells me. "Start with the leaflet and say something like, *Can I talk to you for a minute about a really important subject?*"

Sondra breaks from the rhythm she's already resumed handing out leaflets with a steady stream of talk. "You risk all kinds of nasty remarks with the 'important subject' line—half of them think the only subject worth mentioning is co-ops, or a new take-out deli. And crime, especially muggings. People always want to talk about muggings."

"That's true," I say. In the elevator of my building it's all people talk about. We're scared, that's why. I don't mention being scared, it'll make me sound old-fashioned.

I take a fat stack of leaflets. "Do you know about Spengler's mustard?" I ask each passerby, as if they should. "You'd better read this," I add ominously. The flyer is nicely laid out with a big drawing of a mustard pot and inside the pot a little drawing of women in Guatemala. They're working very hard. When the people on 8th Street start to look the leaflet over, I say, "My friend Nellie in the purple coat right there has a petition you should sign."

Some of them take the leaflets and crumple them up and throw them on the ground, littering and wasting what cost someone, probably Nellie and Sondra, good money. Some people refuse even to take a leaflet, like it's dirt or poison. One man snarls at me, *commie propaganda,* and a pale blue-eyed boy, sixteen, seventeen years old, sneers, *dry up old lady, who gives a shit?* A lot of people ignore me like I'm not there, but pretty soon my stack is gone.

Then we're walking over to my apartment. I don't want my excitement to show. But I haven't made a new friend in ten years, not since Harry got sick and I had to take care of him and by the time he died—not that I'm complaining how long it took, Harry and I had our troubles but I wanted him alive—I couldn't go places by myself anymore. Nancy nags at me, *Ma, why don't you get out, meet some people, you used to love concerts. See the museum exhibits. You used to drool over courses in the New School catalog:* (now comes the punch line) *What are you waiting for?*

I'm waiting to drop dead from getting nagged, I snap. I know she means well, even though it's her own guilt she's trying to quiet. If I'm not busy this bothers Nancy. I can watch her eyes, a lovely blue-grey like Aunt Ethel's, take on a funny sly look.

What am I waiting for? Nothing. I just don't want to go 63 and alone to places I used to go to in my early fifties with Harry.

But here I am waiting for the light to cross Second Avenue with Sondra and Nellie. Sondra cracks jokes steadily, the kind if you heard them on Johnny Carson you'd write to congratulate the network on finally getting a live one. Nellie laughs helplessly, "Sondra, let up, I'll pee in my pants."

"No more control than a little pooper," Sondra teases. Then she points—"Oh, good!"—to a store that sells who knows what, sparklers to stick on your eyelids, colors to spray in your hair, glittery socks. "Let's put green streaks in our hair. You know, for St. Patrick's Day."

"It's May 2nd," I object a bit literally.

"So? I've been a mother more than my adult life. I spent an hour and a half after work giving out leaflets—don't I deserve some fun? Hey, green hair, the kids on my block will say I'm cool."

I think about Nancy's reaction. Nervous, I decide, very nervous. "Ok," I throw my hands up in the air, a gesture so unfamiliar I drop my purse. "It'll make my daughter nervous instead of guilty. I'm sick of guilt. Let her resent me again, like she used to. Here I go."

I march myself into the punk store. "We want green hair spray," I say to the pale skinny child behind the counter, black hair sticking up on top and a purple stripe running through it. Male, I think. "One can— how much in a can?"

"I don't know, people just buy a can. I guess for one head. What do you have in mind?" The young person stares at me with the sudden horrified realization that I'm getting this green hair paint for myself.

"Whatta you think, girls?" I turn to Sondra and Nellie, leaning against the doorframe convulsed with laughter.

"I think one will do," Sondra wheezes.

"Do what?" Nellie chokes.

The person behind the counter purses his/her lips. We are not acting our age. I pay for the green spray. "My treat," I motion grandly to Sondra and Nellie, waving us out the door onto 8th Street.

So this one morning Nellie calls. "Ruthie, come to a party." Someone rich on West End Avenue is giving a party for everyone working on the Spengler's boycott.

"I don't know if I'm up for a party." The whole idea makes me nervous. Nellie will know everyone and within twenty minutes they'll surround her as she explains something important. She'll clang their minds open like a bell, clang, clang. Sondra will make everyone laugh, and the men . . . . I always imagine Sondra surrounded by men.

I will sit off in a corner, invisible and by definition boring.

"Come on Ruthie, it'll be fun, we'll have a great time. There'll be food, wine, deli, nachos. Pigs in blankets if we're lucky." Nellie makes a great nag, she should get together with Nancy. I do have a weakness for pigs in blankets.

Nancy goes shopping with me for this party. I insist I don't care if I'm 123 years old, I will not wear a navy blue pants suit. Finally I buy a crocheted peach sweater and a nice pair of grey corduroy slacks with big pockets. Sitting here in the bagel place waiting for Nellie and Sondra I feel like an old fool.

Finally Nellie arrives in her purple raincoat as usual, and underneath a pink satin blouse and dark red pants. I can see a roll of fat around her ribcage that looks nice through the satin, like you could pinch it.

Not that I mention this. Then Sondra shows up with a heavy-set Black woman with rich brown skin, very short hair a little greyer than Sondra's. Her name's Darrell and she's shorter than Sondra but solid as a rock. I look at them and don't ask me how, I know: Darrell is Sondra's lover. Not only that. When Sondra introduces us, Darrell smiles at me and—there is no other way to describe it—my heart flip flops. We're walking down 82nd Street, and I'm trying to act normal. Beautiful Sondra has a woman lover. I just swooned from her smile, Sondra's woman lover's smile. I have only reacted that way to about three smiles in my life and one was Paul Newman in *The Long Hot Summer* and it's Joanne Woodward he's smiling at.

Next thing I know, Nellie's daughter Emma turns up at the party with her friend Selena. I guess I'm on the alert, I take one look at them and think, *they're lovers too*, though this is not such a psychic experience, no flip flops or anything. It's how they dress: jeans, no makeup, and they're each wearing the same pair of unmatched earrings. Emma, in addition, has a few silver hoops in her ears. She must have about six holes.

The party's sort of a dud, lots of people but light on wine and even the potato chips run out. We find a cab willing to take six of us, no easy feat, and zip up to Sondra's where we order up pizza. Darrell tells stories about work—her job is to get the schools to admit homeless kids. Darrell impresses me, smile aside, and I feel a jealous stab. Beautiful Sondra. I try to find signs of trouble, something wrong with Darrell, tension between them. Not that I imagine myself in Sondra's place, this thing with women makes me nervous. Besides I am no fool, I am 63 years old and plain. And white. In the end I have to admit, Sondra and Darrell look perfectly in love and perfectly happy, and I have to tell myself, *Love is trouble, Ruthie, you forgot already?*

I don't remember what we're talking about when Emma says, "So Ma, the Gay Pride march is June 24th, you're coming?"

I pat myself on the mental back for guessing about Emma and Selena. Then I look at Nellie. You can tell she's crazy about Emma, but she's not happy. Sondra looks at me and raises her eyebrows.

"Oh, I won't have time," Nellie smiles regretfully, "I'm working on Spengler's, then there's War Resisters . . . ."

"You don't have *time!* I can't believe you said that." Emma leans forward, shaking her earrings, every bit as tough as her mother. "You have time for everything, but somehow this march, this once-a-year march, that's too much?"

"It's not that." Nellie scowls. "I'm working on life and death issues, not sex . . . ." A wave of her hand dismisses sex.

"Ma," Emma's pitch rises, "it's not just sex, it's being free to go out on the street without people spitting at you." (Had someone spit at Emma?)

Nellie's lips purse, a new look for her mouth. "It seems self-indulgent to me, all this . . ."

"Self-indulgent!" Emma explodes, practically bouncing in her chair, shouting over Nellie's voice, "What's wrong with sex, fucking hypocrite, you always told me about dignity, bread and roses. Roses! Remember? You said politics takes a big heart. Where's your big heart, Ma? No room for a few queers?"

"I don't feel like I belong there . . . ." Nellie looks cornered.

"Think you're too good for us?"

"No, Emma . . . ."

"You know it's important now, especially, people act like we not only have the goddam plague, we deserve to have it."

Nellie's beautiful dark skin is mottled with red. I

try to change the subject: "Sondra, you got any coffee?"

No one even responds. Emma is sobbing, "She named me for Emma Goldman. Emma Goldman spoke for gay rights. SHE didn't think it was self-indulgent. SHE wasn't too busy . . . ."

"She could afford to, she always had a man," Nellie's voice cuts through, bitter.

Stunned silence. I feel the room expel a huge breath, like when you finally say the one thing you've been trying not to. Suddenly I understand that Emma chose to ask Nellie in front of us because of Sondra and Darrell. I look at Sondra who stares at Darrell who stares at the floor. Selena's eyes fix on Emma. Only Emma, mouth open, looks at Nellie.

Emma speaks first but the anger is gone. "I can't believe you said that." She seems very young, staring at her tough competent mother.

"Emma, baby." Even Nellie's voice sounds deflated. "If I were glamorous it would be one thing. All I ever got was your stupid father, you know what he was like . . . ."

For the first time since I saw the woman in purple in that supermarket I feel tender and protective towards her. "I'll march with you, Nellie," I say out of nowhere. No one should get spit on. Besides, why not? I can paint my hair green. My heart can flip flop from Darrell's smile.

"Nellie," Sondra leans over to put her arms around Nellie's hot pink blouse, "if you were a lesbian, there'd be women kissing the hem of your garment, you know that?"

"I'm a jerk," says Nellie and sniffles.

"I love you, Ma," says Emma. "And you're beautiful. If you only knew."

That night I dream Sondra and I are in a booth at the souvlaki place we go to sometimes after leafletting. She says to me, *Ruthie, if you were a lesbian, there'd be women kissing the hem of your garment.* In the dream I grin, and then I stick my legs out into the aisle and together we carefully check the cuffs of my new grey corduroy slacks.

After the march, Selena and Emma take me up like a protegé and I was definitely somebody's protegé around that march, half the people I couldn't tell who was what. There were men and even some women with whips and chains. Emma and Selena each explained separately, "most gays aren't into s and m." They were embarrassed, so I told them about the magazine I saw at Nancy's when she was still married to that *shlemiel.* It was men and women together. I always assumed it was his, but who knows.

I'm over at Selena and Emma's for brunch, stuffing my face with a cranberry-walnut muffin, when Selena mentions she goes to *shul* every Friday night. I swallow a walnut chunk.

I haven't been to *shul* since I was a girl and then just a few times. My parents were—you know, no to pork, yes to shrimp in the Shanghai Palace around the corner from my Aunt Ethel's. We always did seders, though I never learned the Hebrew and neither did the other girls. But when Ethel died we just stopped. Ethel lived to be 93 and totally right in her mind, not like my mother, who faded slowly like Ophelia in *Hamlet* which I saw twice, once on stage and once on television, and both times Ophelia was sweetly crazy and drowned. The second time I saw it I was shocked that she didn't drown on stage, someone tells about it: I thought I'd actually seen it.

Shul. "Selena, don't mind my asking, why do you go?"

She smiles that slow beautiful smile. "We always went when I was a kid and I loved it. I thought I would be a rabbi."

Pages of history unfold between me and Selena.

She's young enough to have grown up thinking women could be rabbis. Just like that. To me it would be like thinking a woman could be god with that huge white beard in the Golden Book bible I got Nancy when she was five.

"They know about you and Emma where you go to *shul?*"

Selena swallows and I watch the muffin progress down her long dark throat. "It's a gay synagogue. Everyone there is queer."

I never heard of such a thing. To me synagogue means living like your parents or in many cases like their parents. Being gay means living *not* like your parents.

"Do you believe in god?" I have not asked anyone that question in fifty years. I find it hard to believe that people do, believe in god, especially someone like Selena with her two different earrings and her hair sticking straight up.

"That's not what it's about for me. It's my culture."

"I understand that," I say. "It's my culture too." We both laugh, and Selena ducks her head slightly to glance over at me.

"Maybe you want to come with me sometime."

"Maybe." Then I remember the gay part. I actually spill some coffee and blush.

Selena's quick. "You don't have to be gay or anything to come," she says casually.

I busy myself with the spilled coffee. Then I turn to Emma. "What do you think?"

"You know Nellie . . . ." Her grimace implies an entire world view. "I'm pretty anti-religion. I feel weird in a synagogue. I don't know the language, I don't know what to do. It seems stupid."

"You sound just like Nellie." A faint smile curves Selena's mouth. "It's not about religion, it's about being Jews together."

"I don't feel it. Anyway I'm only half-Jewish."

"Tell it to Hitler," Selena tosses off in a surprisingly light voice and starts clearing the table. I stifle the impulse to say *Selena, how can you?* but Emma stifles nothing. "You're like my Aunt Nettie, can't open your mouth without her bringing up the Holocaust. Like it entitles her to something." Emma flicks her wrist, whisking away the Holocaust. "What does Jewish mean now anyway except fussing for holidays and arms for Israel?" A second's pause. Then she adds dutifully, "And a few songs."

I hear rather than see Selena hurl the plates, hear them whoosh across the kitchen where they crash against the sink. She storms out of the room. I hold my breath and keep my eyes on the cleared but not sponged table, willing myself to invisibility. Emma mutters *fuck* and stomps down the hall. A door slams.

I wonder at the waste of plates—do they have so much extra? I wonder at my friend Nellie I admire so much—this is her daughter's definition of Jewishness? I'm tired. I wish I was home in my calm tidy apartment.

My body slumps over the table, its weight pulling my back into roundness. I know Jewish is more than Emma thinks. I picture newsreels I saw when I was younger than Emma of Jews with no flesh on their bones, thinner than I could have imagined a human body, and eyes the size of planets, with Edward R. Murrow's announcer voice choking: *I wish I were not here to see this.* So someone could tell him about it, like Ophelia drowning?

I picture my mother cleaning for *pesakh.* I remember her eyes deep with anger and purpose when she told us about slavery, in Egypt and in the South—*the same thing,* she said. I remember Ethel teaching us the *mizalu.* I think of Moishe, my cousin in Israel, he and his wife work in the Peace Now and their boy went to jail instead of Lebanon.

After a while I walk down the hall to look for Emma. I want to ask her something. She's sitting on the edge of the bed staring at the closet door. It's a double bed, I notice, disconcerted.

"Emma, you're half Greek, right?"

She nods, pathetically grateful for conversation. "Yeah, my father was Greek. Is Greek."

"What does Greek mean?"

"Great food"—she rubs her stomach. I don't smile. "I don't know," she shrugs. "A language, an alphabet. Loud music. Greek tragedy. A country, a culture. Bossy men, beautiful women—why?" she asks, suddenly suspicious.

I ignore the question. "What does Jewish mean?"

She looks at me and opens and closes her mouth twice. "It's not the same, Ruthie, you know it's not the same."

In the living room Selena is curled up on the couch, really a mattress covered with a print bedspread. I go over and put my arms around her.

"Hey sweetie, you'll work it out," I say, wondering how.

Selena begins to sob, long deep sobs. "Why does she hate it? Why can't she understand it's who I am? It's who she is. *Where's your big heart?* I want to ask her . . . remember she said that to Nellie . . . ."

I go to the bathroom for kleenex and when I come back Emma is sitting on the couch next to Selena, holding her hand. I give Selena's other hand the kleenex.

"Ruthie, do you understand?" Selena asks. "It's like in this house, in our *life* there is NOTHING to keep Jewishness—not even alive, just in the AIR."

"Didn't I learn those songs with you?" Emma coaxes. ("Jesus," Selena tosses her head, "two songs!") "Didn't I help you make the seder last year?"

"Look, I have to go out, I just have to walk . . . ." Selena's on her feet.

"I'll come with you," Emma says hopefully, with me going, "That's fine, girls, don't worry about . . ."

"NO!" bellows Selena, "I need to be by myself . . ." and slams the door.

Emma and I are left staring at each other.

I have two rules for getting through awkward situations. First, get the other person talking. Second, bring up history. "Emma, do you and Selena have this conflict often?"

"Once or twice. Sort of. I didn't know she felt so strongly about it." Emma looks ten years old and bewildered.

"Now you know." I put my hands on her sturdy Jewish peasant shoulders, she's just an inch or so taller than me. "So now what?"

Tears enter Emma's eyes and sit there. "I don't understand Selena." She swipes at her cheeks with the back of her hand. Then she crosses her arms over her chest as if for protection.

"Maybe she has a very big heart," I shrug.

A couple of days later I call up Sondra.

"Has Nellie ever talked to you about being Jewish?" I'm a shade nervous. I see the papers are full of how Blacks are against the Jews and Jews are against the Blacks.

But Sondra is Sondra. "Are you kidding? Nellie's from the left, none of them talk about it."

"Why?"

"You tell me, sugar, that's your people. I never have figured it out. My parents pointed it out to me when I was little." I picture Sondra in her huge yellow kitchen curled up on the grey-blue sofa. It's the most wonderful original thing I've ever seen, a sofa in the kitchen.

"Were they socialists?"

"Communists. Twenty-two years. My mother thought it was great there were so many Jewish communists. She could never figure out why they didn't talk about it more." Then she adds as an afterthought, "Of course the rich Jews were hiring our mamas to clean up their dirt."

I cringe. When Harry was sick, Betty came in a half-day a week to do the heavy work. I don't say anything. I imagine Sondra hearing my silence.

"Darrell's waiting for me, hon. You talk to Nellie about it, ok?" and we get off the phone. I feel funny about Betty, not that she helped me with Harry but that I didn't say anything to Sondra, like it was shameful. I feel a sudden longing for a friend who has liked me for at least thirty years and has something invested in me, so even if I say or do something ignorant, wrong or just plain prejudiced, she'll see it in perspective: one rotten fish in a sea of good fresh deeds.

All week I worry about Nellie, like a bad tooth you can't keep your tongue away from. I know sooner or later I'll have to say to her, *Nellie, Emma is ignorant and prejudiced against her own people, why is this?* I'm afraid of what Nellie will answer and what this will do to our friendship. Sometimes I wish she'd retreat back into her purple raincoat, someone I've just met and am dazzled by.

The next Friday I have dinner at Nancy and Ethan's, and the one after I'm going to synagogue with Selena. When I tell Nancy, I can see her sturdy brain ticking away. Nancy has always been very logical even as a child and she's going, *green hair, radical friends, gay march, religion . . . .* I don't tell her it's a gay synagogue. We're getting along better these days. She's not feeling so guilty and to be perfectly honest I enjoy shocking her. Each surprised look on Nancy's face tells me I'm still alive and changing, and it seems I'm changing faster than Nancy. I shouldn't gloat, she's depressed and bored with her life, but she has been nagging me for longer than I care to remember.

Suddenly I have a whole new circle of interests and friends. I remember a family therapist we went to when Nancy was a teenager, Harry was still alive. This woman missed the point a lot but one thing she got right was the name for a certain kind of feeling: *nyah-nyah* she called it, when you feel *serves you right* or *so there* or really like sticking your thumb at the end of your nose and waving your fingers at someone going *nyah-nyah*. That's how I feel sometimes with my daughter, I'm embarrassed to admit. But it's true.

Friday comes. The *shul* is in the basement of a huge apartment complex, you wind around this hall and that stairway and come to a big grey room, cold and dreary, with folding chairs and lots of bright cloths up on the walls. Selena explains they rent the space for Friday nights, and before services people hang the cloths and set up the chairs. Afterwards they undo it. The effort touches me.

Then I notice how many chairs. I count one row and then the number of rows. "Selena," I say, "there's 300 seats."

She grins. I can tell she finds me naive, but she's a sweet girl, she doesn't embarrass me.

"What are there, three million Jews in New York?" she asks.

"Less now. Maybe two million."

"Figure ten percent are gay—"

"Ten percent?" I'm shocked.

"That's a conservative estimate, Ruthie. About 200,000 gay Jews in New York."

"If they all came to *shul*, it'd be crowded."

Selena mills around but I stick in my seat and watch people come in. Mostly men, young, they look like boys. Nobody pays attention to me and I feel kind of like a schmo, though people smile and say *shabat shalom* if you catch their eye (I grew up on *gut shabes* myself). But it doesn't feel like *shul*. There are hardly any kids or really old people, I'm about as old as it gets.

The seats are funny and my legs are tired from the concrete floor. I dread the service.

It begins kind of informal, like a meeting. A woman gets up and introduces herself and welcomes everyone. *Shabat shalom,* she says, and everyone says back, *Shabat shalom,* me too. She makes some announcements, about new members and welcoming two new babies born to members of the congregation. This takes a minute to sink in.

"Selena, is everyone in this congregation gay?"

"I'll explain later," she whispers back.

Another woman gets up and she's the rabbi. She says to open the song sheets and she says a prayer and then everyone sings. It's very strange. I've been in *shul* about five times in my life but this prayer is familiar and the song—like a song you hear on the radio so you know it almost but not quite well enough to sing it by yourself. But you can sing along. That's how it is with me and these songs, like a muscle I forgot to use for a long time but there it is: flexing, ready. Selena sings next to me, her voice low, sweet and clear.

The rabbi is very beautiful in a strong sort of way. Competent. All of a sudden it dawns on me that the rabbi is a lesbian. I look around at the women. Are they all lesbians? Can they tell I'm not? Could I be one? How do you tell? How would I find a woman to be one with? Thank god I'm old enough to know no one can read my mind.

Then the rabbi asks the mourners to stand and say the *kaddish.* She says we will say *kaddish* also for some members of the congregation and their loved ones whose *yahrzeit* this is, which surprises me as this is a young group, and she begins reading, *Harry Gold, beloved partner of James Kriegel; Stanley Feldstein, lover and friend to Martin Bellini, cousin to Aaron Feldstein; Eric Berg, beloved partner of Carl Krauss, dear friend to Larry Miller, Laura Edelman, Eugene Metzer and Stuart Krantz; Gabe Sherman, lover and partner of Adam Rosenblum; Mark Perez, lover to Daniel Morrison, dear friend to Stuart Felman . . . .* And she goes on, thirteen names of men who died a year ago on this day, and around Eric Berg I understand that they died of AIDS and feel the shudder through the community of loss and grief and terror.

Then the rabbi begins the *kaddish* and the sound of *yitgadal v'yitkadash* echoes through me, sounds I didn't know I knew but they sound my grief and I cry for Harry. I cry for Nancy's dull bitter life. I cry for Darrell's homeless children who can't even attend lousy schools, and for the wall between me and Sondra because I wouldn't say about Betty. I cry for my own unshakeable loneliness, and all the time I'm crying for these boys who died and are dying. I think about Ethan, sturdy and frail at the same time, the beautiful deadly world he's growing up into, less and less room for mistakes. I think about people shooting up drugs with shared needles and women doing sex for money and kids doing what kids do these days with their young bodies, touching each other in good and bad ways. I think about the danger and the cost. I sob with the ancient prayer, feeling the grief around me and in me, *v'chayim aleynu v'al kol yisrael. v'imru amen.*

"Ruthie, what's wrong?" Selena puts her arm around my shoulders.

"It's the first born," I sob, "all the first born," not knowing exactly what I mean. I lean into Selena's skinny breastbone, weeping. If I can find the right words I can explain it to Selena; to Nellie; even to Nancy.

some pieces of jewish left: 1987

I grew up in the CP but it was the fifties, people didn't talk about it. At least not my parents. They were worriers as well as Communists. They barely breathed the words "left wing" in my hearing, but they went to meetings practically every night and never shut up about politics. They could analyze the historical roots and class base of absolutely anything: a jar of peanut butter; the nubbly pink blanket I tucked between my legs every night as I drifted off. A desperate lover once screamed at me, *I bet you do class analysis in your sleep.* To her it was an insult, but to me, kind of probable, I never remember dreaming. I'm the only one of my friends who has never seen a shrink— not that I'm saner, I was just raised contemptuous. Three words epitomize my childhood: *Marx, not Freud.* In 1969, when Vivian Kepler, Naomi Berg and I secretly produced in the university print shop and slapped up all over town 10,000 stickers that read

MARX AND FREUD ARE DEAD
TURN TO YOUR SISTERS,

it felt deliciously daring to pair Marx and Freud. Even more so to announce—as simple fact—that Marx was dead.

A few years ago I thought back to when my mother was selling linen at Macy's, on commission no less, and my father was blacklisted, no one would hire him for eight years. Eight years! I once looked for a job for ten months. I was frantic about money—even with my parents, who immediately reach for the checkbook when I need anything. Besides, as much as I knew I deeply didn't want to be a receptionist or bank teller or motel maid, the constant rejection grinds you down. My father was pretty depressed.

"Sam, that's how it is under capitalism," my mother would say. "There's not enough jobs." She knew better, but usually he perked right up when anyone criticized capitalism.

"There are plenty of jobs for history teachers with my experience." My father's voice could chill August in the Bronx. "You seem to forget I have applied for jobs which *do* exist, both at the Board of Education and in the private sector." He would say things like that, *the private sector.* Now everyone says it, but that's Reagan; then it was my father's version of a dirty word.

Or else she'd say, more to the point: "Sam, what'd you expect, you'd organize the workers and the bosses would thank you?"

I think he had expected something like that; not that the bosses would thank him exactly, but someone would. The bosses would be overthrown, powerless, transformed into people you could tolerate, while the workers would carry him around on their shoulders, at least metaphorically.

Suddenly they were home every night. No one called, no one visited except Aunt Lydia, who would spend two hours talking about her daughter Neila's boyfriend, what scum he was. My father started drinking, not a lot but always one and often two or three rye and gingerales a night. He'd sit in the living room reading, once in a while he'd turn the page. Sometimes he'd ask me to fix him "a highball."

Every night after supper my mother sat at the kitchen table. For hours. It was the summer before I started City College, the sky stayed light for a long time. She'd stare out the window onto Franklin Place, where the kids played punchball and the old people sat in chairs dragged out each evening to breathe air. She'd sit absolutely still with her hand on her coffee cup, as if waiting for it to cool, but the coffee would be long cold. The light would drain from the sky, taking all the color. After a while she'd be sitting in total darkness. Once I flipped the light switch just to see if she'd notice. It took her a minute, but then she looked up, bewildered.

"Rosa?" she spoke slowly. "Did you turn on the light?"

"Yeah, Ma, I forgot you were in there," I lied, ashamed.

So a few years ago I asked. "Ma, the year you worked at Macy's, is that when you and Daddy left the party?"

She stands at the sink scrubbing dishes in a pan full of scalding suds. She always saves water by using a dishpan. Suddenly she turns the tap and runs water, uncharacteristically wasteful, concentrating on getting the soap off the soup bowls. Just when I think she's actually going to pretend I didn't say anything, she shoves her hair back with a hot sudsy hand.

"What gave you that idea?"

"Daddy drank and you were depressed."

"Very observant." She's charmed by her genius daughter, just like when I was four years old reading the *New York Post*, a feat always followed by my father's critique of the Post's bourgeois bias: "Rosa, read it but don't believe it."

"Sam," my mother must have responded 200 times at least, "she's only four (five, six, seven, nine, eleven . . .), what does she know about believing?"

Meanwhile, my mother never actually confirmed that they left the party in 1958, any more than she confirmed that they had ever joined.

I figured out when they joined, even though the evidence is less striking, since I wasn't alive to collect it. It was the early thirties, the internationalism-as-celebration-of-unique-people's-cultures phase—folk songs, circle dances, embroidered felt skirts, the works. Before identity got pegged divisive, diversionary, chauvinist, or nationalist, depending. My parents raised me proud of my Jewishness. They sent me to Jewish work camp, we celebrated the big holidays, though always in opposite ways. Passover we had bread with the matzoh. Yom Kippur we ate on purpose, my mother said there was enough hunger in the world, we shouldn't pretend. She taught me to make chopped liver, cabbage soup, *kreplakh*, we'd take the subway into Manhattan to buy matzoh meal. But people are bigger than their ideology—so who knows.

Every Easter I'd get beat up for killing Christ. I'd beg to stay home from school, thus pitting my parents' faith in working class solidarity (not to mention their obsession with education) against their fleshly, bruised, terrified child. Usually I'd win, but not without them carefully placing anti-Semitism in an historical context as a form of racism which would vanish under the dictatorship of the proletariat. *Before or after the state withered away?* I wanted to ask them later, when I understood more and had acquired some of the bitterness they so sweetly refused.

Around 1958, they stopped refusing. A little air went out of both of them, especially my father, though I have to say his sense of humor improved.

The other day I was over for dinner, pot roast, my mother's kitchen has never been touched by tofu. We started to talk about the Black-Jewish split, how serious was it, and I remembered Cecilia. Cecilia was my best friend when we were sixteen and this kitchen table was mine too. Sometimes Cecilia ate over, and sometimes I ate over there. Our school was maybe half Jewish and a third Black, but totally tracked; the Jews took academic and commercial diplomas, the Blacks took general, which were worthless. A lot of kids dropped out, women and Blacks: the women got pregnant and the Blacks got nothing. And the Black women?

Cecilia was the exception, the one Black student in honors classes. I didn't know the word *token*. Her parents were both teachers, like my father, she always had white friends—Jewish because of where she lived. We hardly ever talked about *what* we were, only *who* we were, as individuals. A few times we got called *nigger* and *nigger lover*, once by three drunk men from a car on a dark street. Cecilia grabbed my hand and we ran, hearts thumping, to an alley too narrow for cars. We hugged the damp wall.

Cecilia had broad shoulders and delicate feet and hands with long slender fingers, like a pianist, although in fact she was tone-deaf. In class she was well-behaved, offering precise ample responses. Out of class she cracked uproarious jokes one after another until I and everyone else around her were helpless, convulsed in almost pain. She was, I realize now, astonishingly beautiful, but our cohorts' standard was small, thin and cute. Cecilia was large and stunning.

So was her mother. I loved Cecilia's parents, Mrs. Tucker especially was the kindest woman on earth and very smart. She used to help me and Cecilia with our English homework. We had trouble with *Macbeth*, and Mrs. Tucker would read whole speeches out loud so we could hear them scan, she said. My parents had bizarre interpretations of Shakespeare, really crude Marxist criticism, not like what people do now. Cecilia and I knew better than to show up in Mrs. Donovan's English 6 honors class with Marxist interpretations of *Macbeth*. I used to wonder why my parents bothered with Shakespeare in the first place since they made him mean things even I could tell he never meant— the man was a royalist!

My parents liked Cecilia a lot, almost too much. It was like our friendship validated them. My father tried to make friends with, meaning *recruit*, Mr. and Mrs. Tucker. He kept inviting them to this panel and that forum, probably the only interracial gatherings in the entire metropolitan area. I could smell disaster. I cornered my mother.

"They'll feel uncomfortable, Ma, they know about white people wanting Negroes to show up so they can feel unprejudiced."

"You think that's why he's inviting them?"

Secretly I thought maybe, but I shook my head. "He's always looking to invite someone. He just assumes Cecilia's parents will be interested because they're oppressed. But they're not like that, Ma."

"Like what?" She was getting huffy. My mother had never met Blacks who weren't communists.

"I mean, they know about politics, they just don't think the same as you and Daddy." Though now it occurs to me how much the same they did think, honoring education like it was god (or in my parents' case, Marx).

Mr. and Mrs. Tucker came to one forum. They were extremely curious, adventurous people who'd try almost anything once. Mr. Tucker wore a suit and tie, Mrs. Tucker a blue wool dress, pearls—church clothes, Cecilia called them. Everyone else was very casual, black turtlenecks, peasant skirts . . . . My father in his habitually arrogant way announced to Mr. Tucker, almost as he introduced himself, that bourgeois democracy was a sham, especially when it came to the Negro Question. I cringed. Mr. Tucker never raised his voice, but he mentioned the vote. My father's face turned brick red; he had no tolerance for disagreement.

"How did you like Cecilia's parents?" I knew better than to ask, but I couldn't stop myself.

"Well, they're not exactly enlightened," he sneered and a curtain of blood dropped before my eyes.

I shrieked, "What do you know about anything? You can't even get a job."

The words hung in the living room, as if hummed by a secret chorus: *YOU CAN'T GET A JOB*. He looked stricken, as he was meant to. I felt like a killer, as I was meant to.

He clenched his teeth. "You're right. I don't know anything. Nothing. Nothing at all." He stormed out of the room and down the hall to their bedroom. I heard the obligatory door slam.

Once, after one of my parents' freedom seders, Cecilia and I stayed up late digesting Pharaoh and Moses and forty years in the desert. We wanted to play Paul Robeson's "Go Down Moses"—ironically, both our parents owned Paul Robeson's entire output—but everyone was asleep. We thought we'd do it another time, we were only sixteen and had all the time in the world. Cecilia told me her parents taught her, *when you're in trouble, if you can't find a Negro, find a Jew*. I felt flattered, but unworthy. My parents with their know-it-all politics were okay in a pinch, but I pictured kind Mrs. Tucker with her fabulous enunciation finding my Uncle Manny, for example, and I felt ashamed. Implicated.

Sometimes I wonder if Cecilia and I hadn't lost touch, would we still be friends. The Black women want everything, right now. That's how it was in women's liberation too. Everything, now. And the Jewish women, everything, now. People confuse self-respect, militancy and plain stubbornness. Women turned on each other at exactly the right moment. Why did we suddenly have to be Jewish women, and Black women, and this women and that women, instead of just WOMEN?

But things take me aback. My good friend and neighbor, Larissa—tall blond and Anglo—drops by the other day, and over a cup of coffee she refers to Leon Klinghoffer as a legitimate war target. As if it were perfectly obvious.

My mouth drops. "He was an old Jew in a wheelchair."

"People in struggle aim at accessible targets." Larissa sounds like my parents before 1958. Leon Klinghoffer sounds like a military base. She brushes crumbs from my not very tidy table. "Don't you think people have to be accountable for their government's—"

The curtain of blood drops. Like when my father called Cecilia's parents unenlightened. Like when I was the only woman speaker at an anti-war rally, I'm quoting statistics on prostitution in Viet Nam and some gorilla in the front row leers: *I wouldn't mind getting some of that action, haw haw.* For years I will hear that *haw haw,* see that curtain of blood crashing in front of me as I shriek over the loudspeakers to a crowd of thousands who have no idea what's provoked me, *Wipe that shitty grin off your face, men like you are my enemy . . .* and so on. Thus the image of crazed manhaters was substantiated in similar scenes across the nation.

Thus I shriek at my friend Larissa, "He was an American and so are you, you think every Jew is responsible for Israel, why don't you slit my throat for the Palestinians?" There's a basic flaw in this argument, I know, but I can't think clearly.

Larissa, calm but injured, apologizes with her mouth, "I'm sorry if I upset you," and I can see in her eyes an allowance because I can't help being a crazy Jew.

On the other hand, there's Vivian, with whom I discovered women's liberation. Now she's all involved with Jewish this and that. She used to do terrific work on abortion, rape. Has all that been solved? Women are free, right?

Last Passover Vivian came to visit. The women in my neighborhood had a gathering to celebrate the concept of liberation, and we asked everyone to name a woman she wanted to honor and say something about her. So women named Harriet Tubman, Clara Lemlich, Fannie Lou Hamer, Emma Goldman, Susan B. Anthony (a couple of women hissed—hard-liners who don't understand you can deserve honor and criticism both) . . . on and on. I found the ceremony moving, but I caught Vivian's face a couple of times and it was bleak. Depression hit me. Nothing's ever good enough for Vivian.

Just then she stood up. "I want to honor Ethel Rosenberg. She was a fighter, a communist, and a Jew." Her voice had an edge.

The edge reached to the far wall. The edge was not *communist*. It was *Jew*. Then everyone went on naming different women, and we shared around some matzoh.

On the way home I breathed in and out. Vivian and I have had our "Jewish differences" conversation four times in as many years. I was not dying to reopen it now.

"You didn't like that," I said. Barely a question.

"Rosa. It's *pesakh*." The pain in her voice startled me. "There's matzoh, but there's no seder. No one explained *pesakh*. No one even mentioned the word *Jew* until I named Ethel Rosenberg. Not to describe Emma Goldman, nothing. I can't believe you didn't notice."

I hadn't noticed, though when she said *Jew*, I felt the edge in the room. Like a fart. Something gross. Or peculiar—a political statement from a time warp. She said the word *Jew* and all those blank irritated faces wondered why it mattered.

2. *f r a n*

Men I have always picked blond and *goyish* as possible, it's the calm with which I have tried—and failed—to paper my life. But friends—women—I want full of fire.

The other day Vivian's in town, we're munching

lazy breakfast, good bread, eggs scrambled with onions, endless coffee. Out of nowhere pops a question, "If you don't care about being Jewish, how come all your friends are Jews?"

Vivian is my young friend—you can tell how old I am, she's in her forties—and she thinks about being Jewish on the toilet and in her sleep, as well as every other moment of the day or night.

"I live in New York," I snap, and we both burst out laughing. Mentally I flip through my friends for a non-Jew. Nothing.

She shakes her head. "You're such a Jew. How come you don't know this about yourself?"

My jaw tightens. I feel like people are crowding both sides of me. They grab my sleeve, cram my ears with sounds I don't even recognize, much less choose: *This is your language, speak it, you're ours.*

I don't feel like *theirs.* The Jewish people. I just don't, never have. I never think about it. I could name twenty categories I connect with and Jewish wouldn't even be on the list.

My parents never thought about it either, it was who they were. In Vilna they were Jews and socialists, and when they came here they were still Jews and socialists. They lived among Jews. Everyone spoke Jewish. What was there to think? It was like air, they breathed it. There was Jewish everything. My parents would argue who you could trust less, communists or Democrats, anarchists they never worried about. All Jewish. Orthodox, secular. Owners, bosses, workers. Doctors, teachers, salesclerks, writers, dancers, peddlers, you name it. All Jewish. Movies. Gossip columns. Like I said, you breathed it.

So I grew up breathing it, but I don't feel it. What's to feel? I don't understand what Jews want. Why are they clamoring for attention? They have good jobs, their kids go to college, why do they keep harping about Jewish, Jewish, Jewish?

I live in this city. There's people wandering
around with their toes sticking out of their shoes, no
homes, not even shelters. There's kids can't go to
school because they don't live in a district. My building's going co-op, in a million years I couldn't buy my
apartment and the landlord is pushing me to sell.
Where would I live? I'm not too old for much, but that
I'm too old for, learning a new city. My job is here, my
friends. This is where I've picketed and screamed in
meetings since I was fourteen years old. I can't leave.
On the other hand, how can I stay, with the rents and
the prices and the worrying how you get home at
night when you can't afford cabs and the subway is
the subway.

But these are not Jewish issues, these are human
issues.

Take South Africa. Could they fuss about apartheid? No. If someone mentions Israel sending guns
to South Africa, they whine about anti-Semitism.

I know, everyone working on divestment, if
they're not Black, they're Jews. But not Jewish Jews.

Jewish Jews worry about Jews. I don't see what
there is to worry about. The Holocaust? It's over.
Ethiopian Jews? What about the other Ethiopians,
half of Africa's hungry. Soviet Jews? I have to remind
myself, they're not just tools in the Cold War, but
they're also not the only ones suffering. And over
religion? People are starving. People are dying. I know
Jews did starve and did die and I'm not one to turn up
my nose at history. But sometimes I just want them to
look at the present. The Jewish Jews always focus on
the past, as if it justifies something. Having. We paid
our dues, they say, now we get to be comfortable and
don't bother us about the rest of the world. Except
Israel, there's always room for Israel.

My past is different. I know events don't always
live up to our ideals, I'm a woman, how could I not
know? We were young socialists, and socialism was

about being young. And perfectible. We built perfect
schools and collectives. We cooked for a hundred people at a time. We slept with each other's husbands and
wives. We were not the folk, we didn't live their life:
we lived the life they would live someday. Perfectly
balanced between physical labor and intellectual
stimulation. We ate the healthiest foods. We wrote
the latest poems. This was very far from my parents'
socialism. But it felt free.

Now I look at us and gasp: the innocence. Almost
criminal, that innocence. Thinking what we were
doing was so new when it was only a little new. It was
1953, women got married and raised kids, even socialists. We said marriage would be different for us, and I
guess it was. He cooked too. I had the first affair.

After a few years and a perfect beautiful daughter, I got sick of my clean blond husband, his tidy
emotions, his spareness, like Scandinavian furniture.
We were drinking fine wine at the Sorensons, we had
just come from the Third Wave's production of *Hedda
Gabler*, an avant garde classic, satisfying everyone's
snobbery on two counts. We all had opinions, it was a
perfect discussion.

I looked around the spare elegant room, lots of
wood, lots of glass. In this living room, I thought,
ordinary people, the ones we were supposed to organize and stand in solidarity and build our tomorrows
side by side with, would not feel comfortable.

Suddenly it all seemed lean and pretentious. I
wanted to sprawl in a huge red overstuffed chair with
a little stuffing leaking out and drink a Pepsi. I wanted
to step into the tavern a mile down the road where I
had never gone, not even to pick up a six-pack, and
shoot pool or watch the TV news with my neighbors.
I was sick of our smug harmonious community.

Not that I didn't love those people, most of them.
I stuck around for another couple of years of harmonious conversation and angrier and angrier affairs.

Then I was first to leave. Other couples started breaking up too, and the community dissolved. The men found younger women. The women found feminism or bitterness, sometimes both. The kids went off to be grown-up kids.

Now I live a lot more like the folk. My apartment is too small and too expensive. I'm lonely at least half the time. I have back pain. I worry about money. I have not given up on politics but sometimes I wonder why not. Is it nostalgia? I used to think everything was possible, we all did. Now I wonder if anything is possible.

I've been thinking about Lisa, my daughter. Lisa is half-Jewish, she identifies with it even less than I do, if possible, and I have begun to notice that she is anti-Jewish. I don't want to say anti-Semitic, she doesn't think Jews should die or be discriminated against, but she would never read a Jewish book, or go to a Jewish movie; not even a documentary. And she makes cracks. Like the other day she described her graduate advisor, "He's really smart but he's obsessed with Jewish stuff." Lisa's beautiful chiselled face scrunched up when she said *Jewish*.

"Like what?" I was curious.

She shrugged. "Do I care if T.S. Eliot is an anti-Semite?"

From this I have to examine what I taught or didn't teach her, because while you may say a mother controls very little of how her kids grow up, you can bet if her advisor claimed T.S. Eliot was a racist, and he probably was, Lisa would care.

And while my friends are Jewish, Lisa's friends are not.

After I say *my friends are Jewish*, I almost want to add, *but not typically Jewish*. As though that will make okay something that is not okay. I hate to admit it, when Lisa calls a person *so Jewish* I know what she means. Sleeve-grabbing urgency. Demanding.

Do you think I don't know this is a total contra-
diction? On one hand, I'm only really at home in a sea
of Jewish socialist types. On the other, I'm just plain
tired of the word JEW. I don't feel connected to the
Jewish world. "Which Jewish world?" Vivian asked
me once: I knew the point she was making.

I went on that March on Washington, you know,
against everything bad and for everything good. I
rode down and back with the pacifists, but I met Lisa
there and we marched together for a while under the
ANC Solidarity banner. She had worked very hard
organizing for this march, she had designed the
banner and it was gorgeous, fierce green and wild
brilliant yellow and black—who could compete
against a child raised to think of every breath, every
forkful of chicken as potentially creative? I pulled her
out of line for a minute to watch everyone go by with
their banners, to let the numbers and noise and spirit
infuse me with hope. I put my arm around Lisa and
she put hers around me, and joy filled me: that Lisa,
my cranky independent daughter, was past the stage
where touching me in public was the ultimate in
humiliation; that she had grown into a clear formed
political being worthy of her grandparents.

We're standing there with our arms around each
other, watching the past and present make slightly
possible the future. Banners marched by on human
legs, banners that said *Puerto Rican Solidarity Committee,*
Lesbian Mothers for Human Priorities, American Indian
Movement, Abraham Lincoln Brigade Veterans. As each
group marched by with its banner, we all cheered,
YAY for the Puerto Ricans, YAY for the Lesbian
Mothers, and the Indians, and the old men who
fought in Spain when they were younger than Lisa.
Then came *Jews Against Apartheid.*

I opened my mouth, YAY for the Jews, and I was
alone. No one else went YAY Jews.

Just then I spotted Vivian. I ran up to her and

gave her a big fat hug and pulled her out of line. I dragged her by the hand, "Come meet my daughter."

Lisa's expression froze, polite. Vivian's hand went dead in mine, I had to hold on and squish it. I introduced them.

I know my daughter. Her beautiful face twitched in dismissal: "Hello," she said, cool as blond wood, a modern morality play: *Every Goy meets Every Jew.* Vivian's nod registered bitter unsurprise. I could tell that Lisa didn't understand, didn't even question her response to Vivian, whereas Vivian had clearly met a lot of Lisas. And just for that second I was ashamed of my daughter. Though god knows I raised her.

I got a note from Vivian the other day, actually a leaflet with *it would be great to see you* scribbled on it. I was standing at my mailbox, having climbed down three flights to get the mail, a big event in my day, unsolicited human contact. Well, not always unsolicited and not exactly human, but often behind a piece of mail is a human. At first I took the cheap yellow stapled paper for junk mail, except it was hand-addressed. It said:

JEWS IN PROGRESSIVE MOVEMENTS
a panel discussion

Barry Goldenberg, author, *Anti-Semitism in Progressive Movements, 1919-1945*

Sid Bresloff, editor, *Di Morgn,* frequent lecturer at Workmen's Circle

Vivian Kepler, feminist

Introduced by Mark Sadowsky, professor, CCNY

Vivian had circled the word *feminist* with an exclamation point, to let me know she'd noticed how curt and sexist it was to label her and skip mentioning where *she* frequently speaks. Oy, Vivian and her Jewish. But on her it doesn't bother me.

Why should it? I ask myself in her voice. But I have

to say, I don't understand. *Jews in Progressive Movements!*
I want to blurt out, *Vivian, dolly, why? Why? It's sexist. It's
narrow. There you're a feminist. Here you're a Jew. Don't you get
claustrophobic? What is there to SAY about Jews in progressive
movements? That there were a lot of them? That now there are
less?*

I say this to Vivian in my fantasy, and in my
fantasy she looks at me, eye to eye, and says, THEM,
Fran? A lot of THEM?

3.   c h a v a

This morning I woke up on my lumpy little cot in the
dorm room I normally share with Dorothy except
she's in Israel and I thought:

Everything's already happened. Protests. Getting busted. Psychedelics. Hippies, Yippies. Everything wild. That's why I'm bored. That's why I can't
get my ass to class. It's already happened.

And I'm stuck here in fucking college in 1987. No
wonder.

I fantasize about the sixties, the cool sixties. They
chanted *Power to the People*, they raised their fists. They
sang "We Shall Overcome" with deep voices; I saw
Eyes on the Prize, they meant it. Even my mother went
on freedom rides, she dropped out of college twice.

Last time I was home, I asked her: "Ma, when you
went down south, how did you decide?" She looks at
me with her eyebrow quirked.

"I mean, you're going to Hunter every day on the
subway, one day you get on a bus to Mississippi?"

"Georgia," she corrects. "Lots of people were
going, it was just—time to go." She smiles at me, like
it's simple. She looks about twelve. "Anyway, we
drove, Jeffrey had a car." She's still smiling but with a
difference. I can tell she's remembering. Jeffrey was
her boyfriend. When she and my father split up, she
was on the phone to Jeffrey so fast it was like she'd

been on her mark, ready. They had a short steamy affair.

"So who went, you and Jeffrey?" I've heard this part before, but I like to make her tell it again.

"And Annie, and Marie—you never met Marie, she died in a car accident—"

"I saw her picture." Marie was the pale skinny one with the baseball cap, kind of dykey if you ask me.

"—and your father." I find this part romantic, though sort of disgusting. My mother and father fell in love over Jeffrey's body, so to speak.

"If you had married Jeffrey instead, you think you'd still be together?"

She gives me her *you're so young* look. "Who knows, sweetie." She dumped my father about five years ago. Sometimes I can't tell if she's glad. At least she doesn't mope around and complain like he does.

"Were Grandma and Grandpa upset when you dropped out of school?"

She snorts. "They were livid: *You're throwing it away, you want to be a bum?*" Then it's as if she remembers who's asking. "Why?" Her eyes narrow into me. "Why are you asking about dropping out?" My mother has a capacity for total focus: the Bulldog, my brother and I call her.

"You know why." I try charm, but she glares back. I know she wants me to graduate and take my place in the world as a B.A. "School is so *boring*."

"I thought you loved your Yiddish class. The poetry and all." Now she's trying to trick me out of being alienated.

"I feel like I'm wasting my life on trivia. This 101, that 202. We write exams in bluebooks. The planet could smash into smithereens and I'd be writing in a goddam bluebook. I want to do something important. Like you did."

"What did you have in mind, sweetie?" She smiles. I hate her for knowing I don't have anything in

mind. She told me she used to dream about the thirties, about Spain and organizing strikes. The way I
dream about the sixties. But it's like her dream came
true and mine hasn't. I said this to her once, and you
know what she answered? *You're still young.* That was a
big help.

I do love Yiddish poetry, not to mention my Yiddish teacher, on whom I have the crush of the century, along with every other dykette on campus. But
this drives me up the fucking wall: I tell people I'm
studying Yiddish, they say, *How cute.* They laugh.
Jackie Mason's about to go on, studying Yiddish is the
warm-up.

Or it's all mixed up with their childhoods and
dead relatives. This old guy Morris who came to the
Yiddish seminar last summer. Shelly, my teacher,
gave a lecture on Yiddish songs, tracking them down,
what they mean. She sang, her voice, every note pure.
I got chills. People clapped. Then Morris sticks up his
hand, waving it around like he's six years old and has
to pee.

"Do you know *oyfn pripetshik?*"

oyfn pripetshik. "Row-Row-Row Your Boat" in
Yiddish. My father taught me *oyfn pripetshik* when I
was seven. Everyone's father taught them *oyfn pripetshik,* right? But this asshole has to get some attention.
Everywhere I go there's some Jew has to get
attention.

I complain to Shelly, she shrugs. "If you were
running in *goyish* circles, there'd be some *goy* has to get
attention."

The other day my baby brother came over. I don't
pay attention to men on principle and also by inclina-
tion, but I remember this one being fucking born.
Spindly fingers waving in the air, his little mouth
sucking.

He stares at me, serious: "I need to ask you something, please don't laugh." Of course I think it's going

to be about sex and I'm embarrassed. What do I know about boy sex?

But it's not sex. "What does it mean to be a Jew?" he asks. Sweet. Thousands of years later, my brother David is wondering.

I look into him like my mother looks into me. His eyes are grey like hers. "Why're you asking?"

He was just at an anti-intervention rally. The main speaker attacked Israel for sending arms to Honduras and Guatemala, as if it's the only country that does. He mentioned this to some guy at the dorm, the guy asked if he's Jewish.

"Yeh, why?"

The guy just smirked.

"I keep thinking about the smartass look on his face. He assumed he knew everything about me just from knowing I'm Jewish. And I don't know anything about it. Nothing. They call the Jewish women JAPS. And the Holocaust. It's like I never noticed it before. How could I not have noticed?"

Oy, the Holocaust. That'll do it. I had to go through it. I read a million books, everything Jewish I could get my hands on. I learned Hebrew, I lived on kibbutz, everything. Name a Jewish song, I can sing it. Now I'm done searching. I just like Yiddish, that's all.

So he's searching and I feel trapped. By triviality. By the eighties—how can *anyone's* life matter in the eighties? And Jewish—what does it mean? Yiddish, beautiful gutsy Yiddish. Shelly, Dorothy, women who make me drool. Even my mother, I'm proud of my mother.

And on the other side, Morris with his *oyfn pripet-shik* ME ME ME. I get tired just thinking about Morris. The women they call JAPS—I don't like the term but I don't like the women either, they embarrass me with their thick makeup and ugly expensive clothes. Or Anita, the short skinny one from the summer seminar, whatever anyone mentions, Anita knows the best. The top. The expert on tomatoes. Heart disease. Fiestaware. Nothing but the best.

There's David's grey eyes. *What does it mean to be a Jew?* I used to turn myself inside out over this. Then I went to Israel and it was like I was the only one who cared. *What does it mean?* I was wearing a *magen david*, and after two weeks I unhooked the chain and put the star in my pocket. At home the star meant, *I'm a Jew*, and it took a little courage to say that to every person who could see my throat. In Israel wearing a star meant one of two things: *I'm religious* or *I'm not Arab*.

I got a letter the other day from Dorothy. Things are worse, if possible. The whole country's split down the middle, half for, half against. She says she feels ashamed. She goes to meetings but there's no energy, people feel helpless. Everyone knows it's gonna blow. Palestinians will get creamed. Some Israeli from kibbutz will get his arm blown off. She says the whole country is on valium, like Beirut. Dorothy exaggerates, but I don't know how you live with war, I never have.

Reading Dorothy's letter, I missed her. I took out my old guitar with its hopeless strings and sang Yiddish songs. My mouth formed the sounds as if everyone around me spoke those sounds all day long, *zuntik bulbes, montik bulbes,* eating potatoes every day of your life. When I sing *bulbes* I feel the poverty but also sometimes the metaphor, boredom. I say this to Shelly, she laughs.

"Did you ever go hungry?" she asks. For a second I hate her.

Or *di shvue*. The oath for Jewish Socialists to sing together, *a shvue, a shvue oyf lebn un toyt,* a life and death oath. I try to imagine Bundists who sang *di shvue*, who swore, *mir shvern*. They had a whole huge movement *oyf lebn un toyt*. That's what I want, Life and Death. It should matter.

Once I was going on about the sixties, Shelly's friend Vivian asks if I've ever been slugged by a cop or knocked down by horses. She says they all learned to shoot, they thought the revolution was smack in front of them and they'd have to kill.

"History was in the streets," I say. I like the ring of it.

"You know what my mother says?" Vivian actually shakes her finger at me. *"When history is in the streets it's very interesting, but it's not so good for ordinary people.* You ever breathe tear gas?"

No, I almost snap, *I never did anything. Never went hungry, never got beaten by cops, never even got smacked by my parents. What am I supposed to do, cash it in?*

Instead I announce, "I choose danger over boredom any day."

Vivian gives me a look. "That's because you're safe."

I think about the Bund. Jewish Socialists. They spoke Yiddish so the workers would understand. Some of them were workers and a lot were women. I've seen pictures, young, with glasses. Soft hair and sharp faces. They had to meet in the woods, it was illegal. Even their goddam meetings were brave.

Dorothy and I found *di shvue* in the library, we xeroxed twenty copies for the whole second year Yiddish class, and Shelly taught us the song. I watched everyone's mouths shape the sounds and I swear I could feel them shudder over words like *blut un trern,* blood and tears. I could almost hear them call the people who sang *di shvue* "violent" and "extreme." They shifted around in their chairs, and I could see them relegate the song to a crude past: *That was then, this is now.* When what we wanted, me and Dorothy, was inspiration for now. And they felt not inspired but embarrassed.

Why embarrassed? Shelly and Vivian say words like *revolution* or *sisterhood* without feeling ridiculous.

My Yiddish class can't even sing *di shvue* without looking over their shoulders—to see what? They'd probably have an easier time fucking in public.

So what makes me different? Vivian says in her
first women's group there were three of them who
admitted they couldn't stand picking up their husbands' dirty socks. "My grandmother would've
blabbed it out the window across the courtyard to
fifty neighbors, *It's his socks, I can't stand it,* and they
would've gone, *Right, Malke, I know what you mean.*"

"In Yiddish," I interrupt.

She laughs a snort of a laugh, ponks me in the
arm. "The point is, it took a mass movement to get me
and two other women to admit we hated the socks.
Why was that so hard?"

I blow bubbles into my coke. "Wasn't that a small
group, three?"

"You start where you are," she says authorita-
tively. "Mao went to Yenan with five people. Or
seven?"

Later I think, but Mao knew what to do. China
stretched before him: hungry, poor, exploited.
Besides, he was Mao.

The other night I went into the city to hear
Vivian give a talk. The bus was crowded with students, a couple of mothers with whining kids, men in
suits. I sat next to an old woman with thin, fine grey
hair wisping around a bun. She was reading a bio-
graphy of Virginia Woolf and she looked like Virginia
Woolf. I kept waiting for her to say something but she
only asked if I minded the window being open just a
crack.

Then I hit New York. It was windy, grit smacked
my face. Riding the bus, the subway, walking across
town, zooming up fourteen elevator stories, I felt
dazed; the strange hallway, the grey room opened like
another planet. Everyone sat in metal folding chairs
eyes trained front on some man, I couldn't follow, it

was about Trotsky. Vivian's wearing a shiny red shirt and jeans, her hair sticks out in puffs. She's a great speaker, though I've heard her do this particular riff before, anti-Semitism on the left. I daydream about being her comrade.

Then it's over. Vivian acts glad to see me, she invites me out to eat with her friends, Shelly my heartthrob Yiddish teacher is there, and Vivian's mother. I try to relax, but I feel grasping. I want to know who they are, what they have to say. The small dark woman is Vivian's best friend, Rosa, she's beautiful, with huge dinner-plate eyes like the dogs in the fairy tale. Her hair keeps falling into her face and each time she shoves it back like she's never seen it before. There's an older one, Fran, she has short crisp grey hair. Her cheeks are very full, her eyes sharp blue and you can tell they see everything. Vivian's mother is small and thin, cute, she wears jeans and sneakers. I want her to look like Vivian but no such luck, she just looks like someone I never saw before.

We crowd around a table in the deli and instantly there's a sea of words, they all swim, everyone talks at once, *hostile sectarian CIA Jackson revisionist liberal racist OPEC reproductive . . . .* Rosa and Vivian argue about the point of voting (no point or a teeny little point), Shelly and Fran debate the value of class action suits (a little value or a little more than that). Vivian's mother (Estelle) explains to me what used to happen in the grey room where the forum took place (union meetings for the garment workers). All their feet are planted on invisible soapboxes, but above the table their upper halves ballet in perpetual motion: Fran waves her arms, Shelly slashes the air with a pickle, Estelle nods and shakes her head as she talks, her face so animated I wonder if I'll ever care about anything enough to get my face moving like that. Rosa's style is slow and patient, she tilts her head and gazes earnestly. Vivian nods and animates like her mother *(little Vivian, young Estelle emoting back and forth in some Brooklyn kitchen)*, but when she talks to Rosa she tilts back *(years of friendship, Vivian and Rosa tilting back and forth at each other in a hundred different rooms)*. Rosa's talking to Vivian about her mother who just had a birthday. "I gave her the same tape you gave me, *Jewish Songs of Struggle*. She looked at it and at me like she wasn't sure what was happening. You know that song about the bridge, the *gesher* song?"

"*The whole world is a narrow bridge but the main thing is not to be afraid . . . .*"

"*Kol ha'olam kulo,*" I sing, and the whole table stares at me, *"gesher tzar me'od . . . ."*

"That's it! I forgot the tune." Rosa claps her hands and I'm charmed. "Sing the whole song." I do, lucky it's short, but I'm glad to know something for Rosa.

"She loved that song," Rosa says, "the paradox. I asked her, 'If the world is a narrow bridge, how could you not be afraid?' 'That's just it,' she clapped her hands, remember how she does that? 'Otherwise it wouldn't be the main thing.'"

Estelle and Fran have been arguing about communists and civil rights (strong involvement or total involvement). "The communists practically *were* civil rights until about 1953, 54." Estelle's being chatty, but I suspect her secret goal is to educate the young, namely everyone except Fran, especially me. I can tell by the way Vivian's eyes wander that she's heard all this before, and I guess you always wish your mother would talk less. Estelle and Fran alternate for a while on our education. Fran tells stories about this time she got arrested, that time she got arrested, I want to know how many times but it seems really uncool. Like asking what grade someone got on their poetry.

But there's something I have to know. "Were you a communist?" I ask finally.

Dead silence. Everyone bursts out laughing. If

the words were inside a comics balloon I could haul them back.

Fran pats my arm and says no, she's a socialist and a pacifist. I can't look any stupider. "Were you?" I ask Estelle.

"Oh, I was, I wasn't," on her mouth a funny half-smile. I've seen it on my grandmother in response to practically everything I ever wanted to know. Now I'm old enough, she's dead, and here's Estelle smiling that smile. It fades. "It wasn't so good for Jews, the party."

"Why do you say that?" Rosa leans forward. "Because Jews got blamed?"

Estelle looks at Rosa with a very wise face and Rosa looks back. You could fall into those eyes and swim for a long time. "We always got *blamed*," Estelle shrugs. "The party didn't teach us to take care of each other. Fake brotherhood. We let things pass about our sisters. Our parents, you know? About Jews."

"Why does everyone worry about the Jews?" Fran sounds annoyed. I can't tell if she's kidding.

Shelly's mouth tightens. "I haven't noticed everyone worrying. Fran, what's your problem?"

"I don't have a problem. I just don't think the Jews have it so bad."

Shelly's voice is controlled. She blinks. "What's *so* bad?"

Fran gestures, impatient. "To listen to some of them—"

"*Them*—" Shelly cuts in, two decibels up, "Who's *them?* You ever hear of self-hate—"

"I am not self-hating." Fran's indignant. "I'm so sick of that. It's not myself. I don't identify with those people. Why should I?"

Estelle: "What do you mean, *those people?*"

Silence in which everyone stares at Fran wondering what exactly she does mean.

"Jews who are just Jews," she says at last.

Estelle keeps at it. "What do you mean, *just Jews?*"

"You know, they go to synagogue, they do Hadassah work."

"Fran, this is bad? These are evil people?"

Fran holds up her palms. "Not *bad*. People are ignorant. They only want to hear what's nice."

"Not just Jews," Shelly insists.

"No," Fran slaps the table, everyone jumps. "Jews sit around and suffer."

"C'mon Fran," Vivian's being reasonable, "Who? Who are you talking about? Who do you know? I'm not like that. You're not. Estelle's not. Who is?"

"I don't mean—I mean—" Fran is struggling to say what she does mean, and I feel sorry for her. Finally she breathes. "It's not that Jews are worse, but they're not any better and they think they are."

"Who? Who's this *they?* What do you mean, better?" Shelly and my mother should get together in the Bulldog Club.

"Why do they—" Fran self-corrects "—why do some Jews keep going on about it like they're better—"

"Forget better—*Jewish*," the words explode out of me. "Some Jews like being Jewish. *I* like it. But I want to be both, radical and Jewish. Why is that hard?"— the question I've been waiting all night to ask. "I read about the Bund, they organized strikes, they were so fucking tough. They used to meet secretly, they went to prison, the women too." I gulp my water. I said *fucking* in front of Vivian's mother.

No one bats an eye over *fucking*. My question, the one I always want an answer to and no one can tell me, or else they can and won't—*why is it hard?*—hangs there for a minute. Then it floats up to the ceiling and vanishes, just for now. Just for now it's not hard. Shelly and Vivian start to argue about a new history of the Bund (worthless or better than nothing). I feel happy and kind of weightless.

Then Rosa looks at her watch. It's time to go, suddenly, like a punch in the stomach. I don't know when I'll see anyone again, except Shelly in class.

Then I realize—this will sound ridiculous—I want us to stand up right here around the table in the deli and hold each other's hands and sing *di shvue* together. I want to know we'll come back together to the deli. To grey rooms. To someone's apartment, to secret campfires. I want us to organize strikes and marches together. I want us to shiver on street corners and pass out a million leaflets. I want us to spend our lives together fighting for everything we believe. I want us to swear *a shvue oyf lebn un toyt*. And mean it.

4. *v i v i a n*

We came down in the elevator from the fourteenth floor where the grey room waits for its next forum and stepped out into the damp night air of 22nd Street. Walking along to the deli with my friends, my mother, anxiety dissipated. The talk was over, I had been at least coherent. I wanted to run, to dance, to leap into the streets as if it were all *Singing In the Rain*, though the sky was dark and clear—I'll never forget Gene Kelly running towards the movie camera, jumping for sheer joy. Even the massive buildings seemed protective, ornamental, and in spite of the exploitation which I could fairly well assume took place behind all 10,000, it seemed, windows, I could see beauty in the buildings and proof of human capability.

But by the time we got seats and the waitress brought the food, that fabulous excessive food, all the happiness had drained out of me. I looked around the table at my best friends, my mother—all Jews—and I realized how unusual that was. I don't live in a Jewish world. Who does? New Yorkers, sort of. Israelis, sort of. But where I live I could be the only Jew on the planet for all I know.

"You're talking to yourself," Rosa grins. Years ago she pointed out to me that when I'm carrying on conversations in my mind, I toss my head around and wave my hands. We're on the subway, I'm sleeping over at her house. Tomorrow I'll drive back to Maine.

"I'm thinking about being Jewish." I laugh, so she'll know I'm only partly serious. She's pragmatic, Rosa, and besides she lives in New York. My preoccupation with Jewish identity seems far-fetched to her.

"What do you mean, being *Jewish?*" I hear raw curiosity, as well as faint contempt. "If you were religious, you could tell me you prayed, at least I'd know what you were doing."

We're quiet as the train rattles along. I figured out recently, one of those observations you come to in your forties, when you stop with *I should* and start with *I am.* For me being Jewish, actively Jewish— studying Jewish history, singing Jewish songs, celebrating the holidays—it's like making love or going to a demonstration: I don't know what it's good for. I can't logically prove results. But when I'm doing it, the eternal demand for reason fades, and what stands out hard and brilliant on the stage of my life's purpose is joy. Just joy.

Shouldn't this—halfway through my life, at least—be enough?

Suddenly I know how to explain it to Rosa. "It means learning. Things I would have known and taken for granted, maybe even rejected if . . . ." If what? No immigration. No assimilation. No Holocaust. A chasm.

She looks at me, amused but affectionate. "History's a big *if.*"

"I just want to learn, that's all." For a minute it seemed clear.

She smirks. "You left out about teaching the

world's remaining thirteen million Jews."

"Well, you can't be Jewish alone."

So it's my own peculiar form of hedonism. When I was nineteen my favorite piece of wisdom was a German play about the French Revolution, *Danton's Death*. Danton, before the title event, enrages the prig Robespierre by shouting (male political leaders always shout in plays and often in reality), *We're all hedonists, Robespierre, you too. Your precious Christ was only the most refined hedonist of all.* I still like that, *refined hedonism*. Antidote to self-righteousness.

The subway's crowded for past midnight, at least to my de-urbanized sensibilities. Half the ad placards are in Spanish and I look idly around the car, wondering if half the passengers speak Spanish and how long do they get to keep their language. How many fights between parents and kids, the kids more adept at, bent on, fitting in. How many kids shamed in school for their accent, forced to speak the awkward new sounds.

I have a fantasy of everyone in the car, thirty, forty people, suddenly tumbling back one, two, maybe three, however many generations to the one that spoke something other than English, and speaking, each of us, our people's tongue. What would it sound like? The kid hanging on the plastic pole, I'd guess Spanish, but who knows. The beautiful young woman across the aisle, which African tongue would she retrieve? The Asian man—would he speak Chinese, a dialect whose name I never even heard? Or Korean, Vietnamese, Thai—what do I know? They called it Babel, but everyone could just as easily learn back and forth—everyone here learned how to ride the goddam subway, didn't they, to descend into the rumbling tunnels where urine as often as not reeks; to step aboard, straddling the space between platform and car; to rock back and forth, hands gripping the plastic overhangs; to switch trains, tracks, platforms, the A train, the F, the RR, the N train, millions do it: Is it so easy?

An old woman with black black hair bound up in a wine-colored scarf stands, rocks with the train, about to vanish through the sliding doors. She looks Jewish, Greek, Arab, Italian, Puerto Rican—if she spoke her language, I'd know. I feel like just standing up and proclaiming *I'M A JEW*. Would anyone especially hate me? Or just look away, another subway nutcase?

Anyway, tonight was not sheer joy. There I was with my best friends and my mother, happy they had come to hear me talk. But understand, in some ways this talk *is* my Jewish life. I live ten hours from New York City on the only paved street of a Maine factory town, I make my living grading compositions of students I never meet, and I don't hear the word *Jew* from one week to the next, which might be a blessing. Even when I drove two hours to go to synagogue for *Yom Hashoah*, no one said hello to me or even nodded. I sat alone watching slides about the Holocaust.

Today I'm here, in Hymietown, as Jesse Jackson was stupid enough to call it and never be forgiven for by people every one of whom had heard *schwartze* at least once in her or his life without protest. Tomorrow I drive back to the Jewish void I call home. Pretty bleak. I could burst into a chorus of "Tired of living, scared of dying," from "Old Man River." In Paul Robeson's voice. Did he ever feel bleak, foolish and out of step with history? Or maybe just kind of bummed out? It's not like I won't survive. I read. I think. About politics, anti-Semitism: trying to make the left safe for Jews is what I call it in my jollier moments. I think about my archetypal Jewish position as an outsider. I think about how to rescue an anemic Jewish self, retrieve something of what my mother, even my grandmother tried to dump. Strangely, surprisingly, this is the joy, the senseless joy.

"Are you ok?" Rosa's shouting over the subway clatter. She looks concerned.

"I'm just crashing after the talk," I shout back, "you know how you build yourself up to a pitch?"

The train rocks back and forth and the lights go out. I close my eyes, wrapped in that impersonal noise that counts as silence. I'm not just tired from the panel, I'm overwhelmed. I picture us all sitting around the table in the deli.

Starting with my mother. She's in her seventies and she will not live forever. She doesn't take the greatest care of herself and she has high blood pressure. This is already unbearable. But besides, she thinks people are basically good, like Anne Frank, without the excuse of being fifteen. I want her to be wise and explain things to me. Instead I feel like I need to protect her.

There's Chava, she's only twenty, smart and tough. I can't believe how much adventure she's willing to tackle, nothing fazes her. At sixteen she decides she's a lesbian. At seventeen she gets on a plane to Israel. Each time I see Chava I get a contradictory hit: faith in the future and horror that I have fooled her again into imagining I have answers. I know one day she'll notice I'm a fraud. Once she described how her women's studies teacher had "positively simpered" on a panel with some male scholars. "You always outgrow your teachers," I told her, "some day you'll outgrow me." I felt proud of myself for warning her.

Then there's Fran—at least I don't have to protect her. Fran's like an unwitting walking advertisement for the Jewish people, but she doesn't identify with our collective fate. A mystery, a smart woman like that. Why not? She comes to these events because she's my friend—maybe she's protecting me?

And she wants to keep an open mind. I keep thinking, so if I'm right why haven't I convinced Fran?

Shelly cares like I do but she's got a special goal,

one for which she has been trained: She wants to save
Yiddish. What am I supposed to save? The particular
quality of assimilation I developed in Flatbush and
have since honed to a fine art in the wilds of central
Maine?

And Rosa. I open my eyes to look at my dear
friend Rosa's beautiful, somewhat lined face. She's
dozing. I have watched Rosa grow from Chava's age
into a cheerful middle-aged bustler, the kind of
woman who makes things happen. Pot lucks organize
themselves, petitions get drawn up and signed,
women march to demand a rape crisis center—that
sort of thing. Why hunt for a cause, is Rosa's considered opinion, which she has the integrity to live by:
There's always one staring right at you. She once
confessed what gave her the greatest pleasure was to
confront state power with at least 10,000 other
women. "Expensive taste," I teased her. Now I think,
right, hedonism. But refined.

I close my eyes again. At the table tonight, gloom
clutched my heart. There I was with my best friends
and my mother, having lectured about the Jewish left,
and the truth is, to me my mother's generation *is* the
Jewish left. When she dies—probably before I do—
and Fran, the whole generation, that leaves us and
baby Chava. Can we keep it together—not the cliche
keep it together—I mean literally. Being Jewish and being
leftists. Where does joy fit in? Is there room, or time?
Will they—the eternal insulated *they,* eight-year-old
boys running around in grownup male bodies—blow
the planet into large irregular chunks? Does my Jewish job consist only in hoping Israel doesn't start it?

In my talk I said Jews take history seriously. Take
it where? Everyone in the big grey room listened
seriously to everything I had to say about Jews and
the left. Now I'm riding the subway back to Rosa's, in
Queens, and tomorrow I'm alone with it. Again.

"It's our stop." Rosa's hand on my arm. We stand,

rock with the decelerating train, move towards the doors. Neither of us says anything until we reach the street, the cold slap of real air. Lights from news-stands and neighborhood grocers greet us, still open, infinite availability against the 9 p.m. buttoned-up lips of Maine. We're walking down Hillside Avenue.

"Are you ok, really?"

"I'm worried about my mother." I sigh. I used to think sighing only happened in books, but then I got older. "I mean she's great, my mother. Innocent, but great."

"She is, she's terrific. A *mentsh*."

I pause. I'm ashamed of this part. "But it's also—" I dart a glance at Rosa "—I'm not ready to be the older generation."

Rosa bursts out laughing and puts her arm around me. "Who is?"

"I feel like I should know what to do, like they did. But I don't." I lean against her, laughing and also, I realize, crying.

"Who knows, who in god's name knows?" She rocks me back and forth. "Remember the *gesher* song, the main thing is not to be afraid?"

I nod, her coat rough on my cheek. "But I am afraid." By now I'm sobbing, mucus clogs my throat.

"Even so." Her voice is tender. "Think of it like walking across a bridge, you just put one foot in front of the other, right?"

I sob/sniff/laugh. We start walking again, clums-ily joined, her arm still around me. I'm laughing now at our awkwardness, Rosa laughs too, and we turn onto her street and keep walking forward, putting one foot in front of the other, crossing the perilous chasm which only later gets called history.

all weekend no one mentions israel

1.
Except me, once. In a joke.

2.
It's Sunday night and there's a barbecue at the community house. When I was a kid they built it, first as a wooden platform, for square dancing. Then came the roof, later the walls and plumbing, and now all kinds of events take place here. Just last weekend the Frickies, new members of "the community," this gathering of people who have summered together, many of them for fifty years, threw a party here. They put up crepe paper and flowers, everyone was invited. But my sister Naomi tells me there were complaints.

"You know what people said? *They only paid their dues so they could have their party, cheap, at the community house,*" she mimics, tossing her head. Naomi has such a mop of thick black hair, tossing it is an event. "How do they expect to get new members with that attitude?"

Growing up, this is where I spent my summers. My mother and Naomi still do, a five-minute walk apart, but I skipped it for twenty years, an underemployed vagabond lesbian with no money and a string of supremely difficult lovers. Now I am quasi-normal, "married" to Kate, we both have decent jobs, and I live in the East again: every year we come for July 4th weekend. My father's dead, my mother's getting old—we all are, but here I'm still the child everyone remembers: fat, bright, good, they thought, but really I was secretive.

"Where are you living now, California?" Rose asks.

That was nearly twenty years ago. "Actually, I moved to Vermont last year, from Maine." I smile fondly at Rose. "How are you doing? You look terrific." It's true, she's stopped dying her hair and cropped it, a steel grey brush. Her color's good. She must be eighty years old.

"Oh darling," Pauline hugs me, "you look wonderful, you lost so much weight." This is only true measured against my seventeen-year-old self. Pauline comes up to my shoulder; our hug tucks her head momentarily under my chin. She wanted me to marry her son Arthur and so did I, when I was eleven, but he had his eye on my cousin Adrienne, my sister Naomi, anyone but me. Now I have been a functioning lesbian with the same stocky body for a good fifteen years, but to Pauline—a faithful Communist through the early sixties and now a dedicated troublemaker in her Florida retirement community—I've just lost weight and should have married Arthur.

Indeed, Arthur's wife Vera, who I'm meeting for the first time, is regaling me with stories of her first encounter with Pauline. "I took Pauline off for a walk, you know, so Arthur could have time with his father, and believe me it wasn't easy, she wasn't interested in me. Only has eyes for Arthur. The first thing she did was tell me about how you really loved Arthur, even when you were children, you had such a deep relationship, she always hoped the two of you would marry, on and on—Finally I couldn't stand it, I said, *Pauline*"—Vera pauses here, for emphasis—"*Arthur is married. He married me—Vera. Arthur married ME.*"

I'm convulsed, just this side of pain. "I bet it predisposed you to like me," I gasp finally. It would be funnier if I hadn't loved and suffered over him.

Turning to get another bloody mary, I bump into

Kate. I let my arm press hers while I tell her about Pauline's foiled plans for me and Arthur. Her skin is hot from the day's sun.

"You know something embarrassing—that arrogant sonofabitch probably imagines he could have saved me from lesbianism."

"Listen, I'm sure every single person here has a separate analysis of why you're a lesbian." Kate has a way of stabbing the heart of the unspeakable, not always welcome. But useful.

"You think one of them would come up with the truth, that it's more fun?"

3.

This is the first whole-community event of the season and they're all here. Besides Pauline commenting on my weight loss, and Rose trying to grasp me geographically with a mind schooled only on desperate moves across oceans, Al Rubin in the same plaid bermuda shorts mixes the same potent bloody marys, and Sam's third wife Helaine says, *god, these are really strong, I'm about to get reeling drunk*, as she says every year at every community party, and she does get reeling drunk. Timmy Fried, a couple of years older than I am, but always Timmy and probably a faggot, though closeted as they come—he won't even mention it to me, whose lesbian publications sit on half the community's coffee tables—Timmy says *Hi, hon, how you doing*, genuinely glad to see me, but we never go past hi, not even to observe that our mothers, once best friends, no longer speak. He's got the same dark, wiry hair, the same smile, dazzling against olive skin. We hung out together as teenagers. I wonder if I've changed so little.

These are old people, mostly—Timmy and I, in our forties, are still the younger generation—and each year someone else is gone. This time it's Evie

Melman, breast cancer, and Herb Meyers, stroke. Helen Bierman's in the hospital, too sick to come, but she's at least eighty-five, whereas Evie was barely seventy and vital, cracking jokes and drawing up petitions, eternally herself. Except not eternally since she's gone. Maybe she is eternally herself elsewhere. I imagine her body decaying down to the bone: the skull of Yorick, who dandled Hamlet on his clown knee; the skull of Evie, who lavished special attention—cool, amusing, conversational—on me, the fat secretive child. Evie's husband Abe looks lost.

I glance over at my mother, unsteady on her feet though arguing earnestly with Rose about some pollution disaster. My mother thrives on disaster. The thought makes me feel mean—at least she cares. She's blurry, in movement and in speech, I can't tell if it's the new medication for her blood pressure, Al Rubin's bloody mary, or simply her refusal to walk and exercise. And cigarettes. She lights one, fumbling with her lighter. When she talks her face looks very alive.

4.

In the 1920s, at a place called, officially, Holloway Farm, but really it was Molly's, this community began. Apocryphally, a few stray Jews rambled through the Catskills looking for something cheaper than the Borscht Belt. In one version of the myth, their car broke down. In another, they got lost and were rescued by Molly's colorless husband. In any case, they landed at Molly's and never left. Or rather the men left a couple of days later to go back to work in the steamy city, but the women and children stayed. First, a week. Later two weeks, three weeks. Molly's had room and board in two buildings called the Main House and the Barn, and soon both buildings were filled with Jewish families, hot from summer in Brooklyn and the Bronx and, occasionally, Queens.

My mother's parents were among those first wandering Jews. Her father, a factory owner's son in Poland, was a printer in Brooklyn, but he soon rose to foreman and knew exactly what to do when there was land and he had money: buy and build.

By the time I remember, houses, mostly simple unwinterized cabins, dotted the as yet nameless and unpaved road. Every summer a truck would dump gravel and spread tar, for the sun to pour into until the warm blackness squished under our bare feet and bubbles formed on the surface for us to deliciously pop. Every house had children or grandchildren, and every summer, during the week, the community was practically adult male-free. We, the children, ran wild, in and out of everyone's house, and wherever we landed at lunchtime, a mother would feed us and report back.

Was this a strain on anyone's finances? Probably. I remember the tension around my mother's mouth when a surprise number of kids showed up towards the end of the week, and the range of food reflected our bungalow community's class spread. At the Melmans, it was bologna or salami, kosher—for quality, not orthodoxy; we often drank milk with our thick-sliced rounds of meat lightly slathered with mustard. At Pauline's it was the dread egg salad, while Timmy's mother Selma always served peanut butter, which I adored (without jelly), and which we never ate at home. My mother gave me to understand peanut butter was not healthy. When, years later, in the flood of whole grain technology, I discovered that peanut butter was an excellent source of protein, I confronted my mother.

She was all innocence. *I knew it had good protein, but it was high calorie. You were always watching your weight.* (Four years old, mommy? Five years old? *Who* was watching my weight?)

At the other end of the spectrum were the Poplows, Sandy and Neil's grandparents. We knew they were rich because their house was vast, winterized, living room filled with what we called "city furniture" covered with plastic. They fed us hot beef goulash with noodles and gravy, which I politely smooshed around on my plate for a while before mumbling, *I'm not very hungry*. The truth was gravy or sauce of any kind disgusted me. Even milk on dry cereal made me gag. I liked my wet food wet and my dry food dry.

This childraising collectivity and male absence gave the women a fabulous freedom. Most of them worked during the year, and they expanded into the space of summer. Mornings they'd gather over coffee; afternoons hang out and play cards, mah jong, and their own invented games, costume galas with themes: a kiddie party (they dressed in diapers and pinafores, wheeled one another in carriages constructed from broken wheelbarrows), treasure hunts, movie stars, for which they played both genders and acted out stylized but torrid love scenes. We kids were told to fend for ourselves, but my cousin Adrienne and I would spy. We saw Rose and Belle glamorously tango, my mother demonstrate "that old soft shoe" on a picnic table, happily tapping up and down the planks, and once my grandmother got tipsy enough to strip off her skirt when someone admired it and auction it off for $3.50. Even had we not seen with our own eyes, we heard these stories again and again from our mothers. This was not a big drinking community—true drunks, like Herb Meyers, stuck out like their red noses, but getting "tipsy" or "high" at an occasional social event was admired for the amusing behavior it produced and for the wonderful stories, cherished like heirlooms.

For us kids, the women organized a collective day camp, and took turns teaching square dancing, arts and crafts, nature walks (which I loathed and cut at every opportunity), athletics, and dramatics, for the inevitable play at the end of the summer: I, an early though monotone reader, got starring roles for years until the others caught up. Beside the platform ran a creek, which our parents paid a local farmer to dam up, so every afternoon we splashed magnificently in the bone-cold brook, until late August, when low water threatened polio. A few local kids came to day camp as well—Cookie, Leona, Joyce—blond and different. They were quieter, they ate bologna with mayonnaise, and, unlike us, they never complained. It was for this day camp that the platform, as we called it, was planned and laboriously built.

The women also ran a vigorous cultural calendar. Literary Circle meant they'd all read the same book and get together at someone's house to eat, always eat, and discuss. There were current events afternoons, speakers in the evenings, square dances, and "musicales," which involved someone with a hi-fi inviting everyone over to listen to records, usually piano. Only during the fifties things got a little dicey around the current events and speakers. The non-reds and slightly-pinks backed nervously and acrimoniously away from the pinker-to-reds with a suspicion that lasted through the sixties. Even now I recognize the edge in some of the questions tossed me at these annual barbecues. We are all a little careful around politics.

5.

Egged on by the smell of chicken grilling, I reach for a third bloody mary, and dilute it with the tomato juice Al keeps stashed under the makeshift bar. Women from the community, with an occasional excessively honored male volunteer, used to do all the cooking, turn every chicken, shred every cabbage leaf, but now they hire it out to some catering firm with a chicken on the side of its truck. Two young men stand over the charcoal, and a couple of local women take charge of setting and clearing the table: Marlene, who cleans for everyone up and down my mother's road at least once a summer, and Marlene's sister Georgia, who lingers by the drinks table, hard after the bloody marys under Marlene's benignly disapproving gaze.

Marlene and I move away from the bar to a bench plunked down in the middle of the lawn for some obscure reason. We pick up on a conversation we'd started this afternoon in front of my mother's house on the now semi-paved road. Marlene had just delivered someone's laundry. She was rushed and left her Chevy running, but after a while she turned it off and lit a cigarette. Her three-year-old in the back seat played happily with a rubber toy and I marveled at his good humor.

Marlene herself is exhausted, doing not only her work but work for her other sister, Joanie, who has just nearly died of pneumonia and blood clots, brought on by her fifth miscarriage.

"Why's she getting pregnant again?" Joanie's nearly forty and has three kids, including two teenagers.

Marlene rolls her eyes up. "Beats me. She's going nuts with having to sit still." She lights a cigarette and I love/hate the smell. Once in a while I'm still tempted to smoke.

"You know anyone we could hire to take my mother shopping, once a week or so? She can't stand asking for favors, and there's no food in the house." Even when there was no money for anything else, my mother did not grow up in the Depression and the wake of the Holocaust for nothing. Her cabinets were always crammed with tuna, canned peas, soup, macaroni; the freezer stocked with frozen fish, string beans, french fries . . . . Now she can afford it, the freezer's empty: not even orange juice, not even bread.

"I don't know what's with these people," Marlene gestures with her eyes up and down the crowd, "it's like they're in clans or something. Like Selma Fried, they used to be best friends. What happened?"

"Ukkhhh." I throw up my hands in disgust. This whittling away of old friends through death or carefully nursed feuds depresses me. "They don't even speak anymore."

"What about the Rubins? They're right down the road. I don't know why they don't take her shopping."

"I think my mother doesn't get along with him."

"Maybe it's her being alone. The couples don't like it."

I wonder about widows who get adopted by couples. Lillian Metzer, for example, with her sugary smile, or Tina, with the still-black chignon and apple cheeks. Tina spent practically all her time with Belle and Sol until Belle, a tiny frantic woman with wild red hair and a huge crooked smile, died of a brain tumor. After a while, Tina and Sol got married.

My mother finds this exquisitely romantic, like her favorite movie with Maureen O'Sullivan, whom she has been told she resembles. In the movie, Maureen O'Sullivan knows she's dying and picks a successor for her family. I have never understood the power of this story for my young-woman mother—whether she, a selfish woman, cherished this ideal of self-sacrificing love; if it was her way of reassuring herself that we, her daughters, would be taken care of (my mother had at least a dozen operations while we were growing up); or if the plan represented one last grab at control. Whatever the appeal, it still holds: even on this visit she mentions again Tina and Sol and how she's sure Belle planned it, like in that movie of Maureen O'Sullivan's.

People used to say I looked like her. She arches her neck, inadvertently displaying her profile, which she hates. She's still beautiful. *You*—she would say to me and Naomi—*you have good features. I was always attractive, but you have good features.* She means we have smallish possibly unJewish noses; about hers there is no mistake. Hers separated her from Maureen O'Sullivan, and she will die not recognizing her beauty includes, is partly because of, her nose.

"Last call for drinks," Al Rubin bellows, and I guide my mother to the food line, hand close to her elbow, ready for stumbling, afraid, angry and helpless: I'm leaving tomorrow, who will watch her? Is this someone who should be living alone, and for how much longer? How do you tell?

6.

At our assigned table Kate's already eating, along with Naomi, her lover Mario and my mother. My cousin Adrienne's there with her husband and their two girls, aggressively silent teenagers who gaze everywhere with contempt, except if you talk to them, they melt into smiling children; Arthur's wife Vera (for some reason sitting with us—Arthur himself, Pauline, and Vera's little girl are all at a table across the room); and Sam and Helaine and Helaine's twin sister Blanche, with whom she has been locked in furious unacknowledged competition for every one of their shared seventy-odd years.

I scoot in between Kate and Naomi. We consume chicken cole slaw potato. The chicken skin should be crisper but I eat it anyway. Chemical-rich. It's enough I stopped smoking.

"I know I shouldn't," I complain to Naomi, who carefully trims hers and sets it aside, "but it's my favorite part." Kate cheerfully filches Naomi's discarded morsels.

Tina and Sol, the happy second-time-arounders, stroll by, balancing plates, and sit the next table over. Tina beams. What couple would adopt my mother? She digs into her chicken as if the task demands all her strength.

Ok, Edith, a large woman with a beautiful, humorous, slightly horsey face and long grey braids wound around her head, commands from the stage in front of the room. *Each table now will present a skit based on what's in the paper sack. See, each table has one. You don't have to use what's in the sack, but you must perform a skit. Ok?*

I'm drunk enough to consider it—Helaine was right, the drinks are strong. Besides, it's a request from an adult. I may move back and forth across the continent, live on stolen goods for a solid two years, and kiss my woman lover in front of a crowd of people who've known me all my life, but I still have a goody-two-shoes streak a yard wide. I'm ready to be polite.

The rest of my table has no such problem. "Fuck it," Naomi says, "I'm not getting up there," and Kate snorts agreement. The teenagers huddle at the other end of the table, oblivious. Vera smiles a mannerly smile. Only Adrienne, a little drunk herself, argues, "C'mon, it'll be fun." She's cruising, eager to display her short tight skirt and beckoning sandals. The woman's a health freak. Every time I sit next to her I bloat. She rustles through our table's paper bag. My mother looks dazed. Last year she would have been on stage arching her Maureen O'Sullivan neck, singing and carrying on with the best of them.

The skits begin. Vera's four-year-old is led up on stage by a woman I've never seen before. The little girl holds a wooden spoon as if it were a microphone. *This is Alice,* says the stranger, *and she's going to sing for us and then we'll all sing along.* Alice is beaming. She sings into the wooden spoon

a-b-c-d-e-f-g   h-i-j-k-lmnop
q-r-s t-u-v w-x y-and-z

now I know my abcs
next time won't you sing with me

Then she leads us in a rousing rendition, the entire community mobilizing behind a cute smart child, wavering only on the *next time won't you sing with me* part, since we just did sing with her and wonder if we're committing ourselves to do it again, an infinite cycle of early literacy. The applause is thunderous.

Four of the women, Selma Fried, my mother's ex-best friend, Edith the emcee, Blanche the twin, and Rose with her brillo hair, clamber up on stage and sing, with gestures:

John Brown's baby had a cold upon his chest
John Brown's baby had a cold upon his chest
John Brown's baby had a cold upon his chest
and they rubbed it in with camphorated oil.

Naomi and I make cringing looks at each other. "Never mind," Kate hisses, "that the song goes *John Brown's body lies a moldering in its grave . . . .*"

"What should we do for our skit?" Adrienne's hot to trot.

"Nothing." Naomi tosses her hair, elegant with disgust.

"Listen," I tug Naomi's hair, "we have a multiple choice: A) you, Adrienne and I sing *Ball-in-the-Jack* . . ." (a routine we did when we were respectively four, five and six).

"Would you?" Adrienne interrupts excitedly, but I continue, "B) we get up there and talk about Israel and the Palestinians . . ."

Naomi shrieks with laughter and shakes her head.

"C) . . ." I pause. I can't come up with C). I'm stuck on the fact that in my life at home I read, speak and write obsessively about Israel and the American Jewish community, and here I am in the community where I grew up. Many of them have visited Israel, most are fierce in their support, though some, like my mother and Pauline and dead Evie, criticize the government. The *intifada,* the uprising, keeps right on rising, in bursts or waves or a steady underground flow with only one direction. And no one has mentioned it until now I did, as a joke. As the ultimate in necessary impossible discourse. I imagine little Alice singing *i-n-t-i-f-a-d-a* . . . .

The women are almost done, they're up to
John Brown's (gesture) *had a* (gesture) *upon his* (gesture)
John Brown's (gesture) *had a* (gesture) *upon his* (gesture)
John Brown's (gesture) *had a* (gesture) *upon his* (gesture)
and they rubbed it in . . . .

They're giggling fiercely, proud of their memories, their silliness. My mother's eyes, slightly glazed, wander, meet mine and she smiles, opening her eyes wider, as if to say she's having fun. At least some people are having fun. They used to care about injustice. Do they still? Is it my job to put the Palestinians on their agenda? Can they listen, can they care, are they too . . . too old frightened bitter selfish? And the "young ones"—Naomi, Adrienne, Timmy, Vera? And their kids? Do they feel connected? For them is it one more global horror story, distinguished only by disproportionate media coverage?

The John Brown skit is over and everyone including my mother claps, not as loud as for abc-Alice but loud enough. Someone will be gone next year. Alice will learn to read, write, will grow into a woman who drinks too many bloody marys or not, likes or is ashamed of her nose, loves a woman or a man. Maybe she'll care about Israel, maybe about the Palestinians, maybe both. Maybe the planet in general and the Middle East in particular will last that long. Maybe the damage is not irreparable.

I clear the table, dump chicken bones from plate to plate, and carry the garbage into the kitchen. Marlene, at the oven, is pink with heat.

I shrug, pointing with my eyes towards the stage, where Manny Beck, wrapped in a vinyl tablecloth, makes ballet poses with Lillian Metzer, the merry widow. Marlene shrugs back and grins.

"You know about the cake?" she asks me and Georgia. "They wanted a cake to celebrate, but they couldn't agree what to put on it."

The cake sits on the counter, huge, rectangular, and white. In pink letters it says HAPPY SUMMER.

"Not too controversial," I laugh harshly. These are my people. I am their child, not ready for this adulthood, but too bad. We walk together, Marlene with squares of thickly white cake, some laced with bits of HAPPY SUMMER pink, me balancing the coffee, mostly decaf, out to the table where my people wait.

in the middle of
the barbecue
she brings up israel

It was the skits Edith had us doing at the barbecue, to get us off our *tukheses*. Edith, the community expert on fun. We had skits all right. First Pauline's granddaughter climbs up on stage, one of those kids who wiggles her toe, everyone swoons. She sings the words, the tune, everything. Our bunch—Edith, Blanche, Rose and me—sings "John Brown's Body," you leave out the words and do this with the hands and that with the arms . . . .

Then Nadine, Rose's granddaughter, Marjorie's younger girl, gets up there alone. Nadine is maybe 22 years old, she wears dungarees, like all the kids, kind of dirty on purpose and torn, and sneakers. Her hair is cut short and spiky and some of it is green—not my cup of tea, but that face, she's a Greenbaum, no doubt about it, and smart like the Greenbaums. She's off at college and she studies Islam, and the Arab language. She studies Hebrew too, but "because of the linguistic connection," she explains, God forbid she should just study Hebrew because Jews have studied it for 5,000 years, maybe more. But she's a good girl, Nadine.

She stands up there on stage and she says, "I know this is a holiday weekend and you're all into having a good time. But I need to talk to you about Israel."

You can hear people shifting around on the benches, coughing, and Lil Metzer, looking slightly ridiculous in a bright red blouse with puff sleeves, says "Nadine, honey, it's a party, for a party you don't—it's not . . ." Lil makes a face, a second's pause while she decides "—it's not *nice*," she says.

Vivian, Estelle's younger girl, pipes up, "Lil, let her talk. It's a good thing to talk about Israel." Vivian's hair is just showing grey. I remember her toddling after my Timmy on fat little legs. Now Estelle and I only nod hello if our eyes run into each other. "Go," Vivian smiles at Nadine, "talk to us about Israel."

"Israel and the Palestinians," Nadine corrects. That catches people up, they mumble things like *terrorists, on with it, her community too, just fun, where else?* But no one knows what to do. Besides, it could be a skit.

"I wouldn't be interrupting the barbecue, except it's important," she says so earnestly no one has the heart to stop her. You can see some people agree with Lil, it's not very nice of Nadine. I look to see if Rose is embarrassed.

"I grew up with you," Nadine pleads, "with your children and grand-children. You all know me since before I know myself. That binds us. We're Jews and that binds us, even though we never talk about it. I know you think Israel is a tiny brave miracle. When the world abandoned the Jews, the Jews made Israel. Out of a dream. They said, *we will be a light unto nations.* I know you remember." Her eyes dart around.

"We remember, sweetie," Pauline nods.

I nod too. I heard it on the radio, the U.N. vote, I was in the kitchen of that tiny apartment on Fetterley, the agency furnished it. I sat down hard on the yellow chair, the torn vinyl scratched my leg. I put my head on the table and sobbed. I knew Israel wouldn't bring anyone back but maybe it could bring us forward.

Nadine shakes her head, the little green spikes bounce. "*A light unto nations.* You know what it's doing, our Israel?" She leans forward and sticks her neck out into the audience. "It's breaking the hands of kids, for throwing rocks. I was a kid here. I threw rocks. Should you have broken my hand?"

I hear the gasp, I feel it in my own throat. Never mind it's not the same, she's a girl still, how could anyone break Nadine's hand? She used to play guitar at the barbecues just a few years ago, "Down in the Valley," "*tzena tzena,*" songs for the old fogies.

"You know how you raised us, with room—to be a little wild?" she asks. We remember. Nadine had crying fits for no reason, oversensitive, she got left out by the other kids. We always had to butt in on her behalf. She used to set little fires too, not trying to burn anything up or down, but it was dangerous.

"You saw it on TV," she says, "about soldiers breaking the hands. And the bulldozer, they buried them."

It's enough, I have to say something. "Nadine, darling, you think we don't know about burying? You think I don't miss my mother, my cousin Bessie, the whole family gone in two years? You don't know these things, to be glad that Bessie at least has a grave, the only one. That I have a life. You have a life, and college, where you can study the Arabs or anything. That's wonderful. You stand there in your 22-year-old body, nothing wrong with it yet. And you talk about burying the dead?"

"They buried them alive, Selma," she says, "with a bulldozer. Like the Nazis . . ."

"How *dare* you speak Israel and Nazis in the same sentence. How *dare* you!" Manny's fist pounds *dare* on the table, his red face gets redder. He's an old *pisher*, but he's not the only one mad at Nadine for saying about the Nazis. Nadine's skin glows—like she ate her beets, we used to joke—but this comparing Jews to Nazis will not do.

Edith is talking now, and Manny and Al, *democracy, they don't gas anyone, Leon Klinghoffer, six million . . . .* Everyone gets in the act, people wave their arms and shake their heads back and forth, up and down. Nadine's head droops. The corner of her Greenbaum mouth droops too.

"I'm sorry, sorry, I didn't mean to offend anyone —but listen." She holds up her hands and who among us could resist?

"Have you ever seen a Palestinian?" She pauses. No one answers. "You know what they look like? Some you can't tell them from the Jews. Like us, like Jews, you can't always tell. And the languages, the letters are so close, and the sounds. Only Hebrew letters are squarer. They're practically the same."

"People who speak Hebrew don't blow people up," I snap. I don't forgive Nadine for studying Hebrew for the wrong reasons.

"They do too, Selma," Vivian cuts in. "Listen to Nadine, she's telling the truth. The Israeli Army acts like an army."

"And the Arabs act like animals," snorts Al.

"What about the settlers . . ." Tina's waving her arms in Al's face, "the Gush Enums, I forget, they blow things up. People's houses. They even killed the girl, the Arabs got blamed, remember, Solly?" (She pokes Sol with her elbow.) ". . . a young girl, fifteen years old, maybe younger. They went around shoot-ing Arabs for revenge, Jews did that. And all the time it was a bullet from one of their own guns . . ."

"It was self-defense . . ." Al starts to interrupt, while Tina concludes, slapping the table for emphasis. ". . . killed her."

"You're attacked, you have to defend yourself," Al goes on, "they're like animals."

"That's disgusting," Pauline sneers across the room, "they're just people, human beings, they have a right to stick up for themselves . . . ." and Estelle jumps on the bandwagon, "They want their rights. They want a home. Just like the Jews."

"They have a home," that new young Frickie stands up, kind of pompous. "They have Jordan." He pauses. "If all they wanted was a home they'd stay in

Jordan. They want *us* not to have a home. They want to push us into the sea. That's your Palestinians," he sneers at Nadine, and several of us glare disapproval at him: Who's he to talk like that to Nadine?

"Nadine, darling, you didn't see the worst times of this century." It's Bertha, her son married an Israeli girl, he lives there. She visits at least once a year and takes a million snapshots of the grandchildren to show us. "What do you know? Tell me, you've heard of Adolf Hitler?"

"Who's talking about Hitler, Bertha?" Nadine's rosy face knits with impatience. "I'm talking about Israel and the Palestinians. Jews have to talk about these things."

"Let them stop killing," Bertha tosses off. "They're the ones who kill, children, that schoolbus. The Olympics, the whole world lets it happen."

"They want a state, a Palestine, to point like a dagger at Israel's heart." Edith folds her arms across her big chest, and nods at Bertha.

"Arafat wants Jerusalem. They all want Jerusalem," Bertha nods back.

"Surprise: it's a war." Vivian has never been known for her patience. "The point is, how do you settle a war? You have to talk, right?"

"The Jewish people will never give up Jerusalem," proclaims Bertha, and Manny chimes in, "We refuse to negotiate with terrorists." What does he mean, *we?* He lives in the Bronx.

"I've been to Jerusalem," Nadine says, "have you?"

Several heads nod, I look around to see who.

"East Jerusalem . . . the people look at me with . . . I've seen it in Harlem. I don't belong there."

"So don't go there, who's making you?" snorts Al, and Rose, Nadine's grandmother, cajoles, "Nadine, a good girl like you? She works very hard, scholarships, a Saturday job," she explains to us.

Nadine's voice softens. "It's a golden city, Jerusalem. Light echoes off the stone walls. Golden, like the song . . . ." She breaks into song, *"yerushalayim shel zahav da da da dum . . ."*

She interrupts herself, talking again, very fast, "You can't have gold without peace. We need peace. The Arabs need peace. We need to lie down together, the lion with the lamb, *yea though i walk through the valley of the shadow of death i shall fear no evil for thou art with me thy rod and thy staff they comfort me surely . . . ."* She closes her eyes and sways slightly back and forth. A tear squeezes out of her eye and runs down her face. Suddenly I understand that Nadine is a little crazy, a little lost in the valley of the shadow of death. Everyone's still talking, *Jordan, partition, nine miles across, Peace Now, terrorists, Judaea . . . .* Nadine doesn't seem to hear, her eyes are closed, tears rolling down her cheeks.

"You're my people," she croons, "you taught me right from wrong." She opens her grey eyes wide and looks right into mine.

"YOU HAVE TO STOP IT," she sobs like a prayer; it enters me.

But you know, Nadine's up there with that earnest face as if we can listen to her, when really we think: What could she know? Nothing. She wants the world to be nice, like we taught her, but we lied. We never showed her the world's true face, the one we saw, the one we believe in—I could call it Hitler's face but it's all the faces who liked Hitler, who chose Hitler, millions of them and nobody stopped it. *Take care of your own, chickie,* I want to warn, even though she is right this minute spouting words we taught her, *equal, peace, justice, swords into ploughshares.*

No one knows what to say back to Nadine, not even Marjorie. That it's okay to beat ploughshares into swords? That she should sit down and let us get on with our skits?

epilogue

I wrote "All Weekend No One Mentions Israel" in the summer of 1988. It's a story, though there was a barbecue and no one did mention Israel. Writing the story named something for me. "In the Middle of the Barbecue She Brings Up Israel" was a fantasy designed to untrap me, to unhook the actual from the possible: someone could have disrupted the uneasy peace of "All Weekend."

There's a third story, a true one, but I haven't been able to write it. Still, it should be told. In January, 1989, I was part of a peace delegation that visited Israel and the Occupied West Bank and Gaza. On the weekend of July 4th, 1989, some people who knew about my trip mentioned to my mother that they'd like to hear me speak. Actually, knowing my mother, my guess is, they probably said, *how interesting,* which she passed on to me as grand desire.

But the point is, we set it up. We announced it at the barbecue—though I waited to talk about it till the next night, I have some sense of appropriateness and I am not 22 like Nadine. And the next evening people showed up to hear.

The other point is, they listened and were concerned. They did not say, *what do you know, you're a kid; a woman . . . .* They said things like, *that's terrible.* Their faces were grim. A couple of the women cried.

Of course most people who are rabid or apathetic on this subject know me and didn't bother showing up. One woman, whose son made *aliyah,* said I was presenting one side of things, which is true. Another woman I have always adored, warm, loving, the kind of person who makes *mishpocheh* by walking in the door, said, *I don't care, they should kill them all,* meaning the Palestinians. But another, who spent her girlhood in then-Palestine, half of whose family is Israeli, interrupted this woman, her lifelong friend: *That's horrible,* she said, *you can't say that, you can't do that.*

What I want to name here, and to let stand, is the concern, the horror. Whether these are enough is another story. They asked questions. They were disturbed. They were not immobilized. They were not too anything to care. I had misjudged and underestimated them, and this statement is my apology.

*Event and invention are equidistant from story
and require the same arts.*

Lore Segal,
On the Second Book of Samuel,
*Commentary: Contemporary Writers
Read the Jewish Bible*

notes

INVIOLABLE SPACE

When Words Are Seeds
[p. 46] . . . *little fat girl who refused to stop healing* . . . These words come from a letter by Diane Nowicki, characterizing "Harlem Summer."

She Becomes a Writer
[p. 58] Muriel Rukeyser (1913-80), poet; radical, Jew, lesbian; the relevant lines, "What would happen if one woman told the truth about her life?/The world would split open," from "Kathe Kollwitz," in *The Speed of Darkness* (1968). Kathe Kollwitz (1867-1945), German sculptor and graphics artist; anti-war, leftist; chose often to work in poster and print media, so her work could be cheaply reproduced and available.

WAR STORIES, 197-

[p. 92] *Sister Gin*, wonderful novel by lesbian writer and publisher June Arnold. In it, several women, mostly in their seventies, tie up, strip naked, and deposit in the center of town several rapists (1st pub., Plainfield, VT: Daughters, Inc., 1973; republished, New York: Feminist Press, 1989).

OUR FIRST TALK

[p. 106] . . . *too much acting and being reacted to according to type.* Wording suggested by Enid Dame's "Ethel Rosenberg: A Sestina" (". . . how people usually react according to type"), in *The Tribe of Dina: A Jewish Women's Anthology,* eds. Melanie Kaye/Kantrowitz and Irena Klepfisz (Boston: Beacon Press, 1989).

SOME PIECES OF JEWISH LEFT

Chava
[p. 194] *Eyes on the Prize*, Documentary history of the Civil Rights Movement, widely televised in 1987; the title comes from the Black freedom song, "Keep your eyes on the prize, hold on," which in turn comes from the traditional spiritual, "Keep your hands on the plow, hold on." (Produced and directed by Judith Vecchione; Executive Producer, Henry Hampton; Blackside, Inc., 1986.)

[p. 202] *Jewish Songs of Struggle.* "Jewish Songs of Celebration and Struggle" by Yasmine (Oak Leaf Studios in Berkeley, CA, 1983).
Vivian
[p. 209] . . . *I feel like I need to protect her.* Insight from Vera Williams, "My Mother, Leah, and George Sand," in *The Tribe of Dina: A Jewish Woman's Anthology.*

glossary

(A) Aramaic
(H) Hebrew
(Y) Yiddish

a shvue oyf lebn un toyt (Y) a life and death oath

aliyah (H) literally, go up; immigration to Israel

di shvue (Y) "The Oath," title of the Bundist "anthem"

gesher (H) bridge

goy (Y) non-Jew (pejorative); *goyish* non-Jewish

Gush Enums (H) *Gush Enumin*, Jewish settlers who claim the West Bank (Judaea and Samaria) is biblically Jewish and therefore must be retained for Jewish settlement by Israel.

gut shabes (Y) Good *shabes* (*shabat* in Hebrew; day of rest and celebration, Friday sundown to Saturday sundown; Sabbath)

kaddish (H) prayer; especially of mourning

kibitz (Y) heckle, offer unsolicited, often joking, advice

kreplakh (Y) dumplings

magen david (H) star of David; a Jewish star

mentsh (Y) a human being; a decent person

meshugene (Y) crazy

midrash (H) a story about a biblical event; an explanation

mishpocheh (Y) family, especially extended family

mir shvern (Y) we swear

mitzvah (H) blessing; a deed so good it confers a blessing upon the doer; one of many deeds a Jew is commanded by god to perform, because it is a blessing-conferrer.

oyfn pripetshik (Y) "On the hearth," first words and common title of a popular song (written by Mark Warshawsky, but so well-known as to be considered "traditional").

pesakh (H) Passover; spring holiday, commemorates the planting, and the exodus out of slavery in Egypt.

pisher (Y) pisser

shabat shalom (H) lit., Greetings, *shabat* (see *shabes*); or, greetings to you on *shabat*; peace for *shabat*.

shavuos (Y) a nearly-summer holiday; fifty days after *pesakh*, marks the Exodus; *shavuos* (*shavuot* in Hebrew) commemorates early harvest and the giving of the Ten Commandments at Sinai.

schwartze (Y) black; as noun

sheyne meydele (Y) pretty little girl

shlemiel (Y) a jerk, fool

shmate (Y) rag, scarf

shtetl (Y) small town

shul (Y) synagogue; also school, a place of learning

tukheses (Y) asses

yahrzeit (Y) anniversary of death

yitgadal v'yitgadash . . . v'chayim olenu v'al col yisroel. v'imru amen. (A) opening and near-closing of the mourners' *kaddish.*

yerushalayim shel zahav (H) "Jerusalem, City of Gold," a popular/patriotic Israeli song

Yom Hashoah (H) Holocaust Remembrance Day

zuntik bulbes, montik bulbes (Y) Sunday, potatoes, Monday, potatoes; first words of the popular song *"bulbes."*

Melanie Kaye/Kantrowitz is a long-time activist and writer, currently teaching in the independent study Graduate Program of Vermont College. She is author of *We Speak in Code: poems & other writings*, co-editor of *The Tribe of Dinah: A Jewish Women's Anthology*, and her poems, stories, essays and reviews have appeared in the *Village Voice, Jewish Currents, Sojourner, Tikkun, The Women's Review of Books*, and *The Utne Reader* among other places and have been widely anthologized in such books as *Nice Jewish Girls, Naming the Waves*, and *Out the Other Side*. She is also the former editor and publisher of *Sinister Wisdom*, one of the oldest lesbian/feminist journals.

For some years Melanie has been involved in the cause of peace between Israel and Palestine. She also works with New Jewish Agenda as a member of the National Steering Committee and the Task Force on Anti-Semitism and Racism.

My Jewish Face & Other Stories is Kaye/Kantrowitz's first collection of fiction.

Photo: Linda Vance

The Aunt Lute Foundation is a non-profit corporation that grew out of the work of the Spinsters/Aunt Lute Book Company. Its purpose is to publish and distribute books that have the educational potential to change and expand social realities.

We seek manuscripts, both fiction and non-fiction, by women from a variety of cultures, ethnic backgrounds and subcultures; women who are self-aware and who, in the face of all contradictory evidence, are still hopeful that the world can reserve a place of respect for each woman in it.

Please write or phone for a free catalogue of the other fine books we have published, or if you wish to be on our mailing list for future titles. You can buy books directly from us by phoning in a credit card order or mailing a check with the order form that comes with our catalogue.

Aunt Lute Foundation Books
P.O. Box 410687
San Francisco, CA 94141
(415) 558-9655